Free Draw
A Jake Samson Mystery

Also by Shelley Singer
SAMSON'S DEAL

Free Draw

A Jake Samson Mystery

by Shelley Singer

ST. MARTIN'S PRESS
NEW YORK

Library of Congress Cataloging in Publication Data
Singer, Shelley.
    Free draw
    I.Title
PS3569.I565F7   1984   814'.54   84-11792
ISBN 0-312-30366-1

First Edition

10 9 8 7 6 5 4 3 2 1

For Linnea Due and Sabina Thorne
Week after week

The author is grateful for the help of
Ellen M. Lacroix, attorney at law; Jacqueline Letalien;
Caroline and Michael Norris; and Rosanna Poret.

Free Draw

A Jake Samson Mystery

1

I had not been in a good mood to start with the day my friend Artie Perrine called and told me, in his roundabout way, that he needed my help.

I had a cold. My car was in the shop. The sun had poked through for a while that morning, but the skies were gray with rain again by two. Just another day in a dismal and apparently endless Northern California winter. I couldn't go anywhere and I couldn't settle down to not going anywhere. I was as cranky as a slightly sick kid who has to stay in because the weather's bad. Rainy day coloring books, hot soup for lunch.

My cats, Tigris and Euphrates, were even crankier. The drizzle had driven them inside where they were threatening to shred the living room curtains if I didn't make the rain stop.

The phone rang just as I was deciding to have an afternoon beer.

"I'm afraid," Artie said sadly, "that I won't be able to make it to poker Tuesday night."

Obviously, I was supposed to ask why. "Sorry to hear it," I grunted.

He waited a full ten seconds, then he said he had to see me right away and asked if I could drive out to his house in Marin County.

"Can't do it," I told him. "No car." I started telling him all about it. How my beautiful 1953 Chevy had gasped, stalled, and finally passed out in a cold March downpour in the middle of a San Francisco rush hour. How I'd scraped my knuckles all to hell messing around under the hood. How I'd had to have it towed all the way across the Bay Bridge to my mechanic in Berkeley.

He didn't care. "Borrow one."

1

"Artie, what's going on?"

"Borrow a car. Or take a cab. I'll pay for it."

"A cab?" I was shocked. I don't know anyone who takes cabs from Oakland to Marin. It isn't done. He had to be desperate if he was willing to spend that kind of money just to see me.

"Just come. Please."

Okay, I said. I'd see what I could do. But I didn't feel too great and why the hell couldn't he come to the East Bay to talk to me?

"Because my house is in an uproar. My wife is half crazy. I'm half crazy."

There wasn't much I could say to that. I'd put up as much of a fight as my conscience would allow. Artie and I were old friends. He needed me. He'd get me.

The first thing I had to do was find some transportation. I called my tenant, Rosie Vicente, who lives in the cottage fifty feet from my house. She's a self-employed carpenter and sometimes works weekends, but in the winter jobs are scarce. She was home.

"Rosie? Can I borrow your truck for a few hours?"

"Sure," she replied instantly. "Just get it back by morning."

"No problem."

I dressed in two shirts, a thick sweater, a down vest and heavy work boots, pulled my genuine Basque beret on over my stuffed-up head, and strolled down the path. Rosie was leaning on the sill of the bottom half of her Dutch door. Her black standard poodle, Alice B. Toklas, joined her there, standing on her hind legs, paws on the sill, as I clomped up the steps.

"Hot date?" Rosie wanted to know. Her short dark hair was tousled, her eyes soft. I wondered if she was in the middle of one herself.

"Don't I wish?" I said. I was standing to the side of the door so anyone who might be in Rosie's bed would remain out of sight. Rosie and I are close friends and I want to keep it that way. She likes her privacy.

She handed me the truck keys. I thanked her, said I'd see her later, sneezed once, and headed for the street.

Rosie's pickup truck isn't as old as my car, but unlike the

2

Chevy, it's got its original engine. The truck is fifteen years old and has the personality of a senile housecat. Reliable and tough if you give it special handling with a gentle touch. Soft words to remind it to do right by the human who drives it. Like not drop its gas tank in the driveway, upchuck its oil, or collapse on the freeway.

The truck started after the second try, coughed a little, and purred for me.

In my own car, I can usually make it from Oakland-Berkeley across the Richmond-San Rafael Bridge and on down to southern Marin in about forty minutes. But Rosie's truck gets shaky at anything over forty-five miles an hour, so I was forty minutes into the trip before I passed the San Quentin exit just across the bridge on the Marin side.

I tried not to look at San Quentin. I always try, but it's hard to miss. I used to try not looking at Alcatraz, but of course that island no longer serves its former interesting purpose, and the San Quentin monolith is now the only depressing sight on San Francisco Bay. In a place so beautiful, any ugliness, any misery, is more obvious and somehow more terrible. In the land of beautiful bridges, who wants to believe in trolls?

Traffic was light going south on 101, so in fifteen minutes I was taking the Mill Valley cutoff and heading toward Artie's canyon. The rain was falling softly and steadily. Rosie's windshield wipers needed new blades. My throat tickled and my sinuses hurt. But what the hell, I thought, I was doing it—whatever it was—for Artie. Poker buddy. Old pal. And, in an offbeat way, a business partner. Artie was an editor of *Probe* magazine, an investigative monthly out of San Francisco. The autumn before, we'd made a working arrangement that earned me a nice chunk of money as an unlicensed and under-the-table private investigator and got *Probe* started on a circulation-building series about the radical right. I still carried the credentials that said I was a free-lance writer and gave me the cover I needed to take any other such jobs that might come along.

The road to the canyon twisted narrowly through a tucked-in-the-trees residential area that included everything from old family mansions to log cabins from a kit, most of the homes obscured by trees, shrubbery, and the rise and fall of the land. If there hadn't been a weathered wooden sign that said "Foothill Canyon" nailed to a tree, you'd have thought the graveled entrance was somebody's driveway. A badly maintained driveway, at that, with deep chuckholes from the winter and no place for two cars to pass. I pulled up under a dripping redwood tree, two feet from a miniature rapids cutting into the sides of an overflowing drainage ditch, and swung down from the truck, my boots slipping on the wet clay.

Artie must have been peering through the trees, because I'd just started up the path to his house when I saw him coming down toward me. He met me halfway, about seventy-five feet along.

"The body was down there," he said, pointing toward the frothing ditch. "My nephew found it, and that's how this started."

"Nephew? Body?" I was too busy climbing the muddy trail to react more intelligently. Stumbling over a rock, I grabbed for the base of a shrub, felt something move, and pulled my hand back, wiping the gummy mess off on my pants. Where my hand had been was a creature known in the area as a banana slug. Just picture a green banana covered with slime and crawling along the ground. One of the more prolific residents of the damp and mildewed beauty spots of Northern California. This one was now slightly wounded.

"It's my brother's kid, from Des Moines," Artie explained. "And his wife. And their baby. They're all staying with us until they get settled. I don't know how they're going to get settled now. Stupid kid."

We had reached the slightly more secure footing of the half-dozen wooden steps that led to his front door. I was wondering where Artie was keeping this extraneous family. He and his wife, Julia, had a small house, with just about enough room for them and their twelve-year-old son. Two bedrooms. I was also wondering about the body he'd mentioned.

The living room was a cluttered mess. A pile of luggage, cardboard cartons, and shopping bags huddled in a corner. The sofa bed was folded up, but there was bedding perched on one of its arms.

4

Perched on its other arm was a red-eyed and very young woman.

"Jennifer," Artie said to her, "this is my friend Jake Samson." Her eyes flickered and she tried to smile. A child of about two, with flaming orange hair, was toddle-falling around the room chuckling to itself and trying to get a good grip on the family golden retriever who, motherly creature though she was, looked a bit harassed and seemed to be trying to stay out of the child's way.

Julia was sitting in an overstuffed chair oozing emotional exhaustion, her eyes fixed on the baby as if it were about to go up in a puff of smoke. She turned her head and nodded to me, then spoke to her husband without shifting her gaze from my face.

"Are you going to tell Jake about it, Artie?" The remnants of her New York accent somehow lightened the deeper accent of horror.

"Yeah," he said softly. "We'll go in the bedroom."

"Good. I don't want to go through it again."

"I know," he sighed. "I don't blame you."

I sat down on the bed. Artie paced.

"So," I said. "The body."

2

"Well, Alan found it." Artie's a small guy with a bald spot that makes him look like Friar Tuck. He scratched his bald spot. "Jesus, Jake, it's such a long story." I crossed my legs and picked a pebble out of the sole of my boot.

The long story, or at least the beginning of it, boiled down to this: Alan had found a dead man in the ditch that morning. He'd panicked, screamed, and run away. A neighbor had heard the scream, seen Alan running, and gone down to investigate. She had then called the police and told them she had seen Alan running from the scene of the crime.

"She knew Alan, then?"

"No, not exactly. She described him. The cops started questioning everyone they found in the canyon. No one was here but

Alan. Jennifer was shopping. Julia and I like to go out for breakfast on Sunday. My son, Mike—"

"Go on, Artie."

He sat down on a straight-backed chair and continued. "The cops talked to Alan. He said he didn't know anything about any corpse or anybody running or anything at all. Only he was acting weird, and he fit the description they had, and sure enough, by the time we got home, the neighbor had identified him as the guy she saw."

"Maybe you'd better tell me why he lied to the cops."

"Well, that was just the first lie."

"Oh, good."

"They asked him why he hadn't called them about finding the body and they asked him why he'd lied to them about finding it. And he gave them this long story about how he'd panicked, and how he'd never seen a corpse before, and how he went crazy when he saw the face and the staring eyes . . ."

"Nice."

"Yeah. I don't know how he could be so stupid. Just got carried away, I guess. Like when he got married. He was only twenty when he got married."

"I don't see why what he said was stupid. Sounds like a perfectly reasonable explanation to me."

"Sure. Except the cops then asked him if he knew the guy and he said no."

"And he did?"

Artie began pacing again. "Have you ever heard of Bright Future Correspondence School, up in San Rafael?"

I thought a minute. The name sounded vaguely familiar, and besides being tacky in and of itself, carried a funny smell along with it. I cocked an eyebrow and Artie answered the unasked question.

"We've gotten some hints that there's more than just a little sleaze behind that operation. No real proof, just the possibility. It's one of those multilevel operations, and they suck in a lot of people. That's okay if they keep it legal, but it's tricky stuff—"

"Maybe we can talk about that later," I interrupted. I didn't

6

know what he was talking about and I still didn't know why he was talking about it. "How does this involve your nephew?"

"He was working there for me. Undercover. The dead guy was a Bright Future vice-president." I nodded, waiting for more. "So Alan finds the body and panics. If he gets involved, he reasons, there might be publicity, with Alan identified as living here in the canyon. With me. Which connects him with *Probe*. Which blows his cover. So the first thing he does is lie about finding the body."

"And the second thing he lied about was knowing the corpse."

"Right. Of course, the cops didn't know right away that he lied about that. But they found out fast enough. I guess they put someone on the Bright Future angle right away and found out Alan worked there. That was when they came back to get him. Right before I called you."

"But they can't hold him on that."

"I guess not. But they took him in for questioning and he's not back yet."

My head was beginning to pound. Why wasn't I home in bed? I looked at him. "Artie, I really don't think you've got very much to worry about. All he has to do is explain about the undercover job. You can back him up on that. The cops will think he's an idiot, but . . ."

"There's more. Something the police don't know yet. Or at least I don't know that they do. Another reason why Alan panicked. He'd had a big fight with the guy, at the office. This vice-president, this James Smith—"

"James Smith? Is that an alias?"

"Shut up and listen, Jake. Smith threatened to fire Alan. They had this big argument. Lots of witnesses. It was about a course Alan was working on. Alan told me it was garbage, and that they didn't care what kind of shit they sold, and he just had to say something about it. I told him to for Christ's sake keep his mouth shut and keep a low profile. Dumb kid. This is what I get for giving him work. Fresh out of journalism school. He needed work. What could I do? My brother's kid, after all. I gave him work."

I sighed. Artie didn't notice.

"Okay," I said. "Take it easy. Tell me this. Do you think maybe he could have killed the guy?"

Artie glared at me. "He's a journalism graduate, Jake. What kind of question is that, anyway?"

I shrugged. This was Artie's movie, not mine.

"I was just wondering," I said, "what this Smith was doing hanging around your ditch waiting to get killed."

It was Artie's turn to shrug. "I don't know where he was killed. The cops have been doing a lot of looking around up here and up top. See, that's where the water comes from. There's a ravine up there where it collects, then it runs down the spillway to the ditch." I remembered seeing some kind of stream running down the canyon side when I'd been struggling up the path to Artie's house. "Alan says the body was a mess, like it could have washed all the way down."

"And now you want me to check things out."

Artie smiled hopefully.

I thought about it. Once, for a year or so, Marin County had been my home ground. That was right after I came out from Chicago, a young ex-cop who'd had his trial by fire in the summer of 1968, the summer of the Democratic National Convention and the Yippies and the stink of tear gas and the feel of a kid's blood on my nightstick. Sickened and afraid of myself, I'd fled to California. Flower Land. I'd lived in Marin, and Sonoma, and farther north in Mendocino, wandering around, picking up money where it could be found, falling into and crawling out of a bad marriage, and, eventually, tiring of woods and fields and the role of bitter expatriate and going back to the kind of urban environment I'd grown up in. Not Chicago. Never again Chicago. But the East Bay, with its ethnic neighborhoods and its crime and its vitality.

I didn't know Marin any more. Maybe I knew my way around physically, but it wasn't home. I didn't know the cops. I didn't know the attitudes. I thought of a few more excuses before I cut the bullshit and pushed the sad old memories out of the way. They had nothing to do with Artie's problem. I could handle Marin if Marin could handle me.

Artie was waiting for me to do something besides think and

8

make faces. Suddenly it occurred to me that he hadn't said anything about money.

"Listen, Art. Investigations cost. Expenses. Things like that."

"Sure. Naturally." He waved his hand at me. "I can manage the expenses. If they're not too high." He hesitated. "But, you know, I'm already helping to pay the lawyer—"

"You've got a lawyer already?"

"Well, certainly. The minute they took him in. And you know we just bought this house and the down payment pretty well drained our capital . . ." He let his sentence dribble off into nothing. And nothing was what we were talking about. For me. Artie was looking for a better poker hand without laying out any chips. A free draw.

"This lawyer," I said, probably sneering a little. "I'll need to be in touch with him. If there's really a problem."

"Hey, sure. I'll set it up. Now then," he said eagerly. "What's first?"

"You said the cops were all over the place up here."

"Yeah. They had the whole area up top cordoned off, and down by the ditch, too. And half the canyon on this side. About half a dozen guys."

That sounded about right. A couple of detectives, someone from the coroner's office, a technician, a photographer . . ."I didn't see anyone when I came in. Do you know if any of them are still around?" I wasn't anxious to run into any investigating officers.

"They left right before you got here. And I've been in the house since then. With you."

"Well, the first thing is to have a look around, get my bearings." Artie sighed impatiently, but he didn't argue.

We emerged from the bedroom into the living room where all the actors, apparently suspended in time, were doing exactly what they'd been doing when we left. The kid was still trying to play with the dog, the dog was still trying to avoid playing with the kid, Artie's wife was still sitting in her chair watching the kid and the dog, and Jennifer was still sitting on the arm of the couch looking stunned.

I smiled expansively, like Santa Claus, and told the furniture that I'd be back soon.

It was a relief to get out of that small, crowded house. The rain had slowed to a soft, foggy drizzle, and, looking up through the redwoods, I could see the beginnings of sunlight trying to force their way through the thinning cloud cover. I blew my nose and scanned the canyon.

From where I stood, more than midway up the north side of the canyon amphitheater, I had a good view of the geography. A very pretty view, with fuchsias, hydrangeas, and ferns all over the place and the houses all but hidden by trees.

I was facing downhill, toward the canyon floor. At my left ran the spillway. About twenty feet below me, crossing the spillway, was a wooden footbridge. On the other side of that was another path cut into the eastern face of the canyon, with houses perched on stilts above it. About 200 feet along, that path met the top of a stairway that zigzagged back down to the floor of the canyon just this side of a three-level shingled house.

I turned around and began climbing, up toward the top of the trail and the place where the spillway began.

About fifty feet beyond Artie's was another house, tucked back and well hidden by unmanicured nature. I wouldn't have noticed the house was there, but I tripped over the end of a rough wooden walkway, raised above the clay by half-sunken concrete blocks. That was the last marker of civilization. A few feet farther on, the path dwindled to nothing. And someone was crashing through the underbrush above me.

He was a big man, dressed in boots, heavy cords, a plaid wool shirt with a sweater under it, and a navy watch cap. His eyebrows were dark and shaggy in a weathered, blunt-featured face.

"Hi," he said. "What are you doing up here?"

"Just walking around."

"Oh, yeah?" He dug out his wallet and flashed a badge. "Ricci. Sheriff's department." He was a sergeant.

"Isn't it okay to go up this way yet?" I asked.

"You live around here?"

"No. I've got a friend lives here."

"Mind telling me who?" I told him. He nodded and gazed

thoughtfully at me. "Mind giving me your name and address?" I gave them to him. "Thank you, sir."

"Could I ask you something?" I was using my best earnest and respectful citizen manner, but he just looked at me impassively. "You haven't got enough on Alan to charge him, have you?"

"He came along with us voluntarily for questioning. He's being questioned." He moved past me and headed down the trail. I slogged the rest of the way up.

3

I was looking across a ravine shaped roughly like an arrowhead. At its widest point, about twenty feet, a redwood tree had fallen to form a natural bridge, its roots exposed by the water and the slides of clay and rock that a wet winter brings to land like this. At the upper end of the ravine, water dribbled and splashed down the eroded sides from the woods above. The lower end narrowed to a cut between rocky outcroppings where the wooden trough of the spillway began.

The muddy water made it hard to tell how deep the ravine was. I guessed that it filled and emptied, or nearly emptied, from storm to storm. Although less than twenty-four hours had passed since the last heavy rain, the clay was wet several feet above water level and it looked like that level was dropping fast. If Smith had been killed up here, his corpse had caught the spillway on a good day.

I stood knee deep in ferns, trying to get an imaginary glimpse of what might have happened that morning. But maybe I just wasn't taking Alan's supposed danger seriously enough. The only scene that came to mind was right out of Robin Hood. James Smith and his killer, dressed like Robin and Little John, halfway across the tree trunk, battling for macho domination until one of them won the right to cross by dumping the other one into the water. I think it was Little John who won, but it's been a long time since I read the book.

I also wanted to cross to the other side. Maybe there was

another trail over there. Maybe the cops had missed an important clue. Maybe the killer had dropped his social security card. Maybe there was a whole pile of bodies stacked up over there waiting to be tossed down the spillway. There were two ways to get where I wanted to go: around the upper edge of the ravine or across the log. I picked my way carefully to the upper edge and checked out the terrain. Not so much as a deer trail. Thick, tangled brush. A solid growth of thorny blackberry interspersed with poison oak. Not exactly impassable, but I hadn't brought a machete. I decided the redwood trunk was the lesser of two evils. It was, after all, a good five feet in diameter. Even with a cold and the few extra pounds I was carrying from winter hibernation, I was in pretty good shape. If Robin Hood—or was it Little John?—could do it, so could I.

Using the tangled roots for handholds, I pulled myself up and balanced carefully on the rounded surface. The bark was damp, but the soles of my boots gripped it and I started across, very slowly. About halfway, where the log was some eight feet above the fast-running water, I slipped on a patch of moss. That made me nervous enough to sit down for a minute and take a look around. The water below me was muddy. Nothing to see but brush and branches and other woodsy debris that bobbed to the surface, sank again, and went rushing toward the spillway lip.

I raised myself carefully to my feet and finished crossing to the other side. More blackberry, more poison oak. A few patches of bare ground that might have been part of a deer trail. I poked around for a few minutes, inadvertently terrorizing a four-foot garter snake. Then I climbed up on the tree trunk again and strolled back across, by now being an old hand at crossing raging torrents on a high wire.

Retracing my steps as far as the narrow beginnings of path, I looked across the ten feet or so of canyon wall to the upper stretch of spillway. The trough was built of redwood: eight two-by-twelves, four at each angle of the V-shaped structure, tied together with four-bys and staked and propped in a haphazard fashion with rocks, railroad ties, and concrete blocks. The thing must have needed reinforcement and repair at least every year, but it seemed to be doing the job it was intended to do—containing the runoff and keeping the soil reasonably intact so the houses at this end of the canyon could stay upright on their various and whimsical foundations. The wooden spillway ended about a hundred feet down, where the slope became a little more gradual and the water ran free to the ditch at the bottom.

The space between path and spillway showed bootprints in the muddy clay. Probably from the feet of the law earlier that day. I followed suit, half crawling, half sliding, making a real mess of myself. The trough was nearly three-quarters full of falling water. When I ran my hand along the edge, I realized that it wouldn't take the wonders of modern science to figure out whether the dead man had passed this way. Even if he hadn't left anything of himself behind, the spillway would have left a lot of splinters in him.

I stuck close to the side of the trough and crab-walked down the slope as far as the footbridge. A straightforward enough little bridge, nothing fancy. Solid support beams and a waist-high railing. I hauled myself back up to the path, slithering and scrambling, and returned to Artie's house. The clay had begun to harden on my pants, turning them into a sculpture that cracked with every step. I was chilled. My nose was running and my throat hurt. Artie was sitting on his front steps waiting for me. He jumped up.

"Well?" he said hopefully.

"It wouldn't be hard to kill someone up there and get away without being seen."

"That's right!" he hooted. "That's what I say. So why would a killer run around at the bottom of the canyon yelling so everyone could see him?"

"I don't know about the yelling," I said, "but they might think he went down to the ditch to see if the man was really dead." Artie snorted. "I need," I continued, "some dry pants. Got anything I can wear?"

"Oh, sure. Come on in."

The picture had changed since I'd been in the house before. The dog was sleeping peacefully on the living room floor. Jennifer was sitting alone in the kitchen drinking coffee. "Julia's taking a nap," she explained. "So's Pete." Since the dog's name was

Berkeley, I figured Pete must be the kid.

Artie tiptoed into his bedroom and returned carrying a pair of ratty jeans. I changed in the bathroom. My pants peeled off well enough, but the mud that cracked off them lay in little pieces all over the floor. I found a sponge and wiped up the mess, shook the pants over the bathtub, and cleaned that up, too.

Artie's pants were short in the leg by about four inches, but they covered the rest of me okay. I rolled up my own and carried them out to the kitchen. He was pouring coffee. He took one look at me in his jeans, took mine out of my hand, and tossed them in the washer. I sat down to drink my coffee.

"When you finish that," he said, "you've got an appointment. With the woman who identified Alan. House alongside the stairway, across the canyon. Probably shortest to take the bridge and the eastern path. It's called Hummingbird Lane."

"You're kidding."

He got a little defensive. "We get a lot of hummingbirds up here. Anyway, she thinks you're a reporter. I hope you don't mind, but I thought we should get started right away."

I sipped at the coffee and glared at my friend. "Fine. It's always so hard to get started on a new job."

4

A brass gong about ten inches in diameter hung suspended by two lengths of chain from the low-sloping eaves over the doorway. The hardwood mallet with brass trim hanging nearby looked like a companion piece, so, feeling like the opener in a J. Arthur Rank movie, I used it to give the gong a solid whack. The noise bounced and echoed and lingered in the amphitheater of the canyon. I was wondering how Carlota Bowman's neighbors liked her doorbell when she opened the door.

"Mr. Samson?" she queried.

"Ms. Bowman?"

"Do come in."

14

She was wearing a purple silk wrapper and three-inch pumps. The purple went well with her shoulder-length gray hair. The gray must have been premature because her face hadn't seen more than thirty-five years. I followed her into the house and I couldn't help but watch her walking ahead of me. She was tall and thin and she moved her hips in a way that, if it developed naturally at all, developed in bed.

I felt a little gauche and underdressed in my pedal-pusher length jeans.

The entry door led directly into a small, fastidious kitchen, complete with the requisite butcher block and expensive cookware displayed on the wall beside the stove. I followed her through another doorway into a large living room that looked as if even more money had been spent on it. Everything was in primary colors except the wood.

At the end nearest the kitchen was a round Victorian oak dining table. A baby grand piano squatted dramatically at the far side of the room near the French doors leading onto a deck. There was a bookcase, but it held stereo equipment and a lot of artsy-craftsy items and very few books. The paneled wall across from the stereo was a gallery of clustered drawings and paintings, all of them originals, all abstract or at least not easily recognizable, and all vaguely sexual. I couldn't read the signature. On the same wall, as part of a composition of rectangles, was a full-length mirror. Another mirror, also full-length, hung on the wall with the French doors, near the piano, and next to the mirror was a single painting, about two feet by three. It was a portrait of a dark-haired woman.

Bowman waved her hand at a yellow corduroy loveseat and I sat.

"Would you like a glass of wine, Mr. Samson?"

I said I thought that would be nice. She opened a cabinet under the shelf that housed the stereo turntable and pulled out a cut-glass decanter and two discount store wineglasses. A chink in the perfection. I guessed that she either had a lot of parties or used up a lot of wineglasses herself.

She brought me a glass and sat down facing me in an oak rocker.

I took a sip. Good California burgundy, plain but honest. I didn't recognize the vineyard or the vintage year, but then I never can.

"So, Mr. Samson, you work for Artie Perrine's magazine?"

I explained that I was not regularly employed but free-lanced from time to time. I didn't say what I was not regularly employed at or what it was I did free-lance. "And," I said, "I'm following up on a piece about the company this Smith—that was his name, the dead man you found—the company he worked for. So I need information about his death." I couldn't tell whether she believed me or not, so I added a little something. "And of course if I can learn anything that might, well, clear up the uh . . . ."

The woman wrinkled her forehead thoughtfully, sipped at her wine, and nodded.

"Yes," she said. "Of course." She pursed her lips and sucked in her cheeks. She had more facial twitches than a junky. "I can tell you, basically, what I told the police." She got up and sashayed to the piano, leaning against it chanteuse fashion. "I heard someone shout, I went out on the deck, I saw that young man running up the path. Then I went down the stairs and found . . . it."

I took her through the scene, step by step, slowly. It was pretty entertaining. She acted the whole thing out for me, complete with gestures. The first scene was Carlota Bowman pouring herself another glass of wine. I stayed with the half glass I still had.

She strode to the mirror near the piano and stood facing it, wineglass held at shoulder level. "I was courting a creative spark, a spark I had been trying all morning to coax into flame." Her eyes, reflected in the mirror, dared me to understand. I nodded to show that I did. "I was standing here, at this mirror." She whirled to face me, a drop of wine slopping onto the polished floor. "A mirror is a frame. A frame of the image in the film of my visual life. I have many mirrors."

"Of course," I said.

She turned back to the mirror and struck a new pose—cinema queen, 1939—gazing into her own eyes. "And then I heard the shout."

Because the winter had been a particularly wet one, her first thought was that there was a mud slide, danger of some sort. She had stepped out on the deck and looked down. Here, for my benefit, she threw open the French doors and stepped outside. I went with her. She transferred her wineglass to her left hand and pointed with her right, indicating the area somewhere around the bottom of the steps.

"He was there, running. And he ran up that way." She waved at the path that led up to Artie's house.

She had called out to the man, she said, but he hadn't turned around or answered.

"It was cold outside," she said. I could well imagine that it was. Now, in late afternoon, the fog was wrapping itself around the tops of the redwoods. The giant trees, which even in high summer must have shadowed most of the canyon homes most of the time, were dripping with damp.

Carlota continued. "I came back inside and waited." She led me back into the house.

"Waited?"

"Well, there are other houses down there. I thought surely someone else had heard or seen the man. So I waited. But nothing happened," she said, with just a touch of the sulks in her voice. "No one was doing anything. I began to worry. My foundation is not all that it should be. With the ditch so full and the clay so saturated—well, one never knows."

In preparation for the next scene, she poured another glass of wine. Then she went to a living room closet and got her coat. I held her wineglass while she thrust her arms through the sleeves. We went out the kitchen door to the landing.

She had gone down ten steps or so, she said, to see what she could see. We descended carefully. The steps were worn redwood, slick with wetness and somewhat in need of repair. "I couldn't see anything from here. Not a thing." We descended farther. About thirty steps from the bottom, she paused. "I stopped here to listen, but I couldn't hear anything. Except the water."

She beckoned me on and we went all the way to the bottom, where three planks, nailed to the bottom step and staked into the ground on the other side of the ditch, formed a makeshift bridge.

A few feet to the left of the planking, the stream disappeared into a narrow, brush-screened tunnel the water had cut beneath the surface rock, undoubtedly, I thought, undermining the entire canyon. Carlota and I stood on the second step. She pointed toward the tunnel opening, where the foam slopped over the edges of the ditch and forced its way through the battered branches and exposed roots of the tough native fuchsias.

"It was caught in those branches there."

"That must have been terrible for you," I said.

"Not at first." She laughed madly, lurching a bit and clutching the stairway rail. "At first I thought it was a joke. There are some very macabre people living in this canyon, you know." She laughed again. "I told him to get up and come out of there. Of course he didn't." She drained her wineglass and we plodded back up the stairs. I accepted another half glass of wine when she took her next refill.

"Then what did you do?"

"Well, I've never found a body before. So I wasn't sure what to do about it." She shuddered and frowned. "I decided to call Charles—up there." She pointed upward. I remembered noticing a house behind and above hers, on the up-side of the path, and another one slightly beyond that. Charles, she said, had told her to call the sheriff.

"God, I thought the least he could do was call, or help me call. I was, of course, totally unnerved. He didn't get out of bed at all until the sheriff's men were coming up to see me. I was alone, all that time. It must have been at least fifteen minutes."

Now we were getting to the important part. "About your identification of the man, the one you saw running. Are you absolutely sure it was Artie Perrine's nephew Alan?" Alan had already admitted he had been down there, but maybe someone else had been there, too.

"Oh, yes," she insisted. "It was he." She said "It was he" as though she were very much aware that she was speaking correctly. Occasionally, throughout our conversation, she had tossed in a touch of what sounded like an English accent. I figured she was

18

probably from a small town in Indiana. Maybe Ohio. I was having a hard time lasting through this session with her. Part of the increasing, sandpapery irritation I was feeling came from the confusing signals I was getting from her. They kept leaping out of her skin, sexual signals of some kind. But they didn't quite hit me, if I was, indeed, the target. She just seemed to pop open every now and again like a full seed pod, shooting off in all directions. I got up from the loveseat and strolled around the room, wondering what it would feel like if one of the seeds hit me by accident. Carlota, meanwhile, was making her way, a little clumsily, back toward the decanter. I shook my head when she waved the thing at me.

"Yes," she was repeating, "I'm sure it was he. I'm sorry if this has created difficulty for Mr. Perrine, but the boy shouldn't have lied to the police." I agreed with her. I was standing in front of the artfully arranged exhibit of paintings, wondering if she'd seen anything down there besides Alan and the body, wondering if she would have noticed anything else if there'd been something else to see. How early had she started drinking?

"I see you're enjoying our artwork," she said.

"Oh, yes. Very good. I can't make out the signature."

"Nona Delvecchio." She said the name as if it had special significance. I've been to a few art shows here and there, and I don't think I'm a complete moron when it comes to painting, but I'd never heard of the woman.

"Local?"

"Very." She flashed a crooked smile. "She lives here with me." Carlota pointed at the portrait near the piano. "That's a self-portrait."

I took another look. Dark hair, full lips, angry eyes. "Has she had many shows?" I was just making conversation while I thought about what else I could ask this woman, but she wasn't pleased with the question.

"Not many. It isn't easy, you know, to get recognition."

"I understand that," I said reassuringly. "Was she here when you found the body?"

"No. As I said, I was alone. Nona was at work. She's here

now, but she's painting." She waved vaguely toward a door in the living room wall. "In her studio."

"Who plays the piano?"

"I do." She warmed up again.

"That's wonderful," I said. "Professionally?"

Another wrong move. I was trying to keep her on my side, but paying occupations seemed to be a sore point with her. The room had chilled again.

"I teach. But primarily I am a filmmaker."

I nodded. "It isn't easy to get recognition."

She lifted her chin. She was still standing near the decanter, and stretched out an arm to pull a magazine off the bookshelf. She waved it at me.

"But I'm about to get some," she said. "In this."

I walked over to look at what she was holding. It was a slick little item called *The Marin Journal of the Arts*. A monthly. I cocked my head inquiringly.

"They are going to print a review of my films. In fact, the critic is stopping in to see me later this afternoon."

I was impressed. "Where are they showing?"

"They are being shown twice this month at the film society in Mill Valley."

"That's terrific," I said. "I'll go to see them." I didn't really think I would.

"Yes," she said. But she was not focusing on me, she was frowning at the journal. The pod wasn't popping anymore. She was getting tired of having me around. I thought I'd better get in a quick question or two before she fell asleep or wandered off. She was a little put out when I asked her if she was sure she hadn't seen anything else down around the ditch that morning. She was sure she hadn't. I asked if I could come and talk to her again if I needed to. She wrinkled up her forehead, looked nervous, and said that would be all right. I didn't think the nervous look—or any other of her looks, for that matter—had much significance.

She escorted me to the kitchen door, and I made my way back along Hummingbird Lane, across the bridge, and up the path to Artie's.

He was waiting for me with more coffee, and settled us cosily at the kitchen table. Jennifer joined us, accepted a cup, and gazed pathetically at me.

"Well?" he asked.

I threw another question back at him. "Did you talk to the lawyer?"

"Couldn't reach him. But I did leave a note for Charlie."

"Another witness?"

"Oh, no. No, didn't I tell you he's got a spare room he might be willing to rent? He's a neighbor."

I sipped my coffee. It cut through the coat of wine on my tongue. Carlota had mentioned someone named Charles.

"See," Artie continued, "I figured you wouldn't want to be running back and forth across the bay all the time, and it would be more convenient for you to stay over here when you're working late on the case."

I thought that was very considerate of him, and I told him so.

"You should be able to wrap things up faster that way, and I figure we'll break even by saving on your mileage and restaurant meals and things. Unless, of course, the police find the real killer right away and stop badgering Alan. Then we won't need you."

"Meals? Saving on meals?"

"Sure. You can just plug in a hot plate over there, or come here for lunch. Maybe you could even stay there tonight. If he comes home and sees the note. Or we could put you some-where . . ." he looked around the kitchen.

"No," I said quickly. "That's okay. I've got to get back to the East Bay tonight. I'll come over tomorrow. With my own car."

"Okay." He grinned happily. "But stay for dinner. To seal our bargain."

I stayed for dinner, even though he was the only one who seemed to be getting a bargain.

5

It was after nine when I pulled up in front of my house. The flatlands of Oakland looked awfully damned flat and desolate after Foothill Canyon. Houses all on the same level. Streets. I felt deprived and tried to concentrate on the pluses. Occasionally, even in winter, my yard dried out. I didn't have to stumble down a clay and rock incline or a hundred shaky wooden steps to go to the grocery store. Not to mention going up again.

Also, I had never found a corpse in my front yard. Not yet, anyway.

Rosie's light was on, so I knocked. She and Alice were alone, and she invited me in. Rosie was wearing her favorite at-home outfit: cutoffs, cowboy boots, and Gertrude Stein T-shirt. I handed her her truck keys, she handed me a beer. Now, I do try to control my intake of beer, because in the past couple of years what used to be normal amounts of food and drink have begun to create abnormal conditions in my midsection. Somehow, my spare tire had become more easily inflatable. But my hesitation was brief. I figured that if I was going to spend the next couple of weeks hiking around in nature I could probably afford a few more calories.

I sat down in Rosie's one easy chair, and she sat on her bed, leaning back against the giant pillow that served as a bolster. I began to tell her about my new case. As she listened she grew very still. The look she was giving me could have been misinterpreted as seductive if it had come from another woman, or, more to the point, if the look had been directed by Rosie at another woman. But she was looking at me, her old buddy, and I knew the speculative gleam in her eye was professional.

She'd worked with me once before, on the case of the previous fall, and had come up with some important leads by infiltrating a right-wing campus group. She'd nearly gotten her neck broken in the process, but it looked like old danger hadn't discouraged her from the prospect of new adventure.

Maybe the lack of pay would discourage her, though. She'd gotten a percentage of a nice fee last time for a few days' work.

She'd get a percentage of nothing this time, and I didn't think Artie'd be willing to cover expenses for two. I could get by—I had the rent she paid for the cottage, another small piece of income from a trust fund my mother had set up for me before she died, and a few thousand left over from the last job. Rosie had only what she earned week to week, and maybe a little in the bank. I told her there was no money in it.

She grinned at me. "So? I don't have anything much to do for the next couple of weeks, anyway."

"I thought you had a basement to finish."

"Not until April."

"What about that addition you were telling me about?"

"After the basement."

I explained about the expenses. She told me she could buy her own lunch.

I thought of something else. "Artie's going to try to get me a room over there so I won't have to travel back and forth all the time. Got any friends in Mill Valley?"

She got up to get us both another beer. "I used to," she snapped, "but it doesn't matter. Alice and I can commute." She handed me my beer and put hers down on the table beside my chair. She didn't sit down again, but stood over me, glaring. Now Rosie's not tall. Only about five foot five. And she's not muscular. And she's not mean. But she's got one hell of a powerful personality. And I knew what she was thinking.

"What is this, anyway?" she wanted to know. "Don't you want my help?"

"Of course I do, you know—"

"Are you pulling that protective male shit on me again, Jake?"

"Jesus, Rosie—"

"I thought so." She picked up her beer and sat down on the bed. "Look, you know I can take care of myself. I'm not talking about following you around every damn day. It's your case. But there may be some angle you'll want me to handle, and if there is, I'd be interested. Do you want me to help or not?" The glare had softened a little, but not much.

"Yeah. I do. And I'm not being . . . careful . . . because you're a woman. It's because you're my friend."

She laughed at me. "Drink your beer, friend."

"Yes, ma'am."

"Okay, so tell me more. What about the nephew? Could he have done it?"

I shrugged. "I don't know and I haven't met the kid."

"He sounds like a real jerk. Screaming and running away and lying to the sheriff. What about the woman who saw him running away? Is she a good witness? Is she nearsighted? Did she see anything else?"

I laughed. "I think you'll have to meet her."

Rosie sipped at her beer and nestled a little deeper into the pillow. She was looking pleased. "This is really going to be fun," she said. "Maybe as much fun as the last time."

"Maybe," I agreed. "At least this time it will be far enough away from home so we can escape if we have to."

"Oh, come on. You know it's fun."

I shook my head. "Maybe. But I'm not crazy about risking my life. Not for free, anyway. Let's not forget, in the midst of all this fun, that whoever killed the guy is a killer."

"We can handle it," she said confidently. "Oh, you're not going to need my truck tomorrow, are you?"

"They swear my car will be ready in the morning, so maybe not. Why?"

"I've got a couple of estimates to do in the next day or so. By then you should have a better handle on things, so we can figure out the plan of attack."

Somebody very short scratched on the door about a foot above the threshold. My cats had found me. I got up and let them in. Ignoring me, they said hello to Alice, then to Rosie. The implication was clear. I had been gone for several hours more than what they thought was appropriate. They were wondering if Rosie or Alice knew where I might be, and who was this tall stranger standing near the door, anyway?

"I think I've just been collected," I said. "See you in the morning. Come on, you two." The cats looked at me with sudden recognition and followed me out the door.

24

After slapping some gooey, expensive food in their dishes, I checked my answering machine. A message from Artie that Alan was home but felt as though he were still under suspicion. A message from my father that said I could call any time before midnight, his time. That gave me fifteen minutes. I hoped nothing was wrong. Usually, since he calls collect "just to say hello," he leaves no messages. The man doesn't call collect from Chicago because he's poor, but because he's devious. He says if I can afford to accept a long-distance call, he knows I'm not starving to death.

Anyway, I figured I'd better call him, if only to let him know I was going to be in and out for a while. I dialed his number.

"Yeah?" That was the way he answered the phone.

"Hello, pa."

"Oh, so there you are."

"Yeah. Is everything all right?"

"What's not to be all right?"

"Good. So, you called?"

"Sure I called. Two nights. I tried to call Thursday, too, but I didn't talk to your machine." Thursday night I'd had a date in Berkeley with my close friend Iris. "What's the matter, you're not living at home?"

I explained that I'd been kind of busy, and that I might not be home much for the next couple of weeks because I'd be spending a lot of time in Marin County, across the bay. Working.

"A job? You're sleeping at a job?"

"I work late sometimes, it's a long drive back here."

He grunted. "So, you've got a *nafke*. So what's the big deal?"

"Pa," I said, laughing, "I'm working. I'm not staying with a woman."

"Working, huh? What kind of work this time?"

"Same as last time. The magazine." That was a mistake.

"So how come I never saw the write-up you did before? You're working for a magazine and you don't write anything? Are you ashamed to show it to me?"

I wasn't about to tell him I was investigating a murder. He had nearly disowned me when I'd joined the Chicago police force. When I quit doing that in favor of wandering around California,

25

he was sure I had become a dope fiend. He'd been relieved, in recent years, that I was at least staying at the same address for a while. He's a pain in the ass but I love him and would rather he didn't worry.

"Mostly I just do the research, pa. There's not much to show for that."

There was a brief silence while he decided to drop the job subject. "Listen, your stepmother and I, we're thinking of maybe coming out and visiting around the end of the year. She's got a niece someplace out there, too, we can kill two birds."

"Yeah? That would be terrific."

"Maybe the niece isn't married, you could meet her."

"Sure. Where does she live?"

"Someplace out there. I'll have to ask your stepmother."

She took the receiver from him. "Hello, Jake." "Hi, Eva." I'm fond of Eva. I was glad when my father remarried, some ten years after the death of my mother, because he was a man who needed to be married, needed to have someone to love. He and Eva were close, and, I thought sometimes, almost too much alike. The two of them together could be overwhelming. "Listen," she said, "it's a good thing you called back, he almost called that friend of yours, that Rosie. Your tenant."

A couple of years before, I'd given them Rosie's number for emergency messages. They'd used it once when I'd spent two weeks at Tahoe without calling them.

"She's still there, the tenant? What was her last name again?"

"Yeah, she's still here. Her name is Vicente."

"Such a nice girl. She's good-looking?"

"Very."

"And smart?"

"Yes."

"You're such good friends, maybe you should get married? A forty-year-old man, it's time again. An Italian's not so bad."

"I'm thirty-nine."

She snorted. "Thirty-nine. Like Jack Benny." Then she handed the phone back to my father.

"So? You're going back to this job tomorrow?"

"That's right, don't expect to get me at home for a while,

okay? I'll give you a call in a week or two."

"Okay, okay. Listen, I'm going to say goodbye. Your stepmother's got something she wants to say before we hang up."

"Jakey?"

"Uh huh."

"I mean it. You should think about the Italian. If you got married, you wouldn't have to run to *nafkes* fifty miles away."

"I'll consider it," I told her. "Goodbye, Eva."

"Goodbye, Jake."

6

Alan sat slumped forward on Artie's couch, elbows resting on his thighs, wrists dangling, brown eyes peering out at me through a lock of straight brown hair that hung to his eyebrows. Everything about him drooped: his mouth, his hair, his hands. He was pale and he looked sick and scared.

I hadn't been able to get back to Marin until midafternoon, because it took that long for my mechanic to actually finish working on the Chevy. Neither Alan nor Artie had gone to work, so everyone was waiting for me. Alan, Artie, Julia, Jennifer, Pete, and Berkeley. The twelve-year-old, Mike, had gone to school, probably so he could tell all his friends about the murder.

He was going to be upset when he got home. He'd missed seeing a whole new piece of the action. So had I. Sergeant Ricci had come by around noon to visit Alan again. Just a few more questions. Because the police had found out about Alan's fight with Smith. I managed to drag Alan away from his family for a private talk in the bedroom.

He was sulky. "I don't know why they don't leave me alone. Can you imagine, someone actually told them about that stupid fight?"

"Well, you did lie to them. Maybe you should have told them about the argument before they heard it from someone else. On top of the lies—"

"Look, I know it was dumb, lying that way. But I've explained all that to them, about working for Artie. And shit, I panicked. Who wouldn't?"

I didn't know who wouldn't, I only knew that he had.

"And how was I supposed to know someone saw me? She says she yelled at me, but there was this roaring in my ears, you know? I thought I was having a stroke or something. How could I hear anyone?"

So he'd holed up in Artie's house and hoped for the best, which he hadn't gotten.

"It was terrible, Jake. I've never been in jail. It was an unbelievably brutalizing experience. As a journalist, I guess it's something I should know about, but even so . . ."

"Alan," I said, "this is not Chicago. This is not New York. This is not even Des Moines. Sitting out a few hours of questioning in the for-Christ's-sake Marin County Civic Center in a Frank Lloyd Wright building with a view of the hills is not exactly like ten years on Devil's Island."

He raised his chin a bit and actually stuck out his lower lip.

"Listen, Samson," he said—I wasn't Jake anymore—"I saw some pretty hard cases going in and out of there."

I didn't exactly dislike the kid, and I hoped he'd be able to go through an entire lifetime of privilege and security, but I thought maybe he needed a couple of kicks into the real world where being a nice kid wasn't protection against death, disease, and violence.

"Did you get raped in the toilet during a coffee break?" I asked.

He turned red, jumped up, and paced, first away from me and then back again.

"Listen, I don't need you to patronize me. I know a few things, too, you know." I nodded. "And one of the things I know is that I don't need the help of a middle-aged smartass."

I smiled at him. "I'm not helping you. I'm helping Artie. And I'm not helping anybody by sitting here and listening to your George Raft fantasies." He looked puzzled, and I realized that he wasn't sure who George Raft might be. But he didn't admit it. I continued.

"The first thing I want to know is what you saw when you found the body."

28

He sat down again, narrowed his eyes at me so I wouldn't think he was giving in too easily, and told me.

"Okay. I was just walking around, you know? It was kind of a nice morning. It wasn't raining or anything. So I walked down the path. Thought I'd take a look around the canyon, maybe walk down the road a mile or so. But I noticed this thing flopping around in the ditch, stuck in the brush, so I went over there. It looked like a body, but I figured it couldn't be, so I poked at it with a branch and it turned over to where I could see his face. I recognized him and got sick and scared and ran away. I guess I yelled, too."

"Did you see the wound? A weapon of any kind?" He shook his head. "This fight you had with the guy. What was that about? And when was it?"

He ran his fingers through his hair, brushing back the forelock. It fell right back down again. "It was about his crummy company, Jake." I was Jake again. "You wouldn't believe the way they run things around there. And he was so self-righteous, like they weren't running a scam at all. Maybe I should fill you in a little on the company itself?"

That sounded like a good idea. Since I was working on the assumption that Alan hadn't killed the man, I had to start looking at the victim's life and involvements. "Sure," I said. "Tell me about it. Start with the kind of work you've been doing."

Alan explained that he was an underling in what the company called the communications department. The department produced all the printed materials for the salespeople, he said, and also worked on, and sometimes created, course material.

"You create courses?" I asked. He nodded. "And people buy them and study them by mail? And get diplomas?"

"Yes, except for the high school courses. They're just studying those so they can pass high school equivalency tests where they live."

"And you just kind of—write these courses?" The word "credentials" came to mind. I said it out loud. Alan laughed bitterly.

"Mr. Bowen, he's the president of the company, he got a degree in education back in the forties sometime. Smith used to be a teacher, too. Then there's the rest of the faculty. Some old woman who used to teach fifth grade, a couple of moonlighting high school teachers, a CPA for the accounting course, and a lawyer for the business law. They're all on some kind of retainer. There's a faculty office in the building, but I know some of them don't live around here and I've never seen anyone in that office. When the students send in their course work it gets shipped back out again to the faculty, for corrections. That's mostly all they do, except they're supposed to write any new course material, or at least act as consultants on it. Sometimes Chloe writes to them with questions."

"Who's Chloe?"

"My boss. The manager of the department. She's a burnt-out ex–wire service reporter. About your age."

"So that's what you were investigating? Bad courses?"

"Well, that too. But there's something wrong with the way they're selling the stuff. Kickbacks or something. At least Artie thinks so."

"Yeah, he mentioned something about that. Is that what Smith did? Sales?"

"No. He was academic vice-president."

"So," I said, getting back to my original question, "what was the fight about?"

Alan's first assignment, it turned out, had been to write some kind of study materials to go along with the first two chapters of a history book used in one of the high school courses. He'd churned out the stuff and turned it in to his boss. She had done a little editing and sent it on to Smith, who was her boss. Smith had returned it the next day, while Alan was in her office. Alan asked Smith why his work hadn't been sent to the history teacher. Smith had snubbed him. Despite the manager's warning looks, Alan had kept pushing. In a hurry, I guessed, to get his exposé and get out.

"I asked him if the faculty ever saw the courses before they were printed. He got really pissed off and told me I was 'maligning a fine old company' and I'd better watch myself or I'd lose my job."

"When was all this?"

"Right around the end of the week. Thursday, I think."

30

"And the only witness was your boss?"

"Not exactly. Her door was open. Anyone in the writers' room could have heard. And the receptionist. Maybe even the artists."

I stood up. "Anything else you want to tell me?"

He shook his head. "I don't know. I can't think of anything."

"Okay, relax, Alan. I don't think you've got a real problem." As we walked out I added, "What do you think Smith might have been doing in the canyon?"

"Well, how would I know? I don't think he was looking for me. Sometimes people come here just to walk around. It's a pretty place."

Artie's son Mike was home from school and eating an apple. Jennifer was lying on the couch, the baby sleeping beside her. Julia was doing something in the kitchen. I've never known her to be a particularly domestic woman, so I guessed she was still avoiding the issue of Alan. Artie and Alan and I went out on the deck, with Mike trailing along. We leaned against various parts of the railing and looked at each other.

"The lawyer," Artie said, "says he doesn't see why he should have to repeat things to you he's already told me. So he said you should talk to me."

I swallowed a retort. "Okay," I said. "Does anyone know what Smith was doing here? Where did he live?"

"I don't know why he was here. But he only lived a couple of miles away, closer to town." I gathered that he meant downtown Mill Valley, not San Francisco.

"And what about the murder weapon?"

"He was stabbed."

"With an icepick?" I was getting irritable and I let it show. "With a butcher knife? With a nail file?"

Artie looked helpless and I felt a little sorry for him. But I asked him another question anyway. "When was he killed?"

"I don't know. I guess I just assumed it was in the morning." He was getting embarrassed.

"Forget it," I soothed. "You just don't know what questions to ask. That's why I'm here."

Mike perked up. "You a P.I., Jake?"

31

"No, I'm just helping out." I took out the little notebook I'd stuck in my hip pocket that morning. "What's the lawyer's name?"

"Marty Chandler." He gave me his phone number. Alan was standing there pretending none of this had anything to do with him. I went back in the house to call the lawyer. Unfortunately, I was told, he was not in the office. I left a message for him to call me at Artie's number.

Out on the deck again, Artie was chatting aimlessly with Alan and Mike. Probably trying to take some of the pressure off. Just another ordinary day.

"Yeah," Mike was saying. "I stuck the note on the bulletin board in the kitchen last week, but I kind of forgot to mention it."

"That's okay," his dad said. "I kind of forgot to notice the bulletin board. Did he say what it was?"

"Just some tool or something of yours he had."

Artie smiled at me cheerfully. "Neighbors. Always borrowing something."

I grunted. My throat was getting sore again. I told him about the message I'd left at Chandler's office. And speaking of neighbors, I said, I wanted to sit down with him or Julia and get some background on some of the people who lived in the canyon. Besides Carlota Bowman.

"Uh huh. You'll meet Charlie today. He's the one with the room to rent. He called to let me know he'll be home around five and I should bring you over then. He wants to meet you."

"Does he want references?"

Artie didn't bother to answer that question. "And you'll have a perfect opportunity to meet the rest of them tomorrow night at the meeting." I questioned him with one weary eyebrow. "It's a neighborhood meeting. For the canyon. At Charlie's."

"About the murder?"

He was patient with me. "No, Jake, we have these meetings every so often to work on canyon problems. We have an agenda and everything. And Charlie's got a hot tub."

I laughed. "You meet in the hot tub?" I thought I was joking, but Artie replied, a little defensively, "Well, yes. In a way."

7

"It's over there, Charlie's place," Artie said, pointing across the canyon. I lined my eyes up with his index finger.

"The one with the arch? At the top of the stairs?" It was the house just above Carlota's.

"Yeah. You just cross that bridge and follow the path. It's the one with the sagging gutter. His door's only about twenty steps up from the path."

Or, I thought, about a hundred steps from the floor of the canyon.

I had an hour before Charlie got home. I used it to track down the poker regulars and tell them that the Tuesday night game was canceled for this week.

A little after five Charlie called and said we were welcome to come over. We crossed the bridge and followed the path, only this time I checked out the house a little more carefully. The Asian-looking arch across the bottom step was made of two vertical six-by-sixes and a couple of flat pieces nailed across to form the top, one at the front of the verticals and one at the back. The horizontal boards were jigsawed in a pagoda roof shape. A deck was over our heads. Tucked under it, just above the path, was a small room. The under-the-deck room had its own entrance. Twenty-five steps above the path was the entrance to the house itself, swathed in blackberry and ivy, fresh growth from the passing winter sprouting from the stumps of last year's surgery.

To the left of the entry door was a life-sized statue of a male nude in soft stone.

Artie knocked and Charlie opened the door. He was huge, maybe six foot three and thick in chest, shoulders, and neck. He glared at me and I damned near backed off the deck until I realized the look was one he probably would describe as a shrewd piercing gaze.

"Come on in," he said softly, and we entered the living room. It sloped enough so that a marble placed at the upper end would shoot right down to the lower end, where a sliding glass door led out onto the deck. Not one of the four corners of the room looked like a true right angle. The ancient brick fireplace directly across from the entry looked tilted, but I decided that was because it was vertical and the floor was not horizontal.

The slightly dizzying effect of stepping into a house out of square was the first thing I noticed. The second thing was the art on the walls. It matched the nude on the deck. Naked males everywhere, sitting around in their frames.

Once I got past all that, I noticed the tiny, neat kitchen at the upper end of the living room, the door from the living room to the bedroom, and a steep and narrow flight of steps that led up alongside the kitchen to what was probably some sort of attic room. I also noticed that the view from every window was green and beautiful. The rain had stopped but a damp smell clung to the interior of the house. Like most of the old houses in these canyons, this one had probably been a summer cottage owned by a family living in San Francisco, back in the days when the only way to get to the wilds of Marin County was by ferry boat.

"Nice place you've got here," I said.

"Thanks," Charlie rumbled. He brushed a shock of black hair back from his forehead and smiled proudly. He had small violet eyes that crinkled when he smiled, a large crooked nose, and deep lines from nostril to chin. I guessed his age at somewhere around forty-five. He was a natural for the part of the aging town marshal forced to face the young gunslinger, and he dressed for the part in a worn blue workshirt, nearly new Levi's, and cowboy boots. The pointy kind.

He got right down to it. "How long would you need the room for?" he asked Artie.

"Can't tell—maybe a couple of days, maybe a month. What's your monthly rate?"

"Well, I've never rented it out before. Let's say two hundred dollars."

Artie rolled his eyes. "Let's take a look at this sultan's palace," he said.

Charlie led us back down the steps to the door under the deck, produced a key, and showed us in.

The room was approximately ten by twenty and sparsely fur-

34

nished, with a cot at the far end and a long work table shoved up against three windows that pierced the front wall. In the corner to the left of the door was a small potbelly stove. Its chimney went through the wall, and, I presumed, up from there. I also presumed it rose to well above deck level. The floor was flowered linoleum, with a lot of little dribbles and mounds of crumbly white stuff all over it. I knelt down to rub some between my fingers.

"Plaster?" I asked, looking up at the ceiling to see if more of it was about to fall.

"Of paris," Charlie answered. "The legacy of George. A sculptor." He gestured toward the ceiling, and I realized he was pointing to the nude figure on the deck above. "He left me. And he didn't even clean up after himself."

I nodded sympathetically, and Artie muttered something that sounded like, "Yeah, that's tough."

"Two hundred a month?" I said, looking around the room. I could see black smudges of mildew along the back wall. The dampness I'd felt in the house above was more pronounced here.

"I'd clean it up for you," Charlie offered. "Put in a little chest of drawers. I've got an old chemical toilet you can use. We can share the shower upstairs."

"How much off if he uses the shower at my house?" Artie wanted to know. I wandered out the door and left them to their negotiations. The room was okay for my purposes, even if I had to use it for a couple of weeks. I didn't plan to spend all my nights there anyway. For one thing, I had a date later that week over in the East Bay.

The negotiations were concluded and the two men joined me outside. It had been resolved that I would use Artie's shower. Charlie handed me a key to the room and promised, again, to clean up the residue of George.

"Move in any time," he said.

"You're going to move in tonight, aren't you?" Artie whined.

"Okay. Sure. I'll just run back home and get some clothes and take care of some odds and ends, then I'll come back tonight. If anything happens I need to know about, between now and then, just leave a note on the door."

He nodded gratefully.

I drove back to Oakland and took care of my odds and ends. Like a nice quiet dinner at home, an hour's soak in the tub, and some conversation with Tigris and Euphrates. I also called a neighbor who said, sure, he'd be glad to take care of the cats if neither Rosie nor I could get back to do it. We arranged a signal. I would hang a towel on the fence when I was at home. And I left a note for Rosie telling her about the hot tub community meeting, something I was sure she wouldn't want to miss. Then I tossed some essentials in an airline bag and headed back across the bridge.

I got back to the canyon about nine-thirty, ready to do a little creative thinking about my plan of action. The single street lamp attached to the utility pole in the parking area showed that most of the canyon's residents, or at least most of their cars, were home. I drove up the road, out of the circle of tree-shadowed light, and parked alongside the ditch where Smith had come to rest.

Then I picked my way across the slippery planks that spanned the ditch, tested the handrail gingerly for slimy travelers, and began pulling myself up the stairs through the sweet-smelling mist. Here and there, visible through the trees at various levels of canyon along various paths, lamplight made squares of brightness where houses perched. Music—Haydn, I thought—drifted softly from Carlota's stereo.

I had nearly reached the fuzzy-edged patch of fog yellowed by the coach lamp when I heard Carlota's voice rising above the Haydn.

"But I *want* to. You used to beg me to play for you."

"Not when you were drunk, Carlota. Never when you were drunk. You can't do *anything* right when you're drunk." The voice, I assumed it was Nona's, rose dangerously at her last repetition of the word "drunk."

"I am *not* . . ." I passed their deck, took the next few steps as quickly as I could, and escaped up the path to my little nest below Charlie's house.

A cold, damp little nest. Charlie had indeed cleaned up. He'd placed the chemical toilet in the near right-hand corner, and he'd left me fuel for the stove, too. I jammed some crumpled newspaper, kindling, and a couple of chunks of oak into the potbelly, threw in a match, left the hatch open so I could see the fire and know I was getting warm, and pulled the work table closer to the heat. Then I got out my notebook, spread out a couple of sheets of paper, and began outlining my sparse and inconclusive knowledge about the dead man and the people who might have wanted to kill him. I set up three categories: Bright Future, family, and canyon. Those were the starting places. If I talked to the people he worked with, his family, and the people who lived where he had died, I should come up with some leads. If the killer was someone who even knew the man.

The stove warmed the small room. The mist slid in streamers across the window. If Carlota and Nona were still arguing, I couldn't hear them. Charlie wasn't wearing his cowboy boots, and even his steps across the living room over my head were soft. I was getting some good work done, planning what I like to think of as my interviews, when I heard what sounded like firecrackers, or maybe the cracking of a tree limb. Once, twice. Crack, crack. Or maybe a small handgun. The sound seemed to come from across the canyon, up above Artie's house, but it was hard to tell the source. Sound echoes and dances in a canyon. I listened. I heard Charlie yell, "Oh, shit." Crack, crack. I was sure now that someone was firing a gun. I dropped my pen and crossed the room, opening my door cautiously. Crack.

"Goddamn trees!" Crack, crack, crack. "Goddamn rotten trees!" The bellowing voice, and the shots, were definitely coming from across the canyon and up at the top of Artie's path. I remembered there was another house up there. I slipped out of my room and up the steps.

Charlie answered my frantic knocking by waving me in the door. He was holding the phone and dialing. "Good," I said. "Get the police. Yes." He waited while the phone rang at the other end.

Charlie's party answered. "Listen, Han, that's enough now," he said quietly. "Put the gun away and go to bed." Pause. Crack. Crack. "Goddamnit," his voice got a little louder. "Don't make me call the sheriff." Pause. His jaw tightened, his biceps bulged. He yelled into the phone. "Because bullets don't always go where you want them to, that's why!"

There was a long pause. I couldn't hear a voice at the other end of the phone. No sound in the canyon. Then Charlie hung up. I stared at him.

"It should be okay now, Jake. That happens once in a great while. Nothing to really be alarmed about."

"Gunshots often alarm me. But then, I live in Oakland where they usually have some significance."

He laughed. "It's just Han. Hanley Martin. Up there." He waved his arm in the general direction of the house above Artie's. "He gets drunk, sits in the window, and shoots the trees." Charlie's phone rang. At the same time, I heard a car pull up at the bottom of the canyon.

"Yeah? Oh, hi, Art. Listen, it's not anything you have to worry about. He does that sometimes. You'll see when you've lived here a while. . . . Oh, is that them down there? Can't say I blame you. They'll probably let him off with a warning. They did that last year. Actually, I think he passed out while he was on the phone with me. Yeah. Well, we can talk about it tomorrow night. See you then. 'Bye."

I looked out Charlie's living room window. Two people with flashlights were just visible on the path alongside the spillway.

"Sheriff," Charlie said. "Perrine called them. Han's door will probably be open. They'll stick their heads in and have a look."

"Of course," I said. "And you'll talk about it tomorrow night?"

"At the meeting. Hanley always comes to those. We'll give him some hell and it won't happen again. For months."

I nodded, watching the wavering lights move up past Artie's. "He shoots the trees?" I said.

"Yeah. Well, listen, Jake, I've got a date coming in a few minutes . . ."

"Gee," I said. "Good thing he didn't get caught on the steps during the barrage." Charlie was maneuvering me toward the door. But I did want to ask him one question. "Charlie . . ." He had the door open and was smiling politely. "Why does he shoot trees?"

"I don't really know. I asked him that last year and all he said was that they're too big."

I went back to my plans. A few minutes later the flashlights worked their way down the path across the canyon again. One of the people carrying a flashlight was saying something and laughing. They got down to the bottom, got in their car, and drove away.

A few minutes after that, I heard heavy boots going up the steps past my door. Charlie's date.

8

Some of my plans for Tuesday worked out and some of them didn't.

They were good plans, too: Track down Smith's family, start working on Bright Future, and get background information on the canyon residents.

For one thing, I started the day late by oversleeping. I woke at eleven to the sound of someone banging on my door. I sat up in bed, yelled "Just a minute," and tried to figure out what it was that felt different about this morning. Then I got it. I'd slept off the worst of my cold. Even the maniac at the door couldn't spoil my newfound good mood.

The maniac at the door was Artie.

"What are you doing home from work again?" I asked accusingly, covering a yawn.

"I had to leave work," he gasped. "Guess what's happened?"

"Don't be cute." His panic was getting to me, but I was determined to stay calm.

"They just picked Alan up. At work. Because of the knife. And Julia's not home. She's got this photography class—"

"Then let her take it. She'll find out soon enough. What about a knife?"

He was still wheezing a little, but his breath was coming easier. "His knife. His hunting knife. They found it stuck in the mud in the ditch. I guess they were poking around down there again this morning. It's got his initials and everything."

"It's the murder weapon?"

"I don't know!" Artie howled.

"How about Chandler? Does he know?" The shape Artie was in, I was afraid he might have forgotten to call Alan's attorney. And I couldn't expect Alan to deal with something so basic when he was starring in his own drama.

"I don't know if he knows it's the murder weapon. But he knows they picked Alan up again. I left a message."

"Okay," I said. "Leave another message. Tell him when he's done whatever he needs to do over at the jail, he should call me at your place. You go back there now, make the call, take care of Jennifer, wait for Julia. And relax. There's nothing you can do. And there's nothing I can do until I talk to Chandler. I'll be over in a few minutes."

He nodded and stumbled out the door. I got dressed and followed him back to his house. Where I got undressed again, took a shower, and brushed my teeth.

Then I asked Artie and Jennifer if they were hungry. They both shook their heads. I dug around in the refrigerator until I found butter, eggs, milk, cheese, and some leftover broccoli. I put on the water for coffee and began to create an omelet, big enough for three. It didn't matter whether they ate or not. I was hungry.

When brunch was ready, I called them to the table. Artie came and sat down but Jennifer was listless. She wouldn't eat. I split the omelet two ways and let her wander around the house as much as she wanted.

It was another two hours before Chandler returned Artie's call. He'd just come back from the jail. Artie answered the phone but turned it over to me.

"What are you, Artie's mother or something?" Chandler demanded. I hadn't liked the guy before I ever had a chance to talk to him. Now I could not like him in person. But I decided to be civil enough to get what I wanted.

"Artie's distraught," I said. "I'm helping him out. I've had a small amount of experience along these lines."

"Yeah, sure. Okay, what do you want to know?" He was still cranky, but he, too, had apparently decided to be civil.

"Whatever you know," I said reasonably. "What's the story on the knife?"

"It's Alan's, and it's the murder weapon."

"How do they know it's the murder weapon?"

"Because," he said, veering toward nasty again, "the point was broken off and the point they found stuck in the corpse matches. Real easy, when you know how."

"Why are they so sure it's Alan's?"

"One, it had his initials on it. Two, he admitted it when they showed it to him."

"Well, what the hell was it doing in the ditch?"

"Not to mention in the corpse? Hah. He says he lost it. About a week ago. Says he didn't tell anyone he lost it because it was a gift from his wife and he didn't want her to know."

"Any rust on it?"

He hesitated, as though I'd surprised him by asking an intelligent question. "Not any more. And even if there was, what would that prove? Maybe the kid doesn't take care of his toys."

"Any prints on it?"

"It was washed clean. In the water and in the mud."

"Have they charged him yet?"

"No, not yet. I think they're checking some things out before they take the plunge, so to speak. They can hold him for a while without a charge if they need to. But I think they're going to do it."

"When was the man killed?"

"Close enough to the time Alan was spotted near the ditch. They seem to think he killed him, threw him in the spillway, then ran down to make sure he was dead. They found traces of Smith's clothing up near the top."

"Come on," I said, "maybe a killer would be dumb enough to get himself noticed checking on the victim. But why would anyone use his own knife to kill somebody, with his own initials on it, and then leave it lying around for the sheriff to find? That's really stupid."

He grunted. "It's physical evidence, Samson, stupid or not. And a lot of people do stupid things after they've killed someone. Not everyone's as clever as you are. They figure he left the knife in the body and the trip down shook it loose."

It was my turn to grunt. "Okay. That's it?"

"So far."

"Thanks."

"Yeah."

We both hung up.

As I was telling Jennifer and Artie what he'd said, Julia came in and I had to start at the beginning again. Julia got quarrelsome.

"Oh, hell," she said. "Anyone could have used that knife. They haven't proved anything. I don't see how they can expect to get a conviction on such flimsy evidence."

Jennifer nodded, looking hopeful.

I hated to be depressing, but I didn't contribute to their optimism. "Maybe they'll decide not to charge him. It's not a solid case. Still, if Alan's the best they've got, he may be good enough."

We spent the rest of the afternoon together, going over and over the case. Artie used up a lot of excess energy "helping" me plan my investigation, but no one wanted to turn me loose long enough to get started with it.

I did get a chance to make a call to Bright Future and set up some appointments for the next day. I also managed to get Artie and Julia to talk a little about their neighbors while they were helping solve the case.

We were just finishing dinner when Chandler called.

Alan had been charged with murder.

9

Rosie and Alice showed up at my door a few minutes before the meeting was scheduled to start, and the three of us climbed the rest of the way to Charlie's.

I introduced Rosie and Rosie introduced Alice. "She can stay out on the deck, if you'd rather," Rosie said.

Charlie reached down to stroke the dog's head. "I wouldn't hear of it," he said, looking a little shocked. "I knew a standard poodle once. Very civilized. She's welcome to join us."

When we were seated in the living room with glasses of wine,

Charlie said casually, "Didn't Gertrude Stein always have standard poodles?"

Rosie, who had been looking around the room at the art, laughed and said yes, that was so.

"And her name is Alice?"

"Right again." They smiled at each other.

Now that they had that settled, there wasn't much to do except wait for the rest of the party.

First to arrive were Carlota and Nona, Carlota in a red caftan and Nona in something that looked very much like a karate suit with yellow roses embroidered on the sleeves. Carlota was carrying a bottle of wine flamboyantly, as though any minute she might tuck it under her chin and draw a bow across it. This was the first time I had seen the living Nona. She was remarkable mostly for her smallness. She could not have been five feet tall.

The introductions made, Rosie grinned and stuck out her hand, warm, friendly, and beautiful as ever. Carlota's eyelids flickered and she took Rosie's hand in both her own. Nona scowled, an amazing sight. She looked like a malevolent child with the faint beginnings of crow's feet.

Carlota continued to flicker at Rosie as she asked Charlie about wineglasses. Then she wrinkled her forehead, sucked in her cheeks, and followed him into the kitchen.

"I can't imagine," Nona said, "why either of you would be interested in our little community meeting. But it's very nice of you to come." She was no longer threatening to boil over, but as she spoke to us she gave Rosie only the briefest of glances.

"I've never been to a neighborhood meeting in a hot tub," Rosie said, showing polite and gracious interest.

"Oh, really?" This time she gave Rosie a slightly longer look. "Don't they have them in Oakland? In the hills, perhaps?"

Nona seemed to be playing several roles at once, and I couldn't get a fix on her. She was the fiery woman of deep and explosive passions. She was the gracious hostess, and she was the Marin County snob, which is not much different from the San Francisco snob, the Peninsula snob, or the East Bay hills snob.

"Heck," I said. "We don't know much about the hills. We

live down in the flatlands with the People."

She grimaced, flailing wildly for an appropriate answer—should she be a knee-jerk liberal or maybe even a socialist?—and finally muttered, "Of course . . ." At that moment Carlota and Charlie emerged from the kitchen and Nona regained her balance. She returned to being the fiery woman of deep and explosive passions. I guessed it was her favorite role, and probably the one Carlota appreciated the most. Carlota, too, had regained her balance. She was no longer flickering at Rosie. In fact, she didn't look at her at all.

At one point, when Carlota strode to the fireplace and posed with elbow on mantel and wineglass in hand, her eyes flitting all over the room and avoiding Rosie and Nona as though she were afraid of both of them, I suggested that Rosie might like to get an advance look at the hot tub. She agreed, and we went out through the dark bedroom to the tiny backyard.

The yard was a patch of gravel about ten feet by fifteen, a level spot between a steep downslope to the lane and a damp, forty-five degree upslope, its surface obscured by blackberry and broom, that looked like it was about to start sliding any minute. The upper reaches of the incline were lost in trees and brush a hundred feet or so above the house. Someone had built a three-foot retaining wall at that side of the yard. Comforting. Right up against the retaining wall the hot tub squatted on its decking. It was heating. The cover was still on.

This hot tub was not one of those plastic jobs dropped into a wooden structure like a large sunken bathtub. That kind of thing might be good enough for Oakland, or even Berkeley, but it certainly wouldn't do for southern Marin. This was the real thing. Rustic redwood. The old hand-hewn effect.

The canyon was dark, except for a few house lights showing here and there through the trees. The spillway, reduced after two rainless days to a stream, babbled delicately to itself and maybe to the redwoods. The air was cold and so charged with oxygen it smelled funny. Rosie stood there, staring up at the sharp little sparks of starlight, breathing deeply, and smiling like the Mona Lisa.

44

The place was too damned beautiful. Too beautiful for murder. Too beautiful for some of the types who lived there, like the tree-slayer. Just about beautiful enough, I figured, for me, and for Rosie, and for the few other perfect people in the world. Artie and Julia could stay. I didn't know Charlie well enough to know whether he could stay or not.

I brought myself back from dreamland. "So," I said to Rosie, "What do you make of Carlota and Nona?"

She chuckled. "They're assholes."

"Oh." It was a revelation and a relief. I hadn't known what to do with them and now Rosie had provided a niche.

She turned to face me. "Jake, you're usually pretty good at checking people out. Why did you need me to tell you that those two are jerks? Were you taken in by the too-too-divine act or were you afraid to judge them?"

I could feel myself blushing and I was glad we were standing in the dark. I hesitated. She chuckled again.

"It's okay, pal. I say so and that makes it all right. Yes, these two particular members of my particular minority group are assholes. Okay?"

I laughed with her. "Okay." Then I put my arm around her shoulder and we went back into the house. Artie and Julia—I had convinced them to come to the meeting and get their minds off Alan for a while—had arrived. A short, wiry, nervous-looking blond guy was standing in front of the fireplace warming his left hip. An older couple, early sixties I guessed, were sitting on the couch. She had long gray hair held at the back of her neck with a leather clasp, and wore a wildly colorful dress in reds, blues, and yellows, cinched at the waist with a wide cloth belt. When she crossed her ankles I noticed she was wearing cowboy boots. The man sitting with her also had gray hair. He was wearing a plaid wool shirt over a cotton turtleneck, and baggy worn corduroys.

The wiry blond guy lived in the first house this side of the bridge. His name was Jim something. Jim, I had learned that afternoon, was "in computers." The older couple were Eric and Mary Anderson. They lived next door to Charlie's, just beyond Carlota's and above the lane. Julia had told me that they had a bookstore in

Mill Valley, and that Eric also did "something else intellectual," which she couldn't remember. Charlie, I had learned, was a stockbroker.

Charlie looked at his watch. "We're running a little late. We'll wait another five or ten minutes, then we'll start." Nobody objected. Everyone was drinking wine except Jim, who was dressed in chinos and a sport jacket and looked like a 1958 fraternity boy gone to nerves. He was sucking on a can of beer.

I heard footsteps on the stairs, two kinds, and then a knock on the door. Charlie opened it and greeted two more neighbors. The man didn't look like someone I wanted to know. He was short- to medium-size, about five foot eight, and a little wider than medium across the chest. Stocky, close to the ground, sand-colored hair and beard, blue gray eyes. A physical type you see a lot around the northern California coast. I'm not sure why. I guess that hardy peasant type gravitates toward rugged and primitive land. But he was just a little off. He had pouches under his eyes you wouldn't see up north, and hard lines from nostril to chin that spoke of stress. This was Hanley Martin, would-be killer of redwoods. I had been interested to learn from Artie that afternoon that Martin worked as a gardener.

The woman with him, Arlene Shulman, had long dark fuzzy hair, petulant lips, and a vacant expression in her yellow brown eyes. She was introduced as a friend of Hanley's. Hanley nodded brusquely and sat down. She gazed opaquely into my eyes, said "Hi," and wandered off to the kitchen.

Several small conversations were going on at once. Carlota was saying something about the steps to Rosie. Eric and Artie seemed to be talking about garden tools. "It wasn't your trowel after all, Art," Eric was explaining. "Turned out I'd borrowed it from someone else." Hanley was telling Jim about "some goddamn customer" who couldn't seem to understand that things grew faster in the spring. I noticed that no one was talking about the murder. I wondered if any of them knew, yet, that the cops had arrested Artie's nephew.

"I think we should get started, don't you?" Charlie asked in the style of one who is not asking a question. He was answered

46

with vague nods and murmurs. Charlie turned to Jim. "Give me a hand with the cover, will you?" Jim nodded and followed Charlie outside. The two men had left the back door open and I could just see through the bedroom into the backyard. It looked a little lighter out there now. I guessed the moon was rising just in time for the show. Eric and Mary brushed past me into the bedroom and began to undress, folding all their clothing neatly and placing the pile on the bed. I watched their bare buttocks move outdoors. When I turned abruptly back into the living room I almost bumped into Rosie, who was gazing past me with eyebrows elevated. Then I got out of the way, because Carlota was sweeping through, followed by the dark, glowering Nona. Followed by Artie and Julia. Artie laughed a little nervously at the expression on my face.

"It's a custom, Jake. When in—"

"Yeah," I agreed. "After you, Rosie." She did, indeed, lead the way, past Artie and Julia, who had stopped off in the bedroom to strip. Hanley Martin and his buddy Arlene brought up the rear.

Charlie was in the tub, waiting, with Eric and Mary. Jim, still fully clothed, was leaning against the decking watching the half moon clear the top of a redwood. Nona was sitting on the retaining wall, swinging her short legs. Carlota, standing in the middle of the tiny yard, glanced at Rosie and in one stagy movement, removed her caftan—she was wearing nothing else—and draped it on a shrub. Then she slithered up the steps to the decking that surrounded the hot tub and lowered herself slowly into the water. Rosie coughed. I knew better than to meet her eyes. Arlene had somehow managed to remove her clothing while moving through the bedroom, but she didn't waste much time covering herself up again by getting into the tub. The Perrines minced out the door naked, holding hands. They looked, for damned good reason, goose-bumpy with cold. They also squeezed into the tub. Cosy.

"Bet one more person could fit in," I told Rosie.

"I never take off my cowboy boots in Marin County."

Arlene stared at us blankly. "It's English riding boots, now, you know," she said. "Cowboy boots are out."

"We'll alternate as usual," Charlie said. "Halfway through the meeting, some of us will get out and the rest of you can get in."

Martin nodded sullenly, looking at Arlene, who had seated herself between Charlie and Eric. Jim just waved his hand dismissively and drank some more beer. Nona was still glowering, but I couldn't figure out why. I didn't know how long she'd been living with Carlota but she must have seen this act before. Maybe the heavy frown was a method of limiting the performance. My mother used to do that, may she rest in peace.

Carlota spoke to me, probably because I was Rosie's friend. "Jake, do you remember when I told you my films were going to be reviewed?"

"Yes." Her breasts were bobbing on the surface of the water. I looked resolutely at her face. "*Marin Journal*, right?"

"*Of the Arts*. Yes, well, Eric is going to do the review. He does that sort of thing." She smiled warmly at him. "He has a fine reputation." He shrugged, feigning embarrassment. "When is it coming out, Eric?"

"This weekend," he said. "In time for the second showing of the films."

"So good of you," she murmured.

"Okay," Charlie said crisply. "Let's get down to business." Arlene yawned and stretched. "Let's start with you, Jim. What's happening with the gravel?"

There followed an account of Jim's adventures in attempting to get a couple of loads of rock delivered to fill the winter's ruts in the canyon's entry road. When he finished his report, he seemed to brace himself. Then he turned to Han Martin.

"And I'd like to say a few words on another subject, too," he snarled. Martin raised his chin in a belligerent "c'mon, hit me" attitude. Charlie sighed.

"Okay, Jim, but briefly."

Jim didn't take his eyes off Martin. "I want to know what this jerk thinks he's doing shooting off his goddamn gun again. I thought we talked about that already. I thought we decided he had to stop doing that."

If I'd been Jim, and Martin had been looking at me that way,

I think I would have shut up right then. Jim didn't; but Charlie, who managed to look authoritative even three-quarters submerged, intervened with a few peaceable words.

"Yeah, Jim, that's true. We did decide that. And I talked it over with Han again last night, so how about we think of it as a kind of slip in his good intentions. For the time being." There was just the tiniest note of threat in that last sentence. Martin caught it and sulked a bit.

"Glad to hear about the gravel," Charlie concluded. "Mary? What's new on the parking area? I hear you have some good news for us?"

I had started to shut off my hearing, but halfway through Mary's recital I caught the name "James Smith." Immediately after I caught it I also caught a blow to the ribs from Rosie, who had also noticed that Mary had mentioned the name of the murdered man. I tuned back in again. And I learned that Smith did indeed have a living connection with the canyon.

I got some of the story through Mary's report. Charlie filled in the gaps for the benefit of the guests. It went roughly like this: The area down at the bottom of the canyon, which all the inhabitants had used for parking for, presumably, as long as there were cars, had been threatened by an impending sale, by the county, to a private party named James Smith. Such a sale would have been disastrous. None of the people who lived in the canyon had what is known in real estate as on-site parking, since they were all perched up above the canyon floor. If the lot were sold, and built on, there would not have been enough room at the bottom for the residents' cars. What that meant was that their homes would have become useless, valueless cabins in the sky. The residents couldn't have continued to live there conveniently and it would have been impossible to find anyone foolish enough to buy.

But Mary, who had lived there a very long time, had always had some vague idea that, for some reason, the lot could not be sold legally. She had formed a committee of two—asking Han Martin to help her—and had begun a search of the records, racing against time to prevent the sale.

They had soon found what they were looking for, Mary said:

49

a turn of the century ruling, wherein the county had agreed that the land was to be held in common by canyon homeowners. Forever.

Most of the neighbors nodded knowingly, as though they'd already heard about the committee's success. Only Artie and Julia looked pleasantly enlightened by Mary's announcement.

"We're nearly finished with our report and we're probably going to submit it tomorrow," Mary concluded. "If it's accepted, there can be no more prospective buyers."

"Is there any question that it will be accepted?" Charlie asked.

Mary shook her head. "It's hard to tell. There could be some loophole we don't know about yet. A later ruling, perhaps. But at least now we have time to deal with that eventuality." Mary, it turned out, had checked the day after the murder to be sure the dead man was the James Smith they had been trying to stop.

"Damned good thing, too," Han growled.

"Yes," Mary agreed, not in the least disturbed that Martin had just implied a man's death was a damned good thing. Jim was looking almost happy. Charlie was nodding cheerfully, and Martin was actually smiling. Nobody had the bad taste to applaud, but I could tell that most of them wanted to.

Everything had worked out well for them. Someone had solved their immediate problem—Smith—and barring some as-yet unknown obstacle to their legal rights, the lot was safe. But what if that unknown obstacle existed? And what if another buyer showed up tomorrow? I had a fleeting picture of corpses bobbing down the spillway like logs from a lumber camp.

Again, it looked as though the grapevine had done its work before the meeting. Only Artie and Julia had looked surprised to learn that the murdered man was the prospective buyer. But then, the Perrines had been busy with family problems.

Julia also looked shocked. "Listen, all of you, the man was murdered. And they think Alan did it. And he didn't. And every homeowner in this canyon had a motive for killing him."

That really sobered them up. Jim shrugged, Eric sighed, and Hanley Martin said, "Oh, pig pellets." I guessed the expression was related to "horse pucky" and "dog doo-doo," and felt as though I'd gotten a whole new perspective on his personality. The more you knew him the worse he got. "The cops," he continued, "don't care diddly squat about motive, especially not a silly motive like that. They're into physical evidence. Besides, the ruling will stand."

"Of course it will," Mary agreed. "I'm sure he would have been prevented from going ahead anyway. But Julia does have a point. The man is dead. I'm sure the police won't suspect any of us, but perhaps we can celebrate the survival of our canyon without celebrating a murder, too. Let's just be glad we have a good chance to win and time to fight if we have to."

They were also glad, I was sure, that someone outside their immediate group had been charged with the murder.

"Well," Charlie said, "quite a few of us haven't had a turn at the tub. Let's take a recess and get back to this." I wasn't happy about the interruption. I had been hoping they'd really start arguing, and maybe reveal a little something about themselves. But there wasn't much I could do about it. After a bit of "Oh, no, really, I've been in long enough" conversation, four people got out of the tub and four prepared to take their places. Charlie, Artie, Julia, and Eric went into the house to dry off and dress. Nona, Hanley, Jim, and I took off our clothes and joined Carlota, Arlene, and Mary in the water. I'd never taken a hot tub with more than one other person before, and I thought about leaving on my jockey shorts. But Rosie was trying her best to embarrass me by watching me undress, so I stuck my tongue out, turned around, and removed the last scrap between me and the cold air. If she wanted to laugh at my backside, she was welcome to. Once I was safely in the tub I told her she was really missing something.

"Oh, yeah?" she laughed. "What?"

That was when I felt the fingers on my left thigh. What, indeed, I wondered, was Rosie missing? Both Arlene and Carlota were submerged to their necks in the middle of the tub and both were close enough to touch me. Someone had turned on the bubbles, and I couldn't see anything beneath the surface of the water. I suppose I should have enjoyed the mystery, but I kept thinking about Hanley, on my right, and Nona, on my left. I was not interested in making either one of them jealous. In fact, if I'd had my

51

pick of all the people I would least like to make jealous, those two would have been the big winners.

Charlie had come back outside, dressed warmly in jeans and sweater, and got the meeting going again, unfortunately on a completely different topic. The spillway needed repairing and they had to talk about materials and volunteer labor time. Eric had been asked at a previous meeting to check it out, and he droned on with his report while the delicate touch of someone's hand was raising the hair on the back of my neck. I kept looking cautiously at Carlota, hoping that if I caught her eye she'd stop. I couldn't catch her eye, which was wandering between Rosie and Nona. I switched to Arlene, staring at her until she turned her vacant gaze my way. She blinked once and turned her head again. The hand never stopped moving slowly up my thigh, and whoever it belonged to managed to keep it so disembodied that I couldn't tell where it was coming from. Not so much as the touch of an elbow. The fingers reached my crotch, resting lightly against me. When they began to do more than rest, I thought this was my chance to solve the puzzle. Surely, there would be some small movement to give the culprit away. Then I could look offended and move away from her, whoever she was. But I forgot to look for movement. Then I caught myself beginning to think what the hell, maybe no one would notice anyway. That's when I knew my mind was going, and dealt with myself sternly, sliding my butt off the bench and moving, submerged to my chin, over to the other side of the tub.

No one paid any attention. Not Arlene. Not Carlota. I sat there for a moment, listening to a discussion of the price of redwood, and then got the hell out of that tub and into my clothes. I was almost completely dressed before I realized that I had forgotten to dry myself first.

The meeting didn't last much longer. Although there were occasional surreptitious glances at Artie and Julia, everyone, even Carlota, exercised enough restraint to leave untouched the subject of Alan. A few minutes after I returned, safely dressed, to the backyard, the second shift got out of the hot tub and we all moved back into the house. Everyone milled around for a few minutes, saying goodnight. Rosie was saying something about an estimate to Carlota, while Nona hovered alertly by.

Eric said it was nice meeting me, and wasn't I staying at Charlie's now? I said I was.

"I'm glad to hear it," he said. "Charlie's been pretty lonely since George left." He smiled paternally. I didn't bother to explain that I was not George's replacement, even though Eric seemed to expect me to say something in reply. I just nodded and smiled back.

Rosie followed me down to my room, and asked if she and Alice could spend the night with me.

"See, I've finished my estimates in the East Bay," she said, "and I promised Carlota I'd have a look at the steps tomorrow and let her know what I'd charge to fix them."

I offered her the cot but she insisted on laying her sleeping bag on the floor. I stuck some paper and kindling in the pot belly, got that going, and added a chunk of oak. Then we turned our backs on each other to undress and got into our respective beds. After the hot tub party, it seemed a little silly to return to our former modesty with each other, but it felt right to do it that way somehow.

"So what did you think?" I asked her.

"Weird group." I agreed. "I got the feeling that almost any one of them could stick a knife in someone if they had the right excuse. Especially that Hanley character. And that Jim." She yawned. "He's the kind that neighbors always say seemed like such a nice quiet fellow—until he murdered forty people."

"What about the women?"

"Well, Jesus, that Arlene. Eerie. And of course Nona. Although I would think she'd be more into poisons or curses or something. And Carlota found the body."

"Right. But somehow I can't imagine Carlota taking such direct action. She kind of slides around, you know?"

"You mean she's not violent, she's just sleazy?"

"Something like that."

"She asked me over for a drink tomorrow."

"Carlota? Where was Nona when she did that?"

"In the toilet. I have a feeling only Carlota will be home."

I laughed. "Watch out, babe. She was looking at you like you were her very own birthday cake."

Rosie snorted. "I never mess with married women. Especially if they're total twitches."

"She may also be a mite confused," I said, and told her about the anonymous groper in the hot tub.

"Interesting," she said, once she stopped laughing. "Things like that never happen to me."

"Probably because you refuse to take off your cowboy boots."

"Good night, Jake."

"Good night, Rosie."

10

The Bright Future Home Study Plan Incorporated occupied a two-story office building in an industrial park north of San Rafael. The redwood siding must have looked good a decade before; now it was fading and starting to break loose from the vertical slats that covered the seams. I didn't bother to drive around back to the parking lot. There were plenty of spaces on the industrial park's pseudo streets.

I pushed through the door into the reception area. My attention was immediately split between the smiling receptionist and a real eye-catcher near the right-hand wall: a spiral staircase about three feet in diameter, bolted through the royal blue carpeting to the floor and dead-ending at the solid acoustical ceiling. A sign hanging from it at eye level said, simply, "Bright Future."

I must have stared at this symbol a bit longer than most casual visitors because the receptionist interrupted my musings.

"May I help you, sir?"

I looked at her. Teased hair, molded and sprayed. Dimples displayed by an overwide smile. Long fingernails painted to match her reddish brown lipstick. She looked like she'd just finished eating raw liver.

"Yes," I replied politely. "I'm Jake Samson. I have an appointment with Mr. Bowen."

If she could have smiled wider she would have. I was big stuff. I had an appointment with the president of the company. But the smile was brief. I guessed that my status was only partly resolved. I had an appointment with the president, sure, but what kind of welcome would I get? She buzzed his office. If I was really somebody, Bowen himself would come out to fetch me. If I was nobody in particular, his secretary would appear. The third alternative? Have the receptionist send me back on my own, which could mean I was an old friend—very high status—or they hoped I'd get lost on the way. I was pretty sure I'd get the secretary, since I doubted that someone who'd identified himself as a writer from *Probe* magazine would be left to wander around on his own.

I was there, supposedly, to look over the possibilities for a story on education—the economics and feasibility of what these people called home study, as opposed to other kinds of schooling. As far as I knew, however, no one had ever been interested in said feasibility until one of the company's vice-presidents got himself tossed down a spillway.

Like I figured, I got the secretary. An intelligent-looking middle-aged woman who didn't overdo my welcome. She escorted me back to the presidential suite. The outer office, which she inhabited, was small but carefully decorated with blue carpeting, wood-grain desk, and white file cabinets. The inner office, where Bowen sat, was big enough for a typing pool. White carpeting, blue walls, lots of big windows with blue drapes, a real wood desk with two visitors' chairs upholstered in blue and white tweed, and a conversational group of more blue and white chairs and a white table with a blue ash tray. A blown-up photograph dominated one of the walls, a photograph of an old building on a city street. Screwed to the frame in brass was the legend, "First Corporate Headquarters, 1953, Chicago."

Bowen stood up and walked around his desk to greet me solemnly. He was a short man, thin, with white hair worn medium long. The glasses he wore, and his suit, a slightly wrinkled, brown off-the-rack business suit, looked as though he could have been wearing them since 1953. His face, like his suit, was wrinkled. He had watery, gentle blue eyes. He didn't seem to belong in his office. A formal little man, at home in Chicago in a dead era,

55

transplanted to 1980s California casual. Just a different kind of elegance, maybe, but awfully bright colors for a man in a brown suit.

"Mr. Samson, please sit down. Edna?" The secretary had waited just inside the door. "Would you bring us some coffee, please?" He spoke very precisely, the way teachers used to talk back when they were trying to set a good example.

After he'd finished shaking my hand, he invited me to sit in one of the chairs facing his desk. No conversational grouping for me. Or maybe the decorator's idea of conversation was different from his. He reached for the book of matches lying next to a desk lighter set in a glittering gold ball and lit a cigarette, dropping the dead match in a large blue ashtray that matched the one on the table across the room. There were just a few butts in the ashtray. He offered me a cigarette. An unfiltered Chesterfield. He needed only a brown fedora to complete the time warp. I, being a modern person, declined the cigarette.

"I'm afraid," he said quietly, "that I'm not very clear on why you wanted to see me. Something about a magazine article?"

I leaned forward earnestly. "I'm very interested in the home study phenomenon. Historically and currently." I wasn't sure he was hearing me. "Mr. Bowen?" He looked up. I took out my notebook and a pen, and gestured toward the photograph on the wall. "Is that the year of your founding? 1953?" He swung his chair around to face the photograph and spoke to it.

"Yes. And that was our building."

I counted rapidly. "All five floors?"

He kept his eyes on the photograph. "Well, no. We started with the second floor. But by 1963 we occupied all of it."

"Very impressive. Do you still have an office there?"

He turned around to face me again. "We moved out here in 1975, and consolidated." He smiled sweetly. "Things aren't the way they used to be, you know. A business can only grow these days by paring away the fat. And of course you needed more people back then, just to operate. No computers, that sort of thing."

"So your business has grown?"

"Recently, yes. But we have always kept even with the econ-

56

omy." I wasn't sure, but it seemed to me that keeping even with the economy didn't sound too good, overall.

"And the key to that," I nodded, "is the management team, right? A solid corps of executive talent. Mature experience and fresh new blood." The corners of his mouth turned down slightly in a half-born frown. "And I know—I'm terribly sorry—that you recently lost one of your team members."

The frown was now complete. "Ah, yes. Very sad. A long-time and loyal employee. A young man, too, with a family. But the company goes on." For the first time in our conversation, he looked alert. "It always has." He paused. "Mr. Samson, isn't *Probe* magazine somewhat given to sensationalism? What is sensational about a respectable old company that has dedicated thirty years to the education of people all over this country?"

"Mr. Bowen," I said, gazing directly into his eyes, "*Probe* is a monthly journal that attempts to report on and interpret the significant events and developments of our society." Artie had given me that one, and I'd never had a chance to use it before. "Sometimes, certainly, those events are sensational. But I am not on the staff of the magazine. I am a free-lancer who gets work where he can."

The old man was no fool. "Just the same, Mr. Samson, James Smith's death was a sensational one. He was murdered."

I sighed and shook my head. "Mr. Bowen, I'm afraid that murder no longer qualifies as unusual enough for the national media to bother with. Assassination, yes. Murder, no. Mr. Smith was, undoubtedly, valuable to your company. But his death is of very little interest to a magazine like *Probe*." It was pretty interesting to one of *Probe*'s editors, but Bowen didn't have to know that.

He was, or seemed to be, nearly convinced. "It does seem coincidental that this magazine has not shown interest in Bright Future before."

I affected a world-weary shrug. "Let's say that the murder brought your company to my attention. I pick up ideas from the newspapers. I suggest those ideas to editors."

"Ah." He nodded, relaxing.

"Actually, I rather expected that you'd be pleased by the

possibility of national exposure." I'd no sooner said "exposure" than I wished I hadn't, but he had drifted off and away from alertness again so it didn't matter.

"Perhaps if you'll tell me what aspect of our institution interests you the most, I can direct you to those departments and persons involved," he said indifferently.

"The history, of course," I replied. "And the academic department. Sales. Whatever subsidiary departments those might have. I'm afraid I don't know much about your corporate structure."

He nodded. "Let me give you some printed background materials and turn you over to my executive vice-president. We can talk again another time." He buzzed his secretary, gave her some instructions, and said a polite goodbye.

She, in turn, pulled a few items out of her files, handed them to me, and led me off to another wing of the executive first floor, where she passed me on to another secretary who asked me to wait a moment, please. I sat down and looked at the top sheet of the stuff the first secretary had given me. It was a diagram of the corporate structure. Nothing very unusual about any of it. The president was under a board of directors. Below him were the executive v.p. and the controller. Under the executive v.p. were the sales and academic vice-presidents. Under the sales department were shipping, field staff, and advertising (communications). Under the academic department were faculty, consultants, and editorial (communications).

I didn't remember Alan saying anything about an editorial department or an advertising department. Just communications, which, on this diagram, applied to both. Did two vice-presidents share one department? That alone sounded like a motive for murder. I glanced quickly through the other papers. They were advertising flyers.

The executive vice-president came striding out of his office, a tall thin man with youthful bearing and gray hair. His suit was gray, too, very nicely tailored, and worn with a pale blue shirt and a gray, blue, and red-striped tie.

"Bill Armand," he said, sticking out his hand.

"Jake Samson." I took brief but firm hold of his manicure.

"Sorry to keep you waiting. I was on the phone. Listen, I've got a meeting in just a few minutes. I wonder if I could get you started by taking you over to our sales chief. He knows just about everything there is to know about this place." Armand flashed a smile that was too good to be true. Were those really his teeth?

I was beginning to feel like a marker in a Monopoly game. If the sales vice-president shook the dice again, who knew where I'd end up?

11

"Howard Morton is one of the most knowledgeable people we have," Armand was saying as he walked me briskly toward the end of the hallway. "All aspects of the business. Amazing guy. Absolutely amazing. Joined the company just a couple of years ago and he's done wonders."

We passed a door marked "Controller." I stopped. "I'll want to meet him, too," I said, pointing toward the closed door.

"I'm afraid you can't," Armand said sadly. "He died."

I swallowed hard. Another one? "When was that?"

"Last year." The vice-president looked at me coldly. "He was eighty-two years old. He had a heart attack. I've taken over that end of things for the time being." He touched my elbow and got me moving again.

"Did most of your people come out from Chicago?" I asked. I wondered how far back Smith went with the company and how far back the other executives went with Smith.

"Well, let's see . . ." he wrinkled his handsome forehead as if he actually had to think to answer my question. "Bowen, of course, is the founder. I joined him out there in 1970. Then of course there's our communications manager. She first joined the company back in Chicago. Chloe."

"And what about James Smith?"

He shook his head, sad again. This guy was a total phony. "Oh, yes. He went all the way back with Bowen, back to the fifties. So does old Ed, the man who runs our shipping department." I thought it was interesting that only presidents and

59

vice-presidents had last names. "Old Ed," presumably, was a mere manager. Like Chloe.

Armand was smiling at the sales vice-president's secretary, who was young, pretty, and a little flashy. "Tell Mr. Morton we're here to see him, Sandra." She buzzed her boss.

Howard Morton came bouncing out of the inner office and grabbed my hand. Armand left me with him.

"Come right on in, Samson," Morton said, his arm around my shoulder. "Always happy to tell the Bright Future story. Always. Happy to. Sit down. Can I have my secretary get you anything? Coffee? Or do you press guys only go for the hard stuff?" I was tempted to tell him I was a teetotaler, but I wanted him to think I was just one of the guys.

"Nothing, thanks," I said heartily. "Had a little more than I needed last night." He liked that. Morton had a conversation grouping just like the president, only in white plastic. That's where we sat, leaning back against upholstery etched with some fictitious animal's skin wrinkles.

Morton looked like he should be fat but managed, by sheer strength of will, to keep his belly flat. He looked like he'd just shaved. His light brown hair was carefully styled and I was pretty sure there was spray on it. It looked solid, like it wasn't made up of individual hairs at all. He was wearing a double-knit suit that showed the contours of his bulging thighs and biceps. He looked like a cop wearing a wig.

"Bill says you want to do a little magazine piece on us. Great idea. Tell me more about it." He had small eyes and he kept them well covered with lid. I explained that the story wasn't just about Bright Future, it was about home study generally, and how it stacked up against in-class education. His eyes got even smaller.

"Uh huh. You starting with some kind of premise or are you really open to the true story?"

"Open. Totally open, Mr. Morton."

"Howard."

"Jake."

"Great. Really great. Because you know home study just doesn't have the snob appeal of, say, your trade school or college.

But listen, have you seen any of the stuff we print? About the advantages of working at your own pace?"

"Well, I haven't read anything yet, but I've got a bunch of brochures and things. I thought I'd try to maybe get some quotes from the people who know what it's all about. Tell you the truth," I added confidentially and untruthfully, "I never went to college myself. Always thought it was overrated."

I'd gone too far. He looked suspicious, then covered the look with a smile. "Let's just say that nobody should ever underrate the power and value of any kind of education, Jake. Now what kind of information, exactly, did you want from me?"

That was a very good question.

I wanted information about a dead man; I had to ask for information about the company he worked for.

"Well, let's see," I said thoughtfully, "why don't you tell me a little something about the courses."

"Better than that." He opened a desk drawer and pulled out a handful of brochures. "I'll give you these to take home with you." I took them and thumbed through them. Single-fold booklets, each describing a different course: business English, secretarial, business management, bookkeeping, sales, Spanish, French, and high school subjects. None of the brochures said anything about price. I mentioned that.

He chuckled. "Right to the heart of things, yes sir. Rest assured, Jake. Our prices are competitive, fair, and in the right ballpark. There's a range, of course. Depends on what the student's getting. You just pick one, I'll tell you what it costs."

"Business English."

"That's a good choice. Runs two hundred dollars for the whole thing—twenty lessons, twenty-chapter textbook, and a set of ten learning guides to go with it. Just like having a teacher in your own living room. And tests. They take tests and send them in and get them corrected."

"What about bookkeeping?"

"Depends how far they want to go. There's a beginning, an intermediate, and an advanced."

"Okay, what about Spanish? How do you teach a language by mail?"

61

"There's a book, and some support materials, and tapes. They can go all the way through the equivalent of a two-year program if they want. Starts out at two hundred and fifty dollars for the basics."

"Sounds like a full course could run into some money," I said judiciously. "How do they pay? Lesson by lesson, or everything in front?"

"Well, now, we really couldn't do business on a lesson by lesson basis, could we? We'd have to spend more on record-keeping than we charge for the courses. But they don't have to sign up for, say, a two-year program all at once. It's one course at a time. A serious student doesn't usually have any trouble coming up with two or two-fifty."

"Do a lot of them manage to do it? I mean, how many students do you have?"

"I'm afraid I don't have the exact figures right off the top of my head at any given time. You got sign-ups who don't go ahead, you got dropouts. But you could say we're reaching thousands. Thousands of people."

"Dropouts?" I landed on the word the way I guessed a good reporter was supposed to. "You get a lot of those?"

"Again, Jake, I don't have the exact figures right here. But let's say we've got a solid eighty percent completion rate. Of course, the academic department would know more about that. If you need the exact numbers, we can always run something off on the computer for you."

"Great," I said. "I'll get back to you on that once I've got the big picture." I figured Morton could run off just about anything he wanted on the computer, and as far as I knew, the academic department was dead. But I was glad he'd brought up the subject. "And about the academic side of things—who would I talk to about that now? Is there a replacement yet for James Smith?"

Morton looked pained. "Takes more than a few days to replace a vice-president, Jake. He ran an important area of the company."

I nodded sympathetically. I was thinking that if Alan was right about the care that went into the company's product, they might not bother replacing him at all.

"Speaking of areas," I said, "I've got an organization chart here and I was kind of having a quick look at it. Is it current?" I showed it to him. He nodded. "Okay, then, let's see if I've got this right. You work under Armand, and the three departments under your supervision are shipping, field staff, and advertising." He nodded again. "Now, advertising is part of communications?" He leaned forward in his chair, and clasped his hands together. "And editorial—let's see, that's under the academic vice-president—is also part of communications?"

"Yes, that's right." His lids were covering even more of his eyes than they had before and I decided to skip around a little and come back to that.

"Field staff," I said thoughtfully. "Does that mean sales people or what?"

He relaxed. "That's right. The sales operation. Feeds directly into me, and, of course, into shipping, where the course materials are sent out."

"Okay," I said. "Tell me a little about your sales operation. How it works. How do your people find out someone wants to buy a course?"

He smiled at me patronizingly. "It's pretty complicated, Jake. First, I should tell you about the old way, and how it used to work. Real simple. A potential student would see an ad, like one of these—" He got up, went to a bookshelf, and pulled down a book, which he brought back and opened on the coffee table. It was an album, full of pages cut from magazines, with Bright Future ads on them. The one he was showing me was dated 1963. The ad showed a lot of little photographs of people saying how studying high school at home had changed their lives. There was a coupon at the bottom.

"They'd send the coupon in to the company, and the company would send them out a brochure. They were then a prospect, and their name was given to a salesman in their locality."

"Sounds effective," I said. His patronizing look turned to one of affectionate pity.

He laughed softly. "I'll tell you, Jake, back in the days when costs were low and business was a whole different ball of wax, methods like that got by. But they don't any more. These days, a guy has got to hustle. We're hustling now, and we're growing fast."

I thought about the company's history, its apparent belt-tightening, its move to smaller quarters in California.

Pre-hustle. And pre-Morton.

"I can tell," I said brightly, "that you're a hustler."

He liked that. "That's right. That's absolutely right, Jake. And that's what I'm doing here. I was brought in to modernize the operation, make it flow, get this company the kind of business it deserves."

I put on my most eager face. He got up and began to walk around the office. "It's all in the way you organize things, Jake, and I've got one hot sales organization, let me tell you." Desperately, I tried to think of a way to get him onto the subject of his dead colleague. But it looked like I was going to get stuck with his sales pitch, instead.

He threw a shrewd, appraising look my way. "You really making money at this writing stuff, pal?"

I shrugged. He laughed.

"Well, let me tell you, some of our people are doing just fine. Just fine."

"Great," I said. "I guess everything depends on the product, doesn't it?" I was hoping to steer him around to things academic, but he wasn't having it.

"That's right," he said, nodding. "Absolutely. You take a good product and a right-on sales structure and you've got something, absolutely. And the right kind of sales materials." He scooped the old advertising album off the coffee table and returned it to the bookshelf. He brought back a looseleaf binder and opened that up. "See that? This is the kind of support we provide for our people. Entry level people, so they can move right on up the ladder." I glanced at the pages he was flipping for me. Sales talks or something.

"That's terrific," I said. "What ladder?"

He looked sly. "That's the thing. That is the thing. With my organization a man in the field can move right on up. He sells enough and shows enough promise, he can increase his commissions and get himself a whole new ball game of supervisory duties and privileges. Absolutely. I'll show you something." He scooped this book off the coffee table, and, like the first, replaced it neatly on the bookshelf. He came back this time with a chart.

The chart seemed to have something to do with the navy.

At the top was a box labeled CSO. Below that were several little boxes, each of which had the word "admiral" in it. Under each admiral were several little boxes called "commodores." Under those were captains, and under the captains were commanders and lieutenants. There were various percentages stuck beside each tier of boxes. The lowest percentages showed up next to the lieutenants.

I showed polite interest. "What does this mean?"

Morton leaned toward me, very earnest. "A man starts out as a lieutenant," he said. "As he moves up by showing his stuff, he gets a bigger cut of the pie. At the very top, here, an admiral, well, he runs a whole damned region of the country and he reports directly to me.

"Fascinating," I said. "And what's CSO?"

"Well, that's me, of course. Chief of Sales Operations. Get it? Chief of Naval Operations, Chief of Sales Operations." He smiled broadly.

"There's a lot of numbers here, percentages. But I can't quite tell how much a salesperson makes. Say a guy sells a two-hundred-dollar course. What's his take?"

"Depends. The average retail profit margin here is twenty, twenty-five percent, but there's a lot more to it than that. And that's what the ladder's all about, Jake. The higher you go, the bigger the profits, in volume and in percentages."

"Maybe," I said doggedly, "you could explain some of these percentages to me."

He looked a little impatient. "Well, look here, Jake. It says an admiral gets thirty-five percent plus a ten percent share plus a five percent bonus. Then for a commodore it's thirty percent, seven percent and two percent. Then for captain it's twenty-five percent and five percent, commanders get eighteen and five and lieutenants get a straight fifteen percent. Now what that means is an admiral makes a thirty-five percent retail profit. Then, on top of that, he gets a ten percent share of everything that everybody working below him makes. And on top of that, he gets, from the company, another five percent bonus if all his people make a certain volume quota in a given three-month period."

"Uh huh," I said. All I'd wanted to know was how much a guy made when he sold a course and I was being fed a can of worms. "So admirals and commodores get retail profit, a share of sales, and a bonus, captains and commanders get retail profit and shares, and lieutenants get retail profit."

"That's right, Jake!"

I could see he was proud of me.

"But why does everybody make a different retail profit?"

He got impatient again. "Well, they'd have to, wouldn't they? What you've got here is a differential. The admiral, he buys direct from the company. But everybody else buys direct from the guy above him. You take it on down—the commodore, he runs a statewide area, he buys from his admiral. The captain, he runs a citywide area, he buys from the commodore. And the lieutenants and commanders buy from their captains. See, the captains, commodores and admirals, they're the middlemen. You know, like from the farmer to the wholesaler to the grocery store. Got to have a differential. That's what pays these people for moving the product. They warehouse it, they do the paperwork, they run the meetings and training sessions. So what you've got here is a differential and some added incentives in the form of shares and bonuses."

"And you move up the ladder by . . . ?"

"Creating sales volume and maintaining it. And creating a sales organization in your area."

"Very impressive," I said, very bored. "And you set all this up? This was your idea?"

"Absolutely." I tried to give him back the chart. He told me to keep it.

"This must have meant big changes for the company. How did some of the old guard feel about that? People like Mr. Bowen and Mr. Armand and Mr. Smith?"

Morton stopped smiling and sat back in his chair, folding his arms and crossing his legs. "Well, now, I don't know why you'd want to ask a funny question like that, Jake. Who do you think brought me in to help out? And I don't know why you'd want to bring up poor Jim Smith at all. It was a terrible blow to us, his passing. I can hardly bear to think about that happening to a man like him. A fine, fine, man and I'll say no more on that subject."

"Certainly," I said reverently. "I understand. When did they bring you in, by the way—I mean, how long has this new system been in operation?"

"Oh, I'm the new boy on the block, all right," he laughed, fully recovered from his grief of a moment before. "I set up shop three years ago. Took a while to get things operational, of course. Yes, I'd say we've been fully operational for a couple of years now."

"Amazing."

"No, not really, Jake. We find the best and we give 'em the best to work with. Maybe you'd want to check this thing out for yourself, smart guy like you could make real money. Real money."

"Money's always interesting."

He laughed loudly. "You better believe it. You just give me a call any time you want to get in on the ground floor." He got up and pulled more items off the bookshelf. "Meanwhile, you can take a look at these." He handed me a couple of booklets. He didn't sit down again. Arm around my shoulder, he began to steer me toward the door. Once we got there, he herded me out into the hall and took me back to Bill Armand's office, leaving me in the care of Armand's secretary and telling me again to give him a call any time. Armand's secretary said it wouldn't be a minute until her boss could see me again.

But of course her boss had no intention of actually talking to me. He came striding out of his office and carried me off upstairs to meet the communications manager. "After all," he said, flashing his smile, "you two are kind of in the same business, aren't you?"

12

At the second floor landing, we turned to the right and entered a large, nearly bare room that held a single desk, and a single chair on which was sitting a very young, very attractive blond woman, reading a book. I caught a glimpse of the cover just before she caught a glimpse of the executive vice-president and tucked the book in a partly open drawer. It was a romance.

Armand threw her a tight little smile, glancing at the drawer, and led me across the expanse of blue carpet to an open office door.

Unlike the outer room, this one was small and cluttered. The woman who sat behind the desk didn't quite live up to Alan's "burnt out" description. She was, I guessed, in her early forties. Her eyes were deep blue, and had that tired look people get from years of the wrong kind of work or the wrong kind of marriage. The lids were dark and slightly crepey. Her hair was dark brown and cut straight across at shoulder length. Armand stepped back to usher me in. She smiled.

"Chloe," he said, "this is Jake Samson, the magazine writer I told you about. Mr. Samson, Chloe Giannapoulos, our director of communications." We mumbled at each other. "I'll just leave you two to get down to it, then," he added, disappearing from the doorway. The director of communications waved me to a chair. She dropped her eyes for just a moment to some papers on her desk. When she raised them again they were still tired, but there was also a glint of amusement in them.

"What are you after?" she wanted to know.

I launched into my little spiel about the home study phenomenon. She nodded solemnly.

"I see," she said. "It is a fascinating story, of course. What have you got there?" I was still clutching the papers and booklets I'd gotten from Bowen and Morton. I spread them out on her desk. That was when I noticed the one with the chubby silhouette on the cover. The one that started out, "This man studied at home." The silhouette belonged to Ben Franklin.

The woman sitting across from me tapped an index finger on Ben's nose. "Like this one?"

"Love it."

"I thought you would. It has all the history in it. Of the company. There's really nothing more to know." She tucked all my papers into a neat pile again. I picked them up and stuck them in various pockets.

"Oh, I wouldn't say that. History's important, of course, but it's now that counts."

"That's very good, Mr. Samson. 'It's now that counts.'" She smiled gently. "I would have known you were a writer even if Mr. Armand hadn't told me. Now, where would you like to begin?"

"Communications. What does that mean? What do you do?"

"We produce everything that's printed. Art and copy for advertising, promotional and sales materials. All the paper you've collected so far."

"And the courses?"

"We perform an editorial function. Editing and production."

"Ah hah! Is that why you're listed under both sales and academic? As two separate departments?"

"As two separate functions."

"And one of your functions is under the authority of one vice-president and the other is—or was—under the authority of another vice-president? Isn't that . . . tricky?"

She shrugged. "Maybe, sometimes. For them." She smiled, a woman who had everything under control. Or didn't give a damn. "Would you like to meet my staff, see some of the things they're doing?"

I didn't think she would want me to see all the things they were doing, and wondered how she'd keep that from happening. My wondering didn't last long. She poked at her intercom. I could hear the young woman at the outer desk in stereo, through the door and through the machine.

"Yes, Ms. Giannapoulos?"

"Would you tell the staff to stop throwing food at each other or whatever they're doing? I'm bringing them a visitor."

"Yes, Ms. Giannapoulos."

She didn't get up from her chair. Not yet. I figured she was trying to give her writers time to stash the brain surgery and nuclear physics courses they were writing.

"Perhaps, after that, you'd like to talk to someone in shipping?"

"Actually, I thought I'd ask you to lunch."

She looked at her watch. "It's only eleven-fifteen."

"I'm hungry."

She laughed and got up from her chair.

The receptionist was just returning to her chair from her staff-warning mission. She was about five foot nine and, next to her small, wiry boss, looked like an amazon. I've always kind of liked the idea of amazons, except for the part about cutting off a breast so they could shoot arrows better.

Chloe Giannapoulos guided me first into a well-lighted room where the artists worked. No desks, just big drafting tables and those little side cabinets they call taborets. I knew an artist once who used a taboret as a night table. I've never been able to see one since without imagining it to be full of exotic bed toys.

"This is Arlene Shulman," Giannapoulos was saying. "Our designer."

"Hi," I said.

"Yes," she said vaguely. "Nice to see you." I doubted that she remembered my name. I thought she probably remembered that we had met, since it had been only the night before. She returned to her contemplation of a large sheet of paper with some sort of layout blocked out in rectangles, squiggles, and amorphous forms. Taped up behind her desk was a large travel poster of Manhattan.

My guide also introduced me to two other young artists, a chunky blond man who was laboring over his board, and a thin, fidgety woman with beige hair, beige eyes, and beige skin.

"So," I said cheerfully, "what are you all working on?"

"Personally," Arlene said, "I'm working on becoming a free-lance book designer in New York."

The beige woman giggled. "She always says that, but she'll never leave."

Arlene's eyes showed depth for just a moment in a startling

70

flash of hatred directed at her coworker. Then she shrugged and looked blank again.

Giannapoulos acted as though no one had said anything, and began explaining the various projects the art department was working on: a magazine ad, a drafting course, and, being pasted up at top speed, the revision of a high school history course. Probably Alan's copy, I thought.

"Helen does pasteup faster than anyone we've ever had here," the manager said proudly. Helen was the beige woman.

"She should," Arlene snapped. "She's had years of experience doing those free classified newspapers."

I was not sorry to leave the art department, but it occurred to me that Arlene Shulman might be a woman I'd want to talk to again. I had the feeling she'd be happy to talk about anyone in the company.

The next stop, across the reception area from the artists, was the editorial office. It was a smaller room than the one the artists had. The four desks were jammed against each other in pairs. All three of the people in the room had pencils in their hands and were reading pages of manuscript or pasteups. They all had typewriters but no one was writing anything.

One of the three was more interested in my arrival than the other two. He sat facing the door across the expanse of two desks, one his own and the other an unoccupied one I guessed belonged to Alan. The man was about fifty, or maybe a dissipated forty-five, with greased thin dark hair, pouches under his eyes, and dark, beard-shadowed jowls. His name, Chloe said, introducing us, was Bert Franklin. Bert jumped up to shake my hand and I wished he hadn't. He was carrying the kind of paunch I spend a lot of time and energy trying not to get. Since I figured he was only about ten years older than me, the decay of his sagging physiognomy scared me. He smelled of tobacco and booze overlaid with breath mints. I wondered where he kept his stash.

The other two people in the office just smiled and kept on working, a woman in her early thirties and a young guy who looked about twenty-three. The writing staff didn't promise to be nearly as much fun as the artists. Maybe they were still in shock

71

from having one of their coworkers arrested right in front of them. In any case, the one who interested me was Bert Franklin. He looked like he'd kill for a bottle of sour mash.

Chloe began to explain what her editorial staff was doing. At the moment, she said, they were either editing copy or reading proofs of high school course revisions. Bert volunteered that he was spending most of his time "blocking out a new ad campaign" and working on the newsletter that was sent out to the salespeople. He was in charge of it, he said.

"So I guess you've had a lot of experience at that sort of thing," I said. He nodded, grand-old-man fashion.

We all chatted aimlessly for a while and then Chloe suggested we let her staff get back to their deadlines.

"Where would you like to go to lunch?" I asked as we returned to her office.

She looked at her watch, and I thought she was going to say she didn't have time or maybe that she just wanted a hot dog. She surprised me by suggesting a place in Sausalito that served good seafood and offered a view of San Francisco across the bay. Artie would not be happy with the expense bill for that day.

Fifteen minutes later, we were pulling off U.S. 101 at the Marin City exit down by the houseboats. There's a whole community of them there, and for years it's been the focus of political wrangling—sewage problems, development attempts, even class conflicts between the economically divergent elements of the community itself. I never really tried to understand the issues, but I hope the houseboats stay there forever.

We parked in one of the lots between Bridgeway Avenue and the bay. Parking was even more expensive than the last time I'd been there, and I wondered if there was nothing tourists wouldn't gladly pay to patronize the southern tip of Marin County.

The day was mild and sunny and the bay was decorated with sails of many sizes and colors and shapes. A ferry was docking, spitting out a lunchtime crowd from San Francisco. And Detroit. And Dallas. And Kyoto. We beat them to the restaurant, and we even got a table on the window wall. Chloe ordered Campari and soda. I thought about a nice heavy imported beer, but, with the image of Bert Franklin before my eyes, ordered a glass of Grey Riesling.

"Well, Mr. Samson. Did you get what you needed today?" I answered her half smile in kind. "Call me Jake. May I call you Chloe?" She inclined her head slightly. "Are you a Chicagoan, or did you just work there for a while?"

"Born there."

"Me, too. How about that." We both shook our heads over the mild coincidence. Since I'd lived in California I had met equal numbers of natives and transplanted midwesterners, and I expected that her experience was similar. We talked for a while about Chicago, the neighborhoods, the Loop, the old days of Richard Daley and his magical mayoral machine. Then I got back to the present.

"That's a very dedicated staff you have there, Chloe."

"Yes, aren't they? That's because they're working for such a good cause." She said it with a straight face. I went along with the joke.

"It's important to have a cause."

"It's important," she said, "to have a job."

"And Bert Franklin seems particularly dedicated. Has he been there long?"

"Two or three years. He did the same kind of work for a cosmetics company back east. Do you find him especially fascinating for some reason?"

"I find him fascinating for many reasons," I said truthfully.

She gave me the half smile again. "How nice. For both of you."

"I heard you had a little bit of drama at your office the other day. Must have been pretty upsetting to the staff. The arrest, I mean."

She had stiffened slightly, but she was still smiling. "We were also a little upset about the murder. Is that what you want to know about, Jake? I thought you were interested in the company."

"I'm interested in everything," I told her brightly. "That's what makes me such an interesting guy."

She laughed. Our drinks came and she took a sip of hers.

"The murder," I explained, "was what got me interested in

the company. Naturally I'm curious about it." Naturally.

"Just how interested are you in the company? I know what *Probe* is. What are you trying to prove?"

This was going to be a confusing case, I could see that now. She—and probably everybody else at Bright Future—thought I was after an exposé of the company. There I was, an unlicensed investigator looking for a killer, pretending to be doing a story on correspondence schools, and suspected of trying to dig up a business scandal.

"*Probe* does not," I said self-righteously, "investigate murders. If you know what *Probe* is, you know that. But I do know that one of your executives was killed, and that one of your employees was arrested. It's common knowledge. I was just making conversation, Chloe."

She looked at me for a long moment. "Yes," she said. "One of our executives was killed and one of my employees was arrested. But I really doubt that he did it."

"His knife did it." She shrugged, sipping at her drink and gazing out the window. "And someone at your office told the cops he'd had a fight with Smith."

She turned back to me. "So?"

I raised my hands in surrender. "Okay, I'll change the subject. Why did the company move to California?"

"That's easy, but not very interesting."

"Tell me anyway."

"The company had always done all right, grew a lot in the fifties, stabilized in the sixties, rode out the early seventies. Bowen wanted to expand, open a new shop out here. He just didn't see the economic handwriting on the wall, didn't understand it wasn't a good time to take chances. He sent Armand out here and bought the new building, began to relocate parts of the business. Bowen came out a few times. By the time they realized they couldn't support the expansion, Bowen's old bones—and his wife's—had fallen in love with sunny San Rafael. The building here was smaller and prettier. They pulled out of Chicago entirely. See? nothing to it. Things were tight for a while, now they're fine again. No story there."

74

So that was it, I thought. They'd blown it by making a bad move. And things had gotten tight enough to bring in the razzle-dazzle man. "I had an interesting talk with Morton about the sales structure," I said. "Has it made a big difference to the company?"

"Yes." I waited for more. There wasn't any more. The waiter came again and we ordered lunch.

"Do you have more students than you had before?"

"I have no idea."

"Maybe," I said, "you'd rather talk about the murder."

"I don't know anything about the murder."

"Don't you know anyone who hated Smith?"

She laughed. "I wasn't crazy about him myself."

"Okay," I said. "I'll try again. Tell me about the courses you work on."

"I've got a capable staff."

"You don't trust me, do you?" I tried to look hurt. She laughed once more, but it was a different kind of laugh.

"Look, let's get straight with each other, all right? I used to be in your end of the business. Not much in the way of magazines, but both wire services and a couple of newspapers. Depending on how ambitious you are, the story comes before damned near everything else. I know exactly where you're coming from. And how you got there. You know what you represent to me? One of the five men ahead of me in line for the job, any job. I'm talking about the good old days before the women's movement." Our lunch came and she paused while the waiter served the food. My fried oysters looked good. Chloe stabbed hard with her fork at her crab soufflé and jammed some in her mouth. I ate a small oyster. She chewed, swallowed, and went on.

"There were women back then who were tough enough to push their way through. I was an innocent kid. I didn't have the ego to fight or the humility to take it. I don't know how long you've been doing this, but it's long enough, and long enough means you've stepped over some talented women to get the jobs you've had. I want another drink."

I waved at the waiter and got her another drink. One for me, too. I wanted to tell her I wasn't really a reporter, and that I knew how hard it must have been because my friend Rosie was a carpenter and it hadn't been easy for her, either, even though she was ten years younger than Chloe. I wanted to tell her that I believed women were people. I just looked at her, my tongue stuck to the roof of my mouth. I couldn't feel guilty for being a man. Just grateful.

Chloe lit another cigarette and muttered, "I shouldn't talk about it. It makes me smoke and drink." She took a deep swallow from her glass and settled back in her chair. "Besides, it's not your fault. It was mine. I just wasn't strong enough or smart enough or patient enough or some damned thing. But you asked me if I trusted you? Are you serious? You're doing a job. You could probably justify an exposé even if the company folded and every innocent who works there was tossed out on the street."

I leaned across the table and put everything I had into my disclaimer. "I'm not doing an exposé. Please believe that. I don't know how to convince you, but it's true."

"I don't believe you, because I can't imagine what else you could be doing. If you are doing something else, tell me what it is and don't give me that crap about a nice little piece on home study."

I couldn't. Since we'd started lunch I'd revised my earlier picture of the amazon. Amazons were small and wiry and forty years old. And sometimes dangerous. For all I knew she'd killed Smith herself.

I raised my hands in surrender. "I don't know what to tell you. I wish we could be friends."

"Okay. We're friends. As long as you don't ask me any questions about the company."

"And what it sells?"

She kept her eyes on her drink. "And what it sells."

13

Only a few cars were parked on the canyon floor. Artie's and Julia's were not among them. I climbed the steps to my room, grabbed some clean socks and underwear, and walked over to Artie's.

I knocked. No one answered, so I used my key. Sure enough, no one was there, not even Berkeley the golden retriever. The bathroom was all mine.

Now, there's a myth that macho guys like me, men of action, always on the run, always just a little late for the next adventure, cleanse our bodies and refresh our spirits only in showers hard-driving enough to match our lifestyles. It's not true. Oh, I like a shower as well as the next man. But for real relaxation and real thinking, there's nothing like a long, hot bath. With or without bubbles.

After an entire morning and part of the afternoon at Bright Future, I felt the need for a bath. I filled the tub to the overflow, stepped carefully over a column of ants that was marching from the faucet wall, along the tub, and down to the floor, and settled in with my thoughts.

Bowen, the founder. A living anachronism. Flashes of intelligence in what seemed to be a generally dulled personality. Just drifting. Someone else had to be doing the real work. Howard Morton was easily the most dynamic type I'd met there, with the exception of Chloe. But Chloe had her own cloud cover, her own way of drifting. And she didn't, as far as I could tell, have much power. Morton had been brought in to make things go, and maybe he had also been given the autonomy to do it. He could have an empire out there in the field.

But there was also Bill Armand. The man with two jobs. If his titles meant anything, he held all the power in the company. I'd gotten a chance to spend some time with him, finally, after lunch, when he'd insisted on giving me a tour of the parts of the building I hadn't seen yet, and didn't particularly want to see.

I reached across the rim of the bathtub to retrieve my notebook, which I'd placed conveniently on the toilet seat along with some of the Bright Future propaganda I'd brought home, and knocked about a dozen ants into the water. I scooped up as many as I could get to and put them back in the traffic pattern to dry. The others broke ranks and zigzagged around them, waving their antennae.

Old Ed and his two assistants. The assistants had been busy packing courses into boxes. Old Ed was fumbling around in a pile of orders, but stopped fumbling long enough to shake my hand with his own sweaty one.

A typing pool of bored young women.

Someone sitting in a cubicle doing something with a computer.

An empty conference room with a very long, polished table. Smith's vacant office.

Armand hadn't planned on showing me Smith's vacant office, but when we passed a closed door with his name on it, I asked to have a look.

Armand the Smooth didn't ask me why. He just shrugged and pushed the door open. The office was about the size of Morton's, but the bookshelves were neater. I'd tried to get information about possible replacements for Smith, but Armand had been noncommittal. I'd tried to pump Armand about Smith's attitude toward recent changes in the company's way of doing business, but there was nothing doing there, either.

Some of the ants had dried out and rejoined their comrades. The others remained crumpled up and inert, obstacles the column marched around.

All in all, I had a strong feeling that nobody at Bright Future had told me a damned thing I could use.

I needed to find out more, maybe from Chloe, maybe from Arlene. Did Smith and Morton have a conflict? Where did Armand fit in? Why did the company think its sales force was a navy? Did Bowen care?

I set my notebook aside and reached for the handful of Bright Future paper. The first few items, the sketchy course descriptions I'd glanced at in Morton's office, I skimmed again and tossed on the floor. They were followed by the sales organization chart. That left me with a newsletter of about sixteen pages and a booklet, smaller and thicker than the newsletter.

I started with the newsletter, which was called *Bright Star*. This, I remembered, was Bert Franklin's handiwork. White paper, red headlines, and blue copy. A red spiral staircase on each side of the name. The photograph on the front page also was printed in red. Three guys clapping each other on the back. One of them was Howard Morton, showing pink teeth in a grin. The caption said the other two men were the "numero uno" and "numero dos" captains for the month of January. One of them was captain of San Diego, the other of Seattle. The story, the caption said, was on page 3.

Page 2 had another photo of Morton and a long inspirational piece signed by him. It had to do with "strong, independent business people" and "eagles soaring to the full altitude of human potential."

The story on page 3, which included mug shots of the two supercaptains, was all about how they'd taken their cities to the top of the charts. I noticed no specific amounts of money were mentioned, but there was no way the reader could avoid imagining these guys wallowing in money and adulation.

I thumbed on. A lot of stuff about the value of training. Not much about the value of the courses. Just one page titled "new testimonials." These were quotes from students about how they were getting rich and happy through accounting or how their high school diploma had opened the doors to success. There were many, many hyped-up mentions of commodores and admirals. I took Morton's chart from the pile. Those were the two highest titles under Morton himself.

The most used word throughout was "excited." Everybody was excited about something—the product, the training, the opportunity. I, however, failed to catch the mood. I tossed the newsletter on the floor with the rest of the advertising and picked up the booklet.

It appeared to be some kind of institutional brochure, something they used when they wanted to look classy. The cover was solid blue with a single, silver spiral staircase in the upper right-hand corner. The first page was a sheet of what looked like thick onionskin, blank except for the staircase reproduced like a watermark, this time in the lower right-hand corner. This was followed by a blank page of the same coated paper that filled the rest of the brochure. Then came the history. The old building, with a shot of a crowded, old-fashioned office. A photo of the new building, taken with a wide-angle lens and several shots of the elegant new quarters. Bowen now and Bowen in 1953, maybe wearing the same suit I'd seen him in that day. The heading over the shots of the buildings was "Tradition and Growth Through Caring." The one for Bowen's page was "A Man and a Vision." I didn't read the text. I didn't read anything until I got to the last page, and I couldn't resist that. It was The Bright Future Creed. It went like this:

"To offer to all the opportunity for success through education; to offer to all within our ranks the opportunity to sail freely and speedily to the far horizons of financial security and self-reliance."

If Chloe Giannapoulos had written this, she must have done it with her office door closed so no one would see her cracking up.

I went back to my notebook again, and flipped to the pages on the canyon residents. Hanley the gardener who shot trees. Jim the computer-something who was in charge of gravel. Eric the critic and spillway checker. Mary the bookstore owner and county records searcher. Charlie the group leader. Nona the painter. Carlota the filmmaker and caretaker of the wooden stairway. Which reminded me of Rosie, and her estimate, and her one-on-one cocktail party with Carlota, which had been scheduled for that afternoon. Rosie and I were having dinner together, so I'd find out soon enough how that had gone.

The column of ants had completed its journey or its mission. A few individuals were making erratic circles around the bodies of the ones who hadn't survived their dip in the bathtub. The cleanup crew, or the undertakers. One by one, they picked up the corpses and dragged them off.

I got out of the tub.

Rosie was waiting, with Alice, on the steps outside my room.

"I'm hungry," she said.

"What does Alice want for dinner?"

"She ate. In our new canyon residence."

"Which is?"

80

"Carlota's spare room."

"You're going to share a house with Carlota and Nona?" An amusing idea.

Rosie thought so, too. "Well, only sort of. It's a basement room, lower level. Has its own entrance." She laughed. "And a toilet. And I don't plan to share their kitchen."

"Or anything else, I hope. How was cocktail hour?"

"Very short. I gave her my estimate for the steps, which she accepted, had a quick glass of wine, and escaped to buy the materials. I start work on the job tomorrow."

We decided to try a pizza place she'd noticed on her way to the lumber yard. We took my car, since there wasn't room in the cab of the pickup for two people and a large dog, and Alice was not allowed to ride in the back of the truck.

"This is working out perfectly," Rosie said after she'd eaten her first bite of pizza-with-everything-but-anchovies. "I'll be right there in the canyon where I can keep an eye on things. I should be able to pick up a lot. We can hash things over every night."

"Well, maybe not tomorrow night," I told her. "I've got a date with Iris over in the East Bay. After I've finished tomorrow's quota of running around, I may just head over there to clean up. Visit the cats. You know."

She thought a minute. "I'm going to be over there tomorrow night, too. We could check in with each other, just to see if we've got anything important to pass on. If we miss each other at home, I'll be at Polly's later." Polly's was, depending on what term you prefer to use, a lesbian/dyke/women's bar/club/entertainment center.

"Okay. Got a date with someone interesting?"

"I don't know yet how interesting she is. I've only talked to her once."

I ate a slice of pizza. "So, tell me, what's your information-gathering plan?"

"For starters, I get the feeling that Carlota knows everything that goes on around there."

"What gives you the idea that Nona will give you a chance to hang around talking to Carlota?"

"Carlota gets home from work three hours before Nona does."

81

"And what makes you think Carlota knows anything we can use?"

Rosie grinned. "Let's just say that she seems to be my assignment, so I hope she knows more than anyone you talk to."

"No question about it, Rosie, you've got the most dangerous end of it this time."

14

Just because people live in Mill Valley, it's not safe to assume they like narrow, twisted roads, giant trees, houses on stilts, slugs, and mildew. The town is a bedroom community with equal shares of rustic, quaint, and suburban-civilized.

The Smith house was on an ordinary upper-middle-class street of level lots and mixed architectural styles. There was fake Tudor, brown shingle, redwood siding and glass, Spanish, and California bungalow. The late James Smith's residence was a tidy, medium-size frame house, white with blue trim. It had a small front lawn with no brown spots, crab grass, or dandelions, and the walk was edged with tough, charmless juniper, clipped like a hedge. I'm always suspicious of people who stick juniper in their yards. I figure their second choice would be cardboard cutouts of bushes.

But then, the juniper could have been there before the Smiths moved in.

The doorknocker was the brass head of a harmless looking lion. The woman who answered the door was wearing a gray herringbone dress with a white collar and a white belt. The dress covered her trim, fifty-year-old figure closely and neatly, the way her beauty shop set and brown-rinsed hair covered her head. All very crisp and untouchable. She questioned me politely with cool blue eyes.

"Jake Samson," I said. "I called this morning."

She nodded. "Come in, Mr. Samson. I'm Mrs. James Smith." She did not, apparently, have a first name of her own.

She led me through a formal entry hall into a formal, characterless living room and sat me down in a reasonably comfortable chair that should have had a footstool to go with it, set at right angles to a stiff-looking three-cushion couch. I was facing a fireplace with a nice old mantel of dark wood. There wasn't a speck of dust, let alone ash, beneath the brass andirons.

"What can I do for you, Mr. Samson? You're a writer of some sort?"

"That's right," I said. If I kept this up long enough I might start believing it myself. "I'm doing a magazine piece on Bright Future, and of course I wanted to talk to you about your husband. After all, he was one of the company's guiding lights."

"He certainly was," she said, with a smile as cool as her eyes and an edge of brittle suspicion in her well-modulated voice. "Of course you realize it isn't easy for me to discuss him so soon after our tragedy." That was when I remembered whom she reminded me of. Once when I was a young cop in Chicago I'd been briefly assigned to the Conrad Hilton suite of a big-time evangelist who was playing Chicago that week. The evangelist's wife spoke of her husband with the same kind of practiced reverence. A woman playing the emperor's wife, managing to convey with every word, every expression, that she was proud to sacrifice herself to the greatness of her man. She was as genuine as the emperor's new clothes.

"I understand that," I said softly. "But I just didn't feel the picture would be complete without talking to you." I could be reverent, too.

"Would you like a cup of coffee, Mr. Samson?"

"No, thank you very much. I'll try not to keep you for long. Just tell me about yourself, how you felt about your husband's work, his role in the company. Your family. I believe you have two children?"

Her tiny little smile twitched. "Yes, that's right."

"A son and a daughter?"

"Only the daughter's at home. She's sixteen. She'll be home from school any time now."

"Oh, good, I'd like to meet her." Mrs. James Smith nodded, once. "And your son? Where is he?"

She startled me by laughing indulgently. "Well, my son is thirty-two years old. Naturally, he's off on his own."

"Does he live around here? I'd like to talk to him, too, if it's at all possible."

"Oh, he lives some distance from here, I'm afraid."

"Oh? Where?"

She frowned and said shortly, "Mendocino."

"The town or the county?"

"The town." Her lips were tight.

"And what is his name?"

"You wanted to talk about my husband's work and how his family worked along with him, isn't that right?"

"Yes," I said. "That's right." I heard the front door open. An adolescent girl strolled into the room. I don't know what I expected the daughter of Mrs. Smith to look like, but it wasn't like this. Not that she wasn't neat, trim, and brittle-looking. She was, but in the eerie interplanetary style of the eighties. Plucked eyebrows, dark red lipstick, hair short at back and sides and tossed around on top, tight pants, high-heeled shoes, and a red leather jacket with immense shoulders. Her gaze was also just another version of her mother's, cool, with a touch of the robot thrown in for good measure. She was carrying a book.

Mrs. Smith hesitated—I could almost feel the shudder under her skin when she looked at her daughter—and then introduced us.

"Bunny, this is Mr. Samson. My daughter, Bunny. Why don't you go to your room, dear?"

"Pleased to meet you, Bunny."

Without even glancing at her mother, Bunny replied, leering slightly, "My friends call me Barbara. What's your name?"

"Jake," I said.

"Mr. Samson and I are having a business conversation, Bunny."

The kid's eyes went robotic again, she shrugged and left the room. Mrs. Smith began a monologue about Bright Future and her husband's theory of education, all that stuff about studying at your own pace in the comfort of your own home. I scribbled in my notebook and let her babble on for a while, then pushed back toward more personal topics by asking about the family's move to California, how long they'd lived in Chicago, that kind of thing. Then I got back to the son.

"You say your son is thirty-two, Mrs. Smith?" She looked wary, but she nodded. "And Bunny is sixteen. Was your son—uh, what was his name again?—from a previous marriage?"

She smiled patronizingly. "I've had only one marriage, Mr. Samson, and I expect to live out my days having had only one marriage." I guessed she hadn't liked it all that much the first time. "Bunny was . . ." she paused.

"A pleasant surprise?" I said brightly.

"Exactly."

We had managed to skirt the vile edges of sex, though, and that was a mistake. She got restless.

"Perhaps we could continue this conversation another time, Mr. Samson? I have a lot to do today."

"I understand," I said. "So do I. Just a couple more questions, Mrs. Smith?" She continued to sit on the edge of her seat.

I asked her how her husband felt about the new sales system at Bright Future.

"My husband," she said, "was always loyal to his company and to whatever was good for his company." The woman, I thought, should go into politics.

"I'm sure he was. Mrs. Smith, could you tell me why your husband was in the canyon that day?"

"The police asked me that. It's very simple. We were considering buying a lot there. He walked over to take another look. He was concerned about the water, the runoff. There had been heavy rain. The lot is at the bottom of the canyon. He wanted to be sure the water was contained."

That explained why he'd been puttering around up top.

"I think that will be all for today, Mrs. Smith. Except of course I would like to be able to make some mention of your family members, even those I don't talk to. What did you say your son's name was?" I'd guessed right. Once she thought I wasn't going to try to talk to him, she was willing to give me his name. I wondered why that was so.

She stood up and it was time for me to leave. I thanked her

and allowed myself to be escorted to the door. She didn't waste much time saying goodbye.

As I slid behind the wheel of my car, Bunny-Barbara sidled up. She must have left the house by the back door. She was still carrying her book.

"Uh, hey," she said, "how about a lift down to Throckmorton?"

"Sure," I told her. "Get in." She did. She leaned against the door, one foot up on the passenger seat, and stared at me. I started the car and rolled off in the direction of downtown Mill Valley.

"What's that you're reading?" I asked, by way of opening a conversation I didn't really expect to be very productive.

"I'm not reading anything," she said.

"I mean the book you're carrying around."

"Oh. Yeah. It's my journal. I take it everywhere. You know, so I can keep track of my life." She gave an odd little laugh. "That's what journals are for. Stuff that happens to you. Thoughts. What kind of business you talking with my mother?"

I gave her the line about working for a magazine and told her about my conversation with Mrs. Smith.

"Pleasant surprise, huh? I was an accident and a girl at that. And my brother was an even worse disaster."

"Yeah? How's that?"

"I'm the only one in the family that talks to him. My father wouldn't see him at all. My mother let him in the house once a couple of years ago, but it was so weird I don't think either one of them would let it happen again."

We were getting very close to Throckmorton Avenue and downtown Mill Valley. "Why is that?" I asked her.

"Shit, man," she said eloquently. "You met my mother. My father was worse." I nodded noncommittally. "Don't you get it?" I shook my head. "He's gay, man." She laughed raucously. "He really did 'em in."

"But you're in touch with him?"

She turned cold. "Yeah. Any reason why I shouldn't be? I love him. He's real nice to me, takes me to movies sometimes— weird art ones—and out for dinner. Just let me out in the parking lot."

86

I drove slowly into the municipal parking lot that served most of downtown Mill Valley and the tiny bus station as well.

"I'd like to talk to your brother," I said.

"Why?"

"I want to find out more about your father's life."

"You're a cop."

"No."

She narrowed her eyes at me, thought a moment, and shrugged. "My brother lives in Mendocino. He's got a hotel up there." She told me the name of the hotel.

"Bill Smith?" I stopped the car.

"Did mother tell you his name? That's pretty good." She nodded her approval of my expertise. "You want to go out sometime, Jake?" I gave her a look. She laughed at my discomfort. "No jail bait, huh? Too bad. You want to read my journal?"

"No, I don't think so."

"Sure you do. It's hot."

"It's also private."

"You think so?" She snickered. "Don't you want to know how I felt about my father?"

"Yes, but you've told me that, in a way."

"Come on, have a look. You don't have to be scared. Come on. It's hot," she repeated.

"Okay. Okay. Let me see it."

She handed me the book. Its paper cover was printed in a marble pattern, the predominant color mauve, that favorite of the Victorians. Or was it the Edwardians? I opened it up. The inside front cover still had the price sticker, with the identification "Mary's Bookstore." Which was the name of Artie's neighbor's shop. The price had been scribbled out. The inscription on the flyleaf said the book was a gift to his daughter on her birthday, from daddy. It included the admonition to use the book well and create a structure to her life. The message was dated the week before his death.

I turned the page. And another, and another. The journal was blank. I gave it back to her.

Bunny was looking at me slyly, waiting for me to comment on any one of several meanings the book's emptiness might have. I didn't. She laughed, dug around in her pocket, and handed me a purple card printed with her name, address, and telephone number. "That's my private phone," she said. "In case you want to know anything more about accidents and disasters." Then she got out of the car and strolled off in the direction of the bus station.

15

Over dinner at Sen Ying's that night, I told Iris Hughes about the goings-on in Foothill Canyon, and, since I was trying to be amusing, I leaned heavily on stories of canyon residents.

"I'd love to meet Carlota and Nona," she said, grinning. "I can't believe Rosie is actually staying at their house. I don't know whether to feel sorry for her or envy her the experience. Could be useful in my field."

Iris's field is psychotherapy. She and Rosie had met the previous autumn. They like each other, and I could see that Iris was enjoying the imagined spectacle of good old straightforward Rosie evading the slithery advances of Carlota. Not to mention possible retribution by Nona the intense.

I laughed with her. "We'll get to hear about her first day, if it's okay with you. I told her we might meet her later. At Polly's. Polly's is a—"

"I know what Polly's is," Iris rejoined. "That's great. I can't wait to hear."

I studied her for a minute. "I didn't know you were familiar with Polly's."

She raised an eyebrow at me. "Jake," she said. "I know all kinds of people, just like you do. And I've been all kinds of places."

I wanted to know more, but I'd been seeing Iris off and on for months, and I'd finally conceded that there were going to be a lot of things about her that I'd probably never know. I knew I liked her. I knew that she was beautiful in an Anglo-Saxon way that I find irresistibly exotic. At one point, I'd even thought I was in love with her, but I didn't know how I felt about that now. The attraction was strong, but even when we made love I didn't feel like I was getting, so to speak, to the bottom of her.

Anyway, after we'd polished off the sizzling rice soup and potstickers, and started on the sweet and sour shrimp and Szechuan chicken, we began one of our many traditional debates. I wanted to see a movie about a forties-style detective; she wanted to see a Russian film about love and death among communal farmers on the Kamchatka Peninsula.

"We saw a film last time," I said. "This time we should see a movie."

She couldn't argue with that. Fair's fair.

And Iris is a good sport. She shared a small box of greasy popcorn with me, held hands, and laughed in all the right places.

We got out of the movie about eleven-thirty and drove through South Berkeley into North Oakland. The parking lot at Polly's was full, but I found a spot on the street. We pushed through the padded upholstery-tack studded double doors and were greeted by a large female doorperson who asked to see our identification. We presented our drivers' licenses, were judged to be both well-behaved and old enough to drink, and were waved graciously into the dark, red-wallpapered barroom. We didn't see Rosie at the bar or at the small tables scattered about the room, so we settled in on two recently vacated seats at the bar. The bartender, an acquaintance of Rosie's I'd met once or twice at the cottage, glanced at us and nodded. After she had finished making a couple of margaritas, and had rung up the sale, she cleared the empty glasses off the bar top in front of us and asked what we wanted.

"Have you seen Rosie around tonight?" I asked.

"Uh huh. She's in back. At the show. Cut and Run."

"Huh?" Was she telling me to leave, for some reason?

"Cut and Run. It's a band. New Wave. Should be out soon."

We ordered drinks. About fifteen minutes later, the door to the performance hall opened and a rush of music-high women came through. Rosie was among them. She had her arm around the waist of a pale woman with dark hair. She was about thirty years old and was wearing a blue brocade jacket over faded jeans, which were tucked into the tops of English riding boots. I thought of Arlene, who would have approved. Rosie looked gorgeous in a ratty gray suede jacket, jeans, and, of course, her passé cowboy boots.

I waved and Rosie steered her friend to where we sat at the bar.

Her friend's name was Joyce. She had a hot pink streak in her hair and was wearing a lot of eye makeup. I have never been able to figure out what Rosie's type might be. We mumbled around with the "how are you" stuff for a minute. Joyce looked bored already.

The formalities over, I got right to it. "So? Anything interesting from your end? How's Carlota?"

Rosie laughed. Iris leaned forward, toward her, brandy snifter clutched in both hands.

Joyce frowned. "What are you talking about?" Rosie gave a brief explanation of what she was doing in the canyon. Very brief and not very true. Something about checking on someone who owed a friend some money.

Then she turned back to me. "Carlota was weird, naturally. She flirted and twitched and talked about how wonderful Nona is and what a great painter she is. And how difficult it is to live as an artist. I think that's a direct quote, but may not be. Somehow it doesn't sound phony enough."

Joyce spoke up again. "Really, Rosie," she said. "Don't you think it's a little, well, incorrect, to discuss intimate things about another woman with . . . these people?" Not waiting for Rosie's answer, she leaned over the bar and ordered a bottle of mineral water, orange flavored, and a beer. The beer was for Rosie. Then she excused herself and went to talk to a friend while we finished our "business."

Rosie was blushing, half apologetic, half amused. "Sorry. Joyce seems to lack the social graces."

"Or thinks we do," Iris said comfortably, "since we're interfering in her date with you. What the heck, Rosie, at least she didn't call us 'breeders.'"

90

They both cackled about that, and I tried to get in on the peace-keeping mission. "Maybe it just made her jealous to hear you talking about another woman."

Rosie shrugged. "Who can tell? But listen, something more peculiar than Carlota's personality is going on in that canyon." I was dying to hear what it was, but Polly's on a busy night can be a hard place to have a private conversation with Rosie. She always seems to get involved in a lot of conversational byplay and odds and ends of affectionate greeting. A small woman carrying a large motorcycle helmet came up behind Rosie, hugged her, kissed her on the cheek, and said she knew someone who knew someone who wanted a basement finished. Rosie promised to call her. Polly herself strolled by, her forty-year-old person turned out in bow tie, pegged pants, and a new and wonderfully awful-looking punk hairdo. She put one arm around me and one arm around Rosie, recommended some wine she was selling cheap, and, after being introduced to Iris, asked me why she didn't see us more often. Then she wandered off.

"Now!" I said to Rosie. "Tell me now."

"It's Hanley. He's scaring Carlota half to death. She says he's watching her. She told me he's started using the steps that go past her house, even though the path at his end of the canyon is a quicker route up and down for him. She says he looks in her kitchen window."

"Peeping?" Iris asked clinically.

Rosie shook her head. "She doesn't think so. And while I was working on the steps this afternoon, I saw him standing on that bridge, over on the other side of the canyon. He had binoculars. They seemed to be aimed at her windows."

"Not at you?"

"No, I was a good ten steps below her deck."

I thought about it. "Maybe he's changing hobbies. Maybe he's tired of shooting trees and has taken up Carlota-watching. It could be pretty entertaining." I treated the matter lightly, but I was not happy about nutso Hanley aiming binoculars anywhere near Rosie.

"I think," Rosie said, agreeing with my thoughts and not my words, "that it's pretty damned peculiar."

91

Iris, who had been listening very carefully and with some delight, asked a logical question. "Why doesn't Carlota ask him what he's doing?"

Rosie sighed. "I don't know. Maybe she's afraid he'll tell her."

It was my turn to tell about my day with the Smiths. Since I skimmed over my encounter with Bunny, limiting it to information obtained, the story didn't take very long. Joyce returned to catch the last couple minutes of it. She pretended she wasn't listening, but she knew when I'd reached the end because she took that opportunity to ask Rosie to dance.

Iris and I had one more drink and went back to my house.

Tigris and Euphrates were sleeping on the front porch, curled up together, and followed us into the house yawning, stretching, and complaining. While I fed them, listened to their problems, and scratched behind their ears, Iris built a fire in the Franklin stove. I made coffee and we sank down on the couch to admire the flames and console the cats for my frequent absences. No doubt about it, Iris is beautiful. Sometimes it knocks me out just to look at her. The blond ice maiden with glacier gray eyes that can flash hot enough to pierce a man clear through. She was wearing one of her tailored silk blouses, a lavender one, unbuttoned just far enough down to keep me preoccupied. She folded her hands behind her head, slitted her eyes at the fire, and got me talking about the case. By the time she'd stopped asking questions, she knew everything there was to know, from me anyway.

"So," I said, dragging my eyes away from her mouth, "what do you think?"

"I think you have a problem. Are you sure this young man didn't do it?"

"Pretty sure."

"Well, that leaves only about a dozen suspects," she said.

"Hanley, because he's crazy. That's one."

"And Smith's son," she added, "because his father rejected him."

"I guess." I hadn't thought much about Smith's son.

"And then there's all the people he worked with. Depending

92

on what's going on in that company, there could be some pretty strong motives. Doesn't sound like he was terribly popular. What about that woman—what's her name?"

"You mean Chloe?"

"Yes. Chloe."

"Nah. I don't think so."

"Jake, you can't just cross off people you like. That's not very professional. And you do like her. I can tell by the way you talk about her." Could that be just the tiniest edge of jealousy in her voice?

"So what," I said. "I like you, too. A lot. I would like to like you a lot right now."

She smiled. "Don't you want to talk about the case any more?"

"No."

She turned toward me. It's amazing how warm gray eyes can look.

16

The morning was bright, dry, and clear. By the time I got back to Marin I had decided it was a good day for the long drive north to Mendocino. I stopped at a phone booth and called Bill Smith's to see if I could get a room. The woman who answered the phone said I could.

I packed a bag and had just locked my door and turned to go down the steps when Arlene sauntered up.

"Where are you going?" she wanted to know.

"Won't Chloe miss you at work?" I countered.

"I was waiting for you. I want to talk to you. Can we go inside?"

I was feeling antsy about getting on the road, but you have to take possibly helpful conversation when it comes. I unlocked the door. Arlene walked in and sat on the bed. I put my bag down and leaned against the work table.

"You're investigating the murder, aren't you?" I began to pro-test, but she cut me off. "I don't care what you say. You'll lie. Why shouldn't you?" She took a deep breath. I could feel her tension, but, as always, nothing showed in her eyes. "Hanley didn't do it. I understand why you might think he would, but he didn't. He was with me that night and that morning, so leave him alone. He gets upset very easily and he might get violent if he thinks you're picking on him."

"I guess that's why he shoots the trees. Because they pick on him."

She nodded. "In a way. You have to understand him. He's very sensitive."

I shook my head. "No, Arlene, I don't have to understand him. You have to understand him because you live with him, but I don't."

She looked shocked. "I don't live with him. I stay overnight sometimes. I couldn't actually live with him." She gazed blankly over my shoulder and out the window. "I need my space." I had thought that particular expression had died with the seventies, but apparently some people still found it useful.

She continued. "What people don't understand is that he acts crazy because he's so frustrated by his work. When he shoots a redwood tree, it's a social commentary. Really, he has flashes of genius when it comes to social commentary."

I wanted to get to the point of all this, but my curiosity won out. "How is it a social commentary to shoot a redwood tree?"

"It's his customers. Their ignorance and destructiveness. They're always wanting him to cut down trees and prune things in the wrong season and kill perfectly healthy plants and poison per-fectly harmless bugs. He hates it. He loses a lot of clients by argu-ing with them or 'forgetting' to do things. So when he gets drunk he shoots trees. Big trees with little bullets. Too big to kill with little bullets. It's his way of expressing irony, you see."

I thought about it, and realized I'd have to think about it some more.

"Okay," I said. "Tell me this. Spying on Carlota—is that a social commentary, too?"

She seemed unconcerned. "Oh, is he doing that? With binoculars, I suppose? Well, he has mentioned to me that he doesn't trust her. I don't quite know why. But he won't hurt her or anything."

"I'll try to take your word for it. Maybe you can do something for me, too."

She smirked. "I'm sure I could." I let that go.

"What I mean is, maybe you could tell me some things about Bright Future. No one would ever know you told me."

"I wouldn't care if they did. I could always collect unemployment."

So I asked her about Morton, and his sales scheme. And I asked her about Smith's relationship with Morton, and I asked her to tell me everything she knew about Chloe and Bert Franklin and Armand and Bowen.

She didn't know anything about the Bright Future navy, and said she never paid attention to "things like that." Nor did she know much about Armand and Bowen. She called Armand "frosted glass," which I rather liked, and Bowen, she said, was "totally doddering." All she would say about Chloe was that she had nothing but good to say about her.

"Smith was a—what's a good word—a prig." She laughed. "A male chauvinist prig." This woman really had a way with words. "He was patronizing with women, including Chloe. He had this thing about morality and tradition. He gave me the creeps. He and Morton didn't get along. I saw them talking to each other once in the hall and they looked like a pair of male dogs, circling each other, all stiff-legged and snarly."

She said she didn't know much about Morton except that he was "a classic—you know what I mean," and that he'd come to Bright Future from a cosmetics company that had folded "for some reason no one talks about."

I took hold of that. "Didn't Bert Franklin come from a cosmetics company?"

"Uh huh. Same one. It was called Perfect Day. I think Morton got Bert the job at B.F."

Unfortunately, that was all she had on the subject. I asked her one more question. "Who told the cops about Alan's argument with Smith?"

"Oh, I did. Just in case someone started suspecting Hanley. But I wasn't the only one. Bert told them, too."

I looked at my watch. I really wanted to get started on that 150 miles. "Well, thanks Arlene. Can I talk to you again?"

She got up and walked slowly toward me. I already had my back to the edge of the table, and couldn't retreat any farther. She stood about two inches from me. I could feel her warm breath.

"You will leave Han alone, won't you, Jake?" She reached out and stroked my hand. "I'd be your friend if you'd do that."

The rhythm of her stroke was familiar. And the touch. I pulled my hand away. "It was you, wasn't it? In the hot tub?" I accused. She smiled mysteriously. I slid sideways and got away from her. "I have to leave now," I said sternly. She allowed me to usher her out the door, threw me one more sexy smile—her eyes were still blank—and walked off down the path.

On my way down, I knocked on Rosie's door. No answer. I hadn't seen her truck when I'd first pulled into the canyon that morning, and I guessed she was still over in the East Bay. I hoped she had slept in her own little cottage, alone. A relationship with someone like Joyce could put a real strain on our friendship.

I left a note stuck between door and jamb, telling her where I'd gone and when I expected to be back.

17

Mendocino is one of those places that looks like it was built for the movies. There are towns like that in New England and in the Midwest, too picturesque, too beautiful, too typecast to be real. But they are real. The midwestern towns with big old houses and big old elm trees, where you expect to see Mickey Rooney and Judy Garland turning the corner any minute. The New England towns with saltbox houses and widow's walks and graveyards full of dead sailors and the ghosts of Nathaniel Hawthorne and Lizzie

Borden flashing ectoplasm at dormer windows.

Mendocino is perfect Northern California coast. The town sits on a point of land that juts right out into the ocean like a big tall ship with a deck full of houses. The main street, which is called Main Street, runs along the southern edge of the town, and all the houses and buildings on it have a clear across-the-street or over-the-cliff view of the Pacific. You can walk the length of Main, from highway to westernmost tip, in about ten minutes. North of Main there are a few more parallel streets, intersected by a few side streets, and that's about it.

The inns and shops and restaurants are well kept and what my father would call artsy-fartsy, but most of the private homes look like they're pretty much left to fend for themselves, weathered wood and yards gone to prolific nature.

Every time I visit Mendocino I have fantasies about living there in one of those salt-scrubbed houses. The people who do live there have been known to go to war against whaling ships in small boats, a war of confrontation and harassment. I'd like to confront and harass a whaling ship. I'd like to be able to walk the quiet evening streets of a decent little town, and spend half the night gazing at the Pacific. No muggers, no fear after dark. The only strangers the enchanted tourists, treated like guests, behaving like guests, and representing money in the bank for the town.

I'd love it, but I'm afraid I wouldn't love it for very long. There's always a tradeoff. You can have quiet streets and a beautiful environment or you can have variety, excitement, craziness any time you want it. Maybe an artist's colony like Mendocino, with plenty of creative and intellectual stimulation, is the answer for some people. Artists, anyway. But I'd had my chance at rural Northern California and I'd ended up in Oakland.

I guess some of us are doomed.

So there it was, charming as hell out there on its own little peninsula. I turned left off the highway onto Main, passing some picturesque real estate offices. Just before I hit the business district, I turned off onto the side street that would take me to another side street where James Smith's son maintained what I was sure was going to be a very quaint little inn.

97

I was partly right. The inn was partly quaint; the other part was just old. The building looked to be about halfway along in a renovation and beautification program. It was a medium-sized Victorian house. Not one of those insane castles built toward the end of the era, when architects felt somehow obliged to use up their wildest fantasies before the glory died, but an earlier creation big enough for a big family, fancy enough to satisfy the whims of the time, and solid enough to outlast everything that's been built since 1945. It was half painted in deep blue with white trim. A couple of window frames had been ripped out and had not yet been replaced. Those windows and part of the roof were covered with plastic.

Since Californians don't normally start renovation work in the rainy season, I had my choice of several theories: the project had been started the previous spring and something had happened to stop it, like a lack of money; the owner had gotten the money together late in the season and was so excited he couldn't wait until spring to start working; or the owner always did everything wrong and the place looked this way all the time. The only theory I rejected right away was the third one. A guy just past thirty who'd managed—probably without any support from his family—to get himself an inn in Mendocino is not the kind of guy who always does everything wrong.

I pulled my car up at the curbless roadside, got out and ambled casually up the walk. The front steps were flanked by two big old-fashioned rose bushes that looked like they'd never been brutalized by a prune-it-to-a-dead-stick gardener. Lots of short-stemmed pink blooms, just the way I like rose bushes to look.

But then, I'm a clod. I like paté all right, but I'd rather have fried oysters. I believe that cats are about as mysterious and independent as puppies; I get bored listening to jazz; and I would never buy anything that had someone else's name on it.

I pushed open the front door and walked into a long, high-ceilinged hallway with big sliding doors on either side that once led to parlors or drawing rooms or something. These, I guessed, would be among the Rooms with Fireplaces Bill Smith was charging so much for. I figured that my fifty-dollar room was tucked away somewhere upstairs. Maybe even the attic. There was a stairway at the left and more hallway going past it. At the end was a counter with no one behind it. I pushed the button that had a sign next to it saying "Please ring for service," and a voice called out, asking me to please wait a minute.

The minute lasted only about five seconds. A very pretty young woman with curly brown hair and bright blue eyes appeared, wearing a large white apron over a plaid flannel shirt and jeans. She smiled at me beautifully but impersonally. I smiled back, also beautifully, and with what I hoped was inoffensive and even attractive warmth, and gave her my name. She gave me a key and told me my room was on the second floor, third door on the left. Not the attic, anyway.

"I wonder if the owner's around," I said.

She threw me a suspicious look. "Why?" she wanted to know. And I began to lean toward my first theory of interrupted renovation—a lack of money. She was looking at me like I was a bill collector.

"It's kind of personal," I said. "It has to do with his father."

"He's not here right now," she said neutrally. "But I can leave a message that you wanted to talk to him—about his father?" I nodded. "I'll tell him. But I don't know when he'll be back."

"That's fine," I said. "He is coming back in the next day or so, I hope?"

She nodded. "You said when you called for your reservation you'd be staying a couple of days. Would you like to pay in advance for another night?"

"I'd love to," I said. It seemed to be the only appropriate response, other than "No," to a ridiculous question.

I took my bag up to my room. A small room with blue and pink wallpaper—flowers lined up inside stripes—and a white chenille spread on the high double bed. White lace curtains on the single window. A tiny closet, blue carpeting, and a rag rug beside the bed. I hung up my clean shirt and tweed jacket in the closet, left spare socks and shorts in the bag, and headed out to have a look around.

I turned toward Main Street, figuring I'd hang around the

shops for a while. Once, a few years before, one of the shops along that street had had a collection of music boxes. All kinds, all romantic as hell. The one I liked best was wood with one of those eighteenth-century scenes painted on the lid. You know, the guy in knee breeches and white stockings with the ruffles down his chest and the powdered pigtail hairdo, standing around a garden with a woman wearing a huge wig and a huge skirt, holding a fan over her cleavage. The box played something by Mozart, I don't remember what. I wanted to buy that box, but here's the catch: I wanted to buy it for a woman I loved. At the time there was no woman I loved, unless you count the wife I'd just walked out on because I'd found out she'd been sneaking, lying, and cheating for three years. Even if I had been willing to forgive and forget, I'd had no choice about leaving; she didn't particularly want me to stay. In fact, two days after I left she was already moved in with the latest of her Jake-just-went-to-work-come-on-over gentlemen of the afternoon. So I stood there, I remember, wishing I had someone to buy that damned music box for, and playing the Mozart over and over again. Finally, I put the box back on the counter, walked out of the shop, went to the nearest bar and got drunk.

The shop was still there. It still had varnished Douglas fir floorboards, floor-to-ceiling shelves on all four walls covered with hand-blown glass and other objects of art and otherwise, and glass counters with items that didn't look any more valuable than the ones on the open shelves. There were goblets and bowls and candlesticks. There were scrimshawed brooches and pendants with whales and sailing ships carved on them. There were paintings and chess sets and old photo albums. But there weren't any music boxes. Probably a good thing. I might lose my head, buy one, and still not know whom to give it to.

I wandered farther down the street, past the hotel with its Old West exterior and its opulent Victorian lobby and bar, and checked out a few more shops. An art gallery that sold mostly seascapes. Clothing, books and records, curios and wind chimes and whale sculptures. One shop had a white marble urn, slightly damaged, for only twenty-five dollars. I thought it would look great somewhere in my yard, but I wasn't sure where. I would have bought it, too, but I lost interest when I tried to lift it. Somehow, the idea of carting it all the way back to Oakland and carrying it— or even pushing it in a wheelbarrow—all the way down the path to my house was less than appealing.

I strolled on to the end of the street and walked through the long spring grass to the cliff's edge, where I sat on a rock and watched the ocean crash against the rocks below, indentations in the cliffside sucking the water in and blowing it out again. It was nice to be alone, or nearly alone, with the Pacific. A few other people were walking the paths along the cliff: an old woman with a cane and a small terrier, a young man with a child clinging to each hand, a pair of lovers, and a solitary middle-aged woman carrying an easel, a canvas, and a paint box.

The fog was coming in; it looked like a tidal wave in the distance and I could feel its chill in the first tendrils reaching out for the town. I was warm enough. I was wearing a down vest over a sweater over a cotton turtleneck. But I was also getting cold enough for a brandy.

Abandoning my rock, I headed back to Main, this time walking along the ocean side, and did a slow three blocks to the street that led to my favorite restaurant and bar.

There are fancier and maybe even better restaurants in Mendocino, but I like the Pelican. Good seafood, good prices, and great service. There's a big, friendly bar upstairs that sometimes has live entertainment in the evenings. This was still afternoon, but for the moment, brandy would be entertainment enough.

The bar was on the right, the windows on the left, facing the street. The wall behind the bar sloped up to the beamed ceiling, and all the walls, including the sloping one, were covered with paintings. The paintings, which were new since the last time I'd been there, were mostly very big. The biggest ones looked, at first glance, like some kind of series by the same artist. Since several of them were up behind the bar, I figured I could have my brandy while I got a better look at them.

The bartender was a medium-sized, medium-looking man who was a bonier version of the Han Martin physical type. Sandy, a little tough. He was fast with the brandy and slow to take a tip. I

101

held the snifter cupped in my hands like you're supposed to, to warm the stuff, and looked up at the art work. The first thing I noticed was that the paintings had a few qualities that a lot of the art you see around seems to lack. For one thing, the artist could draw. For another, he or she had worked at the craft, apparently recognizing that art without craft is so much diarrhea. I didn't just like the paintings because the subject matter looked real—whatever that's called. I like a lot of art that is just color and form. I liked these because the artist had talent and discipline. It took me a few minutes to catch on to the series, but once I figured out that the woman getting the stays laced tightly around her wasp waist could only be Scarlett O'Hara, I was able to identify some of the other characters. There was Rick, wearing a trenchcoat, watching the plane take off from the Casablanca airfield. Henry VIII was eating. Tugboat Annie was at the wheel of her vessel.

But there was something odd about the paintings. The faces. They weren't the faces of Bogart or Laughton or Dressler or Dietrich or Lombard or Colbert. Nor were they imagined or idealized. They were real, individual, genuine-person faces.

That was when I noticed the guy three barstools down. He was the Thief of Baghdad.

The bartender caught me looking from the painting to the man and back again.

"That's right," he said. "They're all people who live here in town. The artist's local. Comes in a lot. He's Gary Cooper in *High Noon*."

"You bought all those paintings from him?"

"Nah. Too expensive. We rent them. He needs the money right now. Child custody problems. Rough situation."

"I'm here to see a man named Bill Smith," I said. "Is he up there somewhere?"

"Henry Fonda," he said. "*Grapes of Wrath*." He wandered off down the bar to give the Thief of Baghdad another drink.

I finished my brandy and left the bar. It was still only about six o'clock and I wasn't particularly hungry, so I thought I'd head back to the inn and see if I could catch Smith.

This time there was someone already behind the counter: a

thin young man of about twenty, with his nose in what is usually called a slim volume—somebody's poetry or something.

"Hello," I said affably.

He looked up slowly and spoke coldly and politely. I guessed he was probably reading cold and polite poetry.

"Can I help you?"

"Sure can," I said. "I'm in room 2C—"

"Oh, good," he said, relaxing. "I was afraid you were looking for a room and we don't have any. I hate telling people that."

"Uh huh. Well, I was wondering if the owner was around, because I've actually come all the way up here to talk to him."

The thin young man suddenly became a slender young man, all by raising his eyebrows and tilting his head gracefully. Then he checked the book on the counter. "Samson? Jacob Samson?"

"Right."

"Well, I'll see if he's here, Mr. Samson." I figured that meant he was. The only question was whether he'd talk to me.

He would. The slender young man reappeared in about a minute.

"He's in his office, Mr. Samson. Just go outside and around the house to your right. Follow the wooden walkway through the lilacs."

18

Around the side and at the end of the walkway, there was a door with a sign on it that said "Office." Beyond that, out in the back yard, was a small new building, half glass and half redwood, about twenty by twenty-five, with big skylights. It looked like everyone's fantasy of an artist's studio.

I knocked on the office door and was invited to come in.

I'd never seen James Smith, so I didn't know what he looked like. Mrs. Smith was a fairly good-looking woman, and Bunny, at sixteen, showed a lot of promise. But the painting in the bar was accurate; this man was beautiful.

I don't mean beautiful pretty. I mean beautiful the way—oh hell, not exactly like a Greek god, because his face was too contemporary. He didn't have those Greek god lips that all those statues have, and his nose was longer than theirs and his hair wasn't curly. But he looked like a perfectly handsome man. Perfectly. I would not want Iris to see him. I certainly didn't want her to see him standing next to me.

He had straight, healthy-looking black hair cut short but falling softly over his forehead like the hair of a child. Green eyes, about the color of the Algerian ivy that's pulling down my back fence. His skin had the faded winter tan of the Northern Californian who spends a lot of summer time outside. His eyelashes looked like they belonged on a Walt Disney kitten.

He stood to greet me. About six feet tall, maybe two inches ahead of me. His shoulders, in a soft pale blue sweater, were thicker than mine. His flanks were leaner. Of course, he was several years younger.

He gestured toward a straight-backed chair at the end of his scarred oak desk. I sat. He sat.

"Okay," he said. "I got a message that you wanted to talk to me about my father. But I don't know who you are. Police?"

"No." I pulled out my letter of agreement with *Probe* magazine, the one that says I'm working on a free-lance assignment for them. Smith looked at it and frowned handsomely.

"*Probe*? What exactly are you after? My father wasn't well known. Not even to my mother."

"Well, it's not exactly your father I'm doing the piece on. I mean," I said earnestly, "his death was pretty strange, and certainly belongs in any story about . . ." I hesitated, hoping he'd fill in the blank. He did.

"It's that disgusting company, right? You're doing an exposé on them—on their crooked business. Right?" I smiled and shrugged. "That's terrific. Bunch of hypocrites. Self-righteous crooks. And my father was a real classic. Holy Jim Smith." I managed to look a little shocked. After all, he was speaking of the dead. And his own father. "As you can see, I'm not mourning."

"Yeah. I see that. So you don't think much of your father's

company. And you didn't think much of your father. I've talked to your mother and your sister. Your mother gave me the impression he was a great guy. Honest, hardworking, righteous—"

Smith snorted, but there was no laughter in his eyes. Just a lot of anger, and, not very well hidden behind that, a lot of pain.

"Uh huh. A very righteous man. You want to believe that, go ahead."

"I don't want to believe anything. I'd like to hear what you think."

"Okay. You've already talked to my sister. You know how he felt about me. Anyone who didn't live up to his standards—his high moral standards—just didn't belong in his world, just didn't deserve to live at all. You want to hear a great story about my father?"

"Sure," I said.

"It goes back twenty years. I was twelve, so it's exactly twenty years. Dad wasn't a teacher anymore. He was already working for Bowen. He'd been a high school teacher, see, and Bright Future was mostly just a high school program then. Anyway, he liked to—how did he put it?—keep his finger on the pulse of education. That's what I was for, I guess, pulse-taking. Bunny wasn't born yet. I was the only kid he had. So we used to have these sessions, you know? Maybe every week or two. He'd sit me down and ask me about my subjects and how I was doing. My classes, my teachers. It was a big deal that year, because I was in seventh grade. Middle school. Anyway, he always wanted to know all about my teachers. Were they strict, that kind of thing. You know? Anyway, there was this one teacher, my home room teacher, and I took English from him, too. He was a great guy. I was crazy about him." He shrugged. "I didn't know I wasn't supposed to be crazy about him. I mean, kids hear stuff about that kind of thing, but it doesn't really register as being personal or anything. Not for a while." He was having trouble explaining himself. "Or maybe I was just more innocent than most boys my age." He paused. "You probably don't know what I'm talking about."

"I think I do," I said. "Kids get crushes."

"Yeah, well, it was different for this kid, but I didn't know it yet. And I wasn't any different from the guys I hung out with. I mean I didn't play with dolls or anything." He laughed. "Anyway, I guess I talked a lot about this teacher, or my father didn't like the way I talked about him or something. So pretty soon, when we'd have our little talks, he'd get all casual and maybe toss in a couple of questions about this guy. Where'd he live, was he married, did he have kids, that kind of shit, you know?" I nodded.

"Was he married?" I asked. "Did he have kids?"

Bill threw me a disgusted look. "Yeah."

"So what happened?" I asked, hoping to get to the punch line.

"Okay, so we had this little home room softball team, played against the other home rooms. And after one of those games, he had us over to his house for lemonade or some damned thing. Now you gotta remember I was in love. When I went upstairs to use the bathroom I just had to look around, you know? Get closer to him by sniffing around. The bedroom door was closed, but I opened it and checked it out. Walked right in. And I saw some stuff on the dresser. His brushes, some of his wife's shit, like that. And a little pipe with a piece of screen across the top and a little ash in the bowl. Women didn't smoke pipes, I thought. This belonged to my teacher. This was his. Something of his. I took it. Stuck it right in my pocket, closed the door behind me and went back downstairs again.

"Anyway, my mother found it in my sock drawer and took it to my dad. He took it to some cop friend of his who told him what it was. My dad freaked out, old solid citizen came back to me, not screaming, you know, very calm and cold, and kept at me until I told him where I got it. I guess I even said something about the bedroom. That was the end of my home room teacher."

"Drug bust?"

"Well, they tried. But they couldn't find a trace of anything in his house. All they had was the pipe and they weren't going to get any testimony out of me about that. I already felt shitty enough about letting my father bully it out of me. I shut my mouth and I wouldn't open it again and they just didn't have any proof."

"So how was it the end of him?"

"My father went to his buddies on the school board raving

about dope and seduction. A man like that, he said, had no right to be teaching children. Had no right even to have a child of his own. I actually remember him saying that. Next thing I knew, my favorite teacher wasn't a teacher any more. I heard later his whole life fell apart. And it was all my fault, with a lot of help from my father."

He looked as though he were about to cry. Even now, after twenty years. A long-term load of guilt. I looked at my shoes to give him a second to recover.

He recovered fast. When I raised my eyes again, he no longer looked like he might cry. He looked very hard and very cold, just as his father must have looked when he was making the school system safe and clean for the son he later decided wasn't worth the effort.

Then he laughed. "Sorry. I'm sure you didn't want to hear all this. That righteous bullshit really set me off. The man was a menace. And a hypocrite. There he was, working for that crooked company, and making moral judgments about—"

"You say the company's crooked. Do you know that?"

He shrugged. "Sorry, I can't help you prove it. I wish I could."

I was wishing he could, too. If there was really something illegal going on . . .

Smith interrupted my thoughts. "Listen, I'd like to help you out. If there's anything I can do, all you have to do is let me know. But . . ." He waved a hand over the ledgers and papers on his desk.

"Yeah. I see you're busy. If you come up with anything, give me a call." I scribbled Artie's phone number on a scrap of paper. He stuck it in his pocket. I stood up. "You've got a great place here. Looks like you're doing a lot of work on it. Or were."

He smiled. "Thanks. We're working on it."

Well, I hadn't really expected him to explain that yes, he had some money problems because his savings had gone to hire someone to kill his father. You can't win them all.

"Oh, by the way," I said casually. "Where were you when your father was killed?"

He laughed. "I work on weekends. Always. Even a chance to kill my father wouldn't pry me loose."

I thanked him for his help, said I'd be around for another day or so if he thought of anything, and left him to his business.

Someone was hammering in the backyard. I heard the sound of it before I caught sight of the large man, out in front of the studio, tacking a canvas to a big stretcher frame.

"Hi," I said. He looked up from his work and nodded at me, decided he didn't know me, and went back to his canvas. That one quick look, though, told me who he was. Gary Cooper in *High Noon*. The artist who'd done the old movie series that was hanging in the Pelican bar.

"Hey," I said. "You're the guy that did those paintings, the ones with all the people in town."

He looked up again. Warily. "Well, not all the people in town," he said.

I trotted over to him, the cheery tourist. "I just wanted to tell you how much I like them."

"Glad to hear it," he said, leaning the canvas against the outside wall of the studio and taking his first really good look at me. "Want to buy one?"

"Wish I could."

"Oh." He reached for the canvas again, hesitated, and turned back to me. "You the guy wanted to talk to Bill about his father?"

I nodded.

"You sure you don't really want to talk to me?"

"I don't know," I said. "Who are you?"

He stepped very close to me. He was a big man, and he was threatening me with his size. "Andy Tolberg. If you've got some business with me I'd prefer it if you'd leave Bill alone."

I was finding this conversation very confusing. "I'm sorry, Mr. Tolberg, but as far as I know I don't have any business with you."

He didn't seem to believe me. "What are you doing up here?" he demanded.

I gave him my *Probe* magazine line.

"Bullshit," he said. "You're checking up on me. For my ex-wife. Me and Bill. Our business." He jerked his large chin toward the hotel. "And our life together."

108

That was when I'd remembered what the bartender had told me about this man being involved in a custody battle. And needing money to fight it through. Now I had the explanation for the half-finished renovations. And since he'd said "our life together," I also thought I probably had the reason for the custody problem.

I backed away, hands raised, palms upward. Look, no weapons, nothing up my sleeve. "No. Absolutely not," I told him. "I came up here to find out about Bill's father. I don't know anything about your ex-wife, and I don't care."

He glared at me. "Yeah? Maybe. But get it straight, I love my daughter. I want her with me. We could give her a good, decent home. A hell of a lot better than that damned pillhead of a mother of hers. And her slimy boyfriend." He advanced again, closing the space I'd made between us. "She's my kid, too, for Christ's sake!" Then he turned away abruptly, picked up his nearly stretched canvas, and stalked into his studio.

I walked back out to Main Street, feeling a little stunned by all the emotion I'd been exposed to in the past hour. Bill's hatred. Andy's rage. The town didn't feel as peaceful to me as it had before. But then peaceful wasn't exactly what I was looking for. I'd paid for two nights in Mendocino. That gave me plenty of time to wander around being subtle and clever and finding out a little more about the two men.

I checked out art galleries and I listened to gossip in the bars. The people at the art galleries were more interested in selling art than in talking about artists, and if the locals were talking about Bill's murdered father they weren't talking about him where strangers could hear. Or didn't know he was Bill's father. Or hadn't noticed what might have been, to them, just another murder down in the Bay Area.

By the time Saturday night came around I had myself convinced that I'd achieved nothing but my own depression. It didn't matter that I'd added at least one good suspect to my list, and that I knew more about the victim than I'd known before. What did matter was that I liked Bill a lot better than I liked what I'd been hearing about his father. I was sure that whoever killed the guy had a hell of a good reason for doing it. If Bill was the killer, I sympathized with him. But then, my sense of justice sometimes doesn't square with the law.

Like James Smith. The big difference between us, I told myself, was that my heart was in the right place.

On my way back to my room to shower and change for dinner, I stopped at the desk to have a chat with the slim young man. Smith had told me he'd been in Mendocino the day his father was killed. I wanted to check his story.

"Yes?" The young man lifted his eyes reluctantly from an L.L. Bean catalog.

"Hi. Thought I'd stop by and pick up my coupon."

He looked blank. "Coupon."

"Yeah. When I called in my reservation—let's see, that was last weekend—Mr. Smith told me I would get a discount coupon for my next visit." I'd talked to a woman when I'd called. Maybe he wouldn't know when the reservation had been made.

He smiled with one side of his mouth. "Somebody must have been playing with you, Mr. Samson. This is not a food store. We don't use coupons."

I contrived to look puzzled. "But that's what he said, and I'm sure it was Mr. Smith I talked to."

He stopped smiling. "Now I think you're playing with me," he said. "Was there anything else you wanted?"

I hate it when people don't follow the script I write for them. He was supposed to say something like, "Well, Mr. Smith was here on Sunday, but he wasn't answering the phone." Or he could have said, "Mr. Smith couldn't have told you that because he was in San Francisco last weekend."

But it was not to be. I showered and changed and went to the Pelican for oysters. Then I went upstairs to the bar to hear a country and western group.

The group was good, but my mood of futility carried over through the evening, and I couldn't bring myself to talk to any of the attractive women who were in the bar that night. I was sure they wouldn't follow my script.

110

19

Rosie had left a note on the door of my room. If I got back before six, I would find her in her own room at Carlota's. After that, she wrote, she would be out for the evening. It was a little before five. I dumped my bag on my cot and went down the steps to see her.

Since I'd left on Friday, she'd added a Styrofoam ice chest to his furnishings. She gave me a cold beer and settled down on a floor cushion, after offering me the seat-sprung easy chair, to hear about my trip.

She didn't think Bill had killed his father.

"It doesn't make sense, Jake. After all these years? Why would he decide to kill him twenty years after the fact?"

"But it hasn't been very long since the man rejected him for being gay," I objected. "He's not welcome in his parents' home. Or wasn't while his father was alive. That's pretty heavy stuff."

Rosie just shrugged. "Look, maybe that kind of behavior isn't as common as it once was, but nearly everyone is afraid of it. You come out to your family, you're taking a chance. Even now. But I've never heard of anyone killing because they lost the toss."

I thought about that. For just a minute, I tried to imagine what it would feel like. I didn't succeed very well.

"What about Andy?" I shifted to the second Mendocino suspect.

"That's a possibility. Sounds like he's feeling pretty ragged around the edges about this daughter thing. If Bill's father had anything to do with his problems . . . but that's another chance people have to take."

My Mendocino depression was settling over me again. "Kind of a high price," I mumbled.

Rosie smiled. "Switch to men or you'll lose my friendship."

"Point taken," I said, but I didn't feel like smiling back.

"Cheer up, Jacob. It's a lot like being Jewish in some places, at some times."

I laughed. "And the ones who can't take it pretend to be Christians?"

We had another beer. Rosie said she knew people who would be sure to know all about any custody fight with a gay angle. Movement people. Attorneys. Parents who had won or lost in the past. She agreed to start nosing around right away.

We were silent for a moment, companionable, sipping at our beers. Alice had her head in Rosie's lap and had begun to snore.

"I like your new refrigerator," I said, waving a hand at the ice chest.

She made a face. "I tried keeping beer in their refrigerator." She glanced at the ceiling. "But Carlota kept drinking it all. And speaking of Carlota—" she started to get up but decided to let Alice sleep undisturbed. "I've got a copy of that magazine with a review of her films. It's over there on the bed."

I got up and found the new issue of *The Marin Journal of the Arts*. Rosie was looking at her watch.

"Better start getting ready," she said. "I'm due in the East Bay at seven."

"Got a date with Joyce?" I hoped not, but I couldn't very well say so.

"No. I didn't like her either. It's someone new."

"Good. Good," I said noncommittally, heading for the door.

"Oh, Jake? That review? It's a rave." I turned back to look at her, unbelieving. She laughed. "Well, I guess you never can tell, huh?"

I took the journal with me to a Mexican restaurant in San Rafael, ordered a margarita, enchiladas verdes, beans and rice, and turned to the table of contents. Films, page 23. I found page 23. "Powerful Showing by Mill Valley Filmmaker," by Eric Anderson. There was a nice mug shot of Anderson that looked like it had been taken about ten years ago, and a larger shot of Carlota leaning against a tree. Down at the bottom of the page there was a blurb about Eric that mentioned he was co-owner of Mary's Bookstore in Mill Valley. Nice publicity for the shop.

The margarita came. It was made from a mix and tasted like chemicals.

Carlota couldn't have written a better review herself. It was kind of vague, with a lot of stuff about allegories and metaphors,

112

but the main impression it left was that Carlota Bowman was a sensitive artist with full control of her medium, and that she had created some very avant garde work indeed.

The food was pretty good, so I ordered another chemical margarita to go with it.

Knowing Carlota, I couldn't believe she had control over anything. But there it was, in print. I decided to give the rest of the journal a pass until some other time. I stuck it in my pocket and pulled out my notebook.

While Rosie was getting what she could on Andy and Bill, I had a few things I wanted to do. One item: I still wasn't satisfied with what I knew about the residents of the canyon. Too many holes unplugged, and a couple of important questions I hadn't asked them yet. Then there was Bright Future. Probably the most likely nest of suspects in the case.

So first I thought I'd have a talk with Hanley. After all, there was still the issue of the parking area, and he and Mary had been doing the work in that fight. Hanley, I figured, was nuts. And nuts have been known to end less important disputes in violent ways. I also wanted to talk to Mary. Although I had no reason to believe she was a nut, she was involved in the canyon's crisis. By the time they'd made their report at the hot tub meeting, Smith was a dead man. Maybe the committee of two had decided not to mention something—like having had a face-to-face confrontation with the victim.

As for Bright Future, Bert Franklin seemed to me to be a logical source of information about the company, and, most important, about Howard Morton's past business dealings. I figured the price of a few strong drinks could take me one hell of a long way with Franklin.

I ordered some coffee and sat over it for a while, running over the list in my mind. The people in the canyon, threatened by financial loss. Some of them probably had nothing but their homes. Someone could have panicked. Bright Future tied for first place. If something funny was going on there, and Smith knew about it and was threatening to expose it . . .

Next came Andy and Bill. I didn't know that Andy had a

motive. And maybe Rosie was right about Bill.

So where did that leave me? Still groping around looking for hard, incriminating facts. And there was always the possibility that Smith was killed by someone outside my neat categories, someone I didn't know anything about.

Anyone could have found Alan's knife. Anyone could have used it.

I finished my coffee, paid the check, and went back to the canyon.

Hanley's gardening truck was parked near the bottom of the steps. I headed up the path, but I didn't make it past Artie's house.

"There you are!" Artie crowed at me from his front door. "Rosie told me you went to Mendocino. Come on in, tell me what's going on, have a glass of something or maybe some coffee. Have you eaten? Can I give Alan any news?"

"Whoa, Artie. Tell you what. I'm going up to Hanley's for a while, just checking out something. Then I'll come down and talk to you. Okay?"

He looked more eager to hear my news than my news deserved, so I said, "Still just feeling my way. No solution yet."

Hanley was home. I saw him, in the dim glow of a front-porch bug light, through the thick shrubbery that screened the entry to his house, before he saw me. He was sitting on his front steps drinking beer from a can, his eyes half closed and a dreamy look on his face. He jumped up, startled, when I broke through the last of the brush, and for a second, I thought he was going to throw his beer can at me.

"Hi," I said, tactfully ignoring his unmanly fright. He plunked his butt down on the step again and nodded to me.

"Nice evening," I said.

"It's going to rain."

I looked up at what I could see of the sky between the towering redwoods. Didn't look like rain to me, but I squinted my eyes and nodded, old farmer style.

"What are you doing up here?" he wanted to know.

I shrugged. "Just walking. Thought I'd see if you were around."

114

"Want a beer? I'm about ready for another one, myself." I accepted his surprisingly friendly offer, but I hoped he didn't plan on having several more himself. Just because he'd never shot anything but a tree—or so people said—didn't mean he never would.

When he came back out with the beers, I took a space on the steps beside him, and took a cue from his silence. We both sat there, stoically drinking from cans, gazing at nature. He burped. I burped.

"How come you're hanging around the canyon?"

"Doing a magazine piece."

"On the murder?"

"No. Well, that's a little part of it. It's about the company the guy worked for."

"Where Arlene works."

"Yeah."

"Why?"

"Might be interesting."

"Uhm." He burped louder.

"What do you know about the guy, Han? Besides the fact that he wanted to buy the lot?"

"Wanted to build a house."

"You found out his name before he was killed, right?"

"Right. Wanta make something out of it?" He said it casually, half smiling, so I laughed.

"Not really. But can you tell me anything about when he first made an offer, and how? I mean, there wasn't any 'For Sale' sign on it, was there?"

He shook his head. "Nah. Nearly as we could figure, he went looking in the records for the owner, found out it was the county, and made an offer to someone down there. Maybe he had friends or something. I don't know. Anyway, that was a few weeks ago. Maybe less. Jim's the one who found out about it. He works for the county some way or other."

"Computers."

"Yeah. Anyway, he found out about it, and Mary and me offered to check it out. That was maybe, I don't know, two weeks ago we started. Maybe less. Had to do something."

115

Right, I thought. Something.

I sure as hell couldn't complain I had nowhere to go in this case. I had about twenty places to go. With odds like that, I figured, something had to turn up. Some day.

"You know, Han, I've been kind of wondering. You live up here, close to where the man was killed. Didn't you hear anything or see anything that morning?"

"Uh uh. I spent the night at Arlene's. I wasn't home. Not until the cops were already here." He got up abruptly and went back into the house. Since he hadn't said goodbye, I thought I'd wait and see if he came back out. He did, with one can of beer.

"This is all I've got left. Want to share it?"

I declined. Then, by way of introduction to a change of subject, I leaned back and chuckled. Hanley looked at me with a blankness reminiscent of his girlfriend.

"My friend Rosie—you know, the carpenter who's working on the steps?" He nodded solemnly. "She says Carlota thinks you're watching her."

"Watching who?"

"Carlota."

"Yeah. I am."

I chuckled again. "What for?"

He looked at me coldly. "What do you care?"

"Just curious. Couldn't help but wonder."

"You ought to watch that curiosity of yours. You know what they say about cats. Let's just say I don't trust her. She's weird."

"You think she killed the guy?" It wasn't easy, but I think I managed to continue looking only mildly curious.

He finished his beer and stood up.

"I didn't say that, did I? I got some things to do now. See you."

He went inside and closed the door. I walked slowly down the path, trying to digest what he'd said before I got to the Perrines'.

Jennifer answered the door. She looked at me accusingly.

"You spent the weekend in Mendocino," she said.

"Working on the case, Jennifer. Went to see the dead man's son."

116

She looked skeptical but she invited me in.

Julia, Artie, and Mike were watching TV. Artie got up and led me into the kitchen. He filled the kettle, got out a coffee filter and a bag of coffee, and put the kettle on the stove. Then he sat down across from me and looked expectant. I told him everything I'd learned so far. We spent an hour on Mendocino, and fifteen minutes on Hanley. From time to time during our conversation, Mike wandered casually into the kitchen—during commercials, probably. The third time he did that I spoke to him.

"Mike, you know I think it's best if you don't tell your friends what you hear about this case. Best to keep things kind of quiet until we get it figured out. For Alan. Okay?"

He looked disappointed, but he agreed.

Artie didn't think Hanley was worth pursuing. "He's just a nut, Jake. There couldn't be anything in it. That stuff about Carlota."

He sighed. "We don't seem to have very much yet, do we?"

"Got a busy day planned for tomorrow, though. I'm pulling a lot of threads together," I said optimistically.

He didn't look encouraged. but he reached over and clapped me on the shoulder. "I know you're trying, buddy. I know that."

"How's Alan doing?"

"He's not real happy in jail. Maybe you should go see him."

I didn't want to. "I think it's best," I said, "if I spend my time trying to get him out."

20

Even though Hanley's alibi was meaningless—Arlene would lie for him—I decided to let it stand for the time being. There were other questions that needed answering first. They had to do with the time lines he'd given me on the committee's work, and one matter of timing I hadn't asked anyone about yet. So first thing Monday morning I took a drive to the county building.

The Marin County Civic Center is a real landmark. It sprawls like a growth in a pocket of the green hills of central Marin, hills that turn yellow with summer and, often as not, are black-patched at the end of the dry season by the inevitable and frequent grass fires. Designed by Frank Lloyd Wright. Spawned by a mutant mushroom. Somewhere between pink and tan with a turquoise roof. The building houses everything the county needs to house, from the welfare department to Alan's current home, the jail.

I found a spot in the parking lot not too far from the main entrance and pushed through the doors.

Marin County is not just another pretty place. It's got class. Even though the building looks like a fungus from the outside, the inside looks less like a bureaucratic beehive than any government building I've ever seen. An island of greenery runs down the middle of the ground floor, with offices on either side. Not just your everyday ferns and bushes. No, this is a real garden, with trees reaching up through the railed hallways above, toward the skylight.

I found the recorder's office on the first floor. The county employee who offered to help me was very helpful indeed. Within an hour of my arrival, I had what I needed. Yes, the lot belonged to the county. Yes, a private party had made an offer for it about three weeks ago. And yes, some people who lived in the area had been searching the records on the lot recently. Basically, Hanley had told it right.

I told the clerk that I knew the community organization had found an old ruling that said the county couldn't sell the land. Was she aware of that?

"Well," she said, "there was an old file we found. Not right away. It was so old, it wasn't quite in the right place. Would that be it? The woman seemed very happy about something, but she didn't say . . ."

"Do you remember when that was?"

She thought a minute. "Oh, yes, now I remember. It was last Monday or Tuesday. That's when we finally found the file. Yes, probably Monday. At the beginning of the week."

"Really? Not the week before?"

"No. They'd come in once or twice before then, but we didn't

118

find the file until the beginning of the week."

I thanked the woman and left. Although Mary had never actually said that she and Hanley had found the old records before Smith's murder, she had, it seemed to me, tried to create that impression. She had made a special point of saying, at the hot tub meeting, that they had succeeded in their search "soon" after they began it, and that their report was almost finished. The efficiency of the canyon grapevine—nearly everyone seemed to hear news within a day or two—hadn't hurt. But the truth was, Smith had been killed just before they found their legal remedy to the sale.

Mary was busy with a customer when I walked in the door to her cheerful, white-paint-and-potted-ferns bookstore. She waved at me and I smiled back. I spotted some familiar-looking items on a table to the right of the door and walked over to have a look. The journal books, just like the one Bunny had been given by her father.

Mary finished with the customer. "Hi, Jake. Here to buy or to visit?"

"Thought I'd have a look at your mystery collection. I also wanted to talk to you."

"Sure. What do you need?"

I told her about my visit to the county building and what I'd learned there. She didn't look guilty. Only embarrassed.

"Yes, that's so. Monday. But I didn't see any reason to make a big point of when we actually knew . . . I was sure it was there somewhere in the records . . . certainly you don't think anyone . . ." She got a grip on herself. "No. It doesn't make any sense. Everyone knew we were looking. Everyone knew that I was sure we'd find what we were looking for. Even if someone decided that the way to solve the problem was to kill the man, why take a big step like that until they were sure we had no other way out? I'm sorry, Jake, but I think you're grasping at straws."

"That's a possibility." The problem was, I didn't have much else to grasp at. Mary picked up on what I suppose was a fleeting look of weariness. I liked her. I wasn't convinced, but I didn't feel like arguing with her. And she made me like her even more by offering me a cup of coffee. I accepted. She also offered me a chair

119

behind the counter, near the stool she used. I sat down. Nice guys shouldn't try to solve murders. Mary went off into a back room and returned with two mugs.

I sipped my coffee. "You know," I said, "you might have met Smith."

She had just enough time to raise her eyebrows before two more customers brought books up to the register. She made the sales and turned back to me.

"I don't think so. Not that I know of, anyway. Why do you say that?"

"He bought a book in here, for his daughter. Probably the week before he died."

She looked up at the calendar on the wall. "I wasn't around much that week. Eric was pretty much on his own. Last week, too. I'm thinking of opening another store, in The City, and I've been spending a lot of time across the bridge, looking at sites. In fact, that's why I'm working today, to give Eric a break. Monday's my usual day off."

I sipped my coffee. It was good. "Business is good, then?"

She smiled. "For a bookstore, we're doing very well."

I liked sitting around and talking to Mary. She was a restful person. "Have you always done this kind of thing?"

"Oh, my, no," she laughed. "I used to be a social worker. Have you ever thought about how many people have changed their lives all around since the sixties? Divorce, remarriage, career changes. People who were lawyers, teachers, social workers, executives—"

"And cops," I laughed, tapping my chest. "I guess there really was a revolution, after all."

She sobered. "Yes, and so much of it was good. But there were the bad things, too. We saw a lot of that at the welfare department. Kids, desperate, homeless, strung out . . . that's how I met Eric. He was looking for a runaway daughter. Of course, he was already divorced by then."

I finished my coffee, bought a paperback P. D. James, and said goodbye.

Stopping at a phone booth, I put in a call to Bert Franklin at

120

Bright Future. He remembered me, but he didn't sound all that happy to hear from me until I offered to buy him drinks after work. He didn't even ask why I wanted to see him. We agreed to meet at a place just off 101 north of San Rafael. Then I had lunch at a hamburger place on Miller and drove back to the canyon.

Rosie wasn't around, but I found a note on my door from Julia that said I'd gotten a call from Chloe while I was gone. It said please call back as soon as possible. I crossed the footbridge to Artie's side of the canyon and knocked on his door. No answer. I went in and made a second call to Bright Future. Chloe was at her desk.

"Jake," she said, "I have to talk to you."

"Okay, I'll come right over."

"God, no. I'll meet you tonight. Do you know the Pink Salamander in Sausalito?" I didn't. She gave me directions. I told her I'd see her there at eight.

The rest of the afternoon I spent hanging around the canyon waiting for Rosie, but by four-thirty she hadn't showed up and I decided I'd better start north for my date with Bert Franklin. He'd said he'd get to the bar a little after five, and I didn't want him to have to buy his own first drink. Might put him in an off mood. Also, I knew that the commuter traffic from San Francisco across the Golden Gate and into Marin, Sonoma, and Napa, had been building for at least an hour.

The ten-minute drive took twenty minutes, and I arrived at the Hearthstone Inn well ahead of Franklin. The dining room was deserted. This was not the kind of place where people came in for an early dinner so they could get the kids to bed by seven. The bar, on the other hand, was filling up for happy hour.

It was a nice bar, one of those where everything seems to shine in the dim lighting. All the bottles and glasses sparkled. The dark wood bar top glowed. The mirror caught dazzling reflections of candlelight from the booths. The red plastic barstools looked polished and so did the people sitting on them. Middle management. Young to middle-aged people on the way up. Somewhere. Somewhere in the hierarchies that inhabited the industrial parks of Marin and the financial district of San Francisco. I had a little time to watch while I sipped my Napa Valley white, and decided that none of the people who gathered here had gone as far as they wanted to go. They were restless, and trying too hard to look successful.

Funny place for Bert Franklin to pick, I thought. Hard to believe he was a regular in this bar. My guess was that since someone else was paying, he wanted to go someplace where they served more than shots and beer. Just for a change.

He walked in the door about ten after five, spotted me immediately at the bar, and, belly foremost, unsmiling, lumbered toward me. Despite the belly, despite the graceless walk, his rigidly squared shoulders gave him the look of an aging, overweight tom, scared of the new cat on the block but determined to maintain his dominance. What I had to do was convince him that I wasn't out to rip his ears.

He was wearing a green and yellow plaid jacket, green double knit pants, and Hush Puppies.

I smiled happily, like I was glad to see him, and asked if he'd like to take a booth.

"Bar's fine," he grunted, plunking himself down on the stool next to mine. To the bartender he said, "Jack Daniels black. Rocks." I put a five on the bar.

I asked about all the nice people at Bright Future. Franklin sucked down half his drink before he said everything was "terrific." I ordered another drink for him, and he swallowed the rest of the first one fast enough to be ready when the second one arrived. I kept the chatter light and sociable through the second drink. He began to relax a little with his first sip of the third.

He took one of his elbows off the bar and swiveled slightly toward me.

"Listen, Samson, you didn't invite me here for a friendly gossip. This is real nice and everything, but why don't you 'fess up?" He leered at me. "I don't think you're after my body—though these days it's hard to tell—so order me another drink and get down to it."

Controlling an impulse to gag at the thought of anybody wanting his body, I laughed and ordered him a double.

"Hell, Franklin, it's just the same old journalistic shit. You know how it is. The editor wants a story, I see what I can dig up."

He snickered. "Sure. A story on correspondence schools. What is it, a humor piece?" He started working on the double. I was on my second glass of wine.

"Okay," I said. "I'll level with you. It is a story about correspondence schools." He laughed, spraying Jack Daniels in my face. "No, really. You've got to admit that Bright Future is quite a phenomenon. An old, traditional company that's got itself some hot new people"—I punched his shoulder—"and a hot new marketing plan that's going to take it right up there. A success story. It's good stuff." He narrowed his eyes at me suspiciously, and I added, remembering the operative word in the company literature, "It's exciting."

"Marketing plan's not that new," he muttered. "But I see what you mean." He was still watching me, assessing me. Wondering if I was as dumb as I sounded.

"That's right," I said. "You're kind of an old hand at this sort of thing, aren't you? Didn't you work for another company that ran along the same lines?" I was fishing. I didn't know that Perfect Day cosmetics, where he'd worked with Morton, had been the same setup. But I figured that the more I found out about that business that had gone under in some peculiar way—according to Arlene—the more I'd know about what Morton was doing at Bright Future. Which might lead me to the reasons for Smith's death. Might. But what the hell.

Franklin had turned away from me again, casually, and put both his elbows back on the bar. He finished the double. I ordered him another one. "Whole different ball game," he said.

"What?"

"I said I don't know where you heard that. Completely different kind of company." He glanced at me sideways, and tilted a little in the process. He was not altogether sober. "No resemblance at all." He spoke softly, and with careful control.

"Guess I got it wrong," I told him. "But isn't that where you met Morton? I just figured maybe he ran things the same way when he was there."

"Not at all. Not the same at all." He was still speaking very quietly.

"What was the name of the place? Perfect Day, something like that?" He swallowed the second double in two gulps.

"Thanks for the drinks, Samson. I got to go now." He lurched off the stool, caught himself, and marched through the bar and out the door.

I took a look at the menu, decided Artie couldn't afford the place, and stopped off in San Rafael for Chinese food. Then I got back on the freeway—still jammed going north—and turned south toward Sausalito.

21

Chloe was waiting for me at a table in the back of the bar. I picked up a beer on the way. She was drinking a straight-up martini, and there were three cigarette butts in the ashtray.

"What's up?" I asked, searching her tired face for some clue to what might be wrong.

"I need to know what you're doing," she said, lighting another cigarette.

I stalled. "Why is it more important for you to know this week than it was last week?"

"Because if I'm going to lose my job I'd like to know what I'm losing it for." I waited for her to go on. "I know you called Bert Franklin today at work. I know you invited him for a drink. Morton knows, too. The minute Franklin got off the phone with you he went to report to his buddy."

"That's not exactly a big surprise. I thought he might. What's that got to do with you?"

"I'll take it slowly so you understand," she said with what I thought was unnecessary superiority. "Last week, you asked me out to lunch. Bert of course noticed. Bert of course told Morton." I nodded to show I understood her so far. "Morton didn't think much about it at the time, but this week you made a date with

Bert. Obviously you are sneaking around trying to pump employees. Bert the loyal employee reported this fact to Morton. I, on the other hand, did not."

"Ah hah!"

"Ah hah, indeed. Morton called me in right after he talked to Bert. He wanted to know what you and I talked about. He wanted to know why I hadn't given him a full report. And the son of a bitch wanted to know—as he put it—how close we are. Was I seeing you? What happened at lunch? I want another drink." I got it for her and brought it back to the table.

"Pretty paranoid stuff," I said. "What did you tell him?"

"The truth. That you asked a lot of questions about Smith and about the company and I didn't tell you anything. I also said I assumed he knew what you were doing since you'd also talked to him."

"And he didn't think that was reasonable."

"No. He didn't make any direct accusations, but he made a little speech about the importance of corporate security. Then he got all jovial and made a 'joke' about how maybe I wanted a job with your magazine. So what are you doing, Jake?"

I told her I was trying to find out who killed Smith.

She looked surprised. "Really?"

"Really."

"For *Probe*?" Her expression made it clear that she wouldn't swallow that.

"Well . . ."

"You're not a reporter, are you?"

"No."

"You're Sam Spade." I shrugged modestly. "Why didn't you say so in the first place?"

"Because everyone who knew him is a suspect."

She smiled, and then she started laughing. "You're right. Anyone who knew that jerk could have wanted to kill him."

She sipped at her drink, still smiling. Then she sat back and studied my face. "Maybe Morton did it." I didn't say anything. "Did you know that Smith resigned just a few days before he was killed?"

I tried to look cool and knowing, but I don't think I succeeded.

"Do you know why? Do the police know? Who else knew about it?"

"I didn't think you knew," she laughed. "Now, one question at a time. I don't know why. I'm only middle management. Bowen just let me know that one of my vice-presidents was leaving. As for the police, they must know. They certainly spent enough time around the office before they decided to arrest Alan. Who else knew? Besides Bowen, and me, Armand and Morton would have had to know."

I drank some beer to gain thinking time. "I've gotten the impression that Smith and Morton didn't get along. Wouldn't Morton be glad he was leaving, glad to be rid of him? Why would he kill him?"

Chloe shook her head at me. "Jake, you're not thinking clearly. How much money do you think people can make selling correspondence courses? Multilevel marketing is based on a pyramid-shaped collection of busy little people selling—something—and pumping money up to the top. The higher up you go toward the point the higher your commissions are. The more people you have below you, the more money you've got coming in."

I nodded.

"Do you also understand that the key is recruiting? And do you understand that making money from recruitment alone is against the law? That you can't make people pay a little something to the guy who brings them in—just for bringing them in? And that you can't pay people a little something for recruiting more bodies to recruit more bodies?"

"Are you saying that's what's going on there?"

She looked away from me. "No. I'm not saying that at all. How would I know anything about that? I'm certainly not involved in anything like that and I don't know it's happening. But I do know that fortunes have been made that way, other times and other places. That sales of actual product had very little to do with those fortunes. That's why there are laws now. Because a lot of little people got suckered into paying their money and taking their

126

chances. And lost. Does Morton strike you as an honest man? He runs his own shop. Nobody interferes. Not even Armand."

"And Smith was a moralist."

"Right. Not enough of a moralist to object to the hype or even the useless course material. But outright lawbreaking? Maybe he was delivering an ultimatum when he delivered his resignation. In all the years I knew him, I never knew him to shaft anyone without warning them first. It was part of his code of honor."

"Clean it up or I blow the whistle."

"If there was anything to clean up." She'd returned to her hear no evil, see no evil approach. I couldn't blame her.

"And you can't prove that Morton's running a crooked operation."

"No."

"Can you tell me more about why you think he might be, and how you think he might be doing it?"

She was very quiet. "Give me a day or two," she said softly. "I'll see what I can dig up."

"Why are you being so helpful all of a sudden?" I demanded. Her help might be valuable, if what she was saying was true, but that didn't mean I could be absolutely sure I could trust her. Maybe she was just throwing a complicated, time-consuming, and smelly red herring at me.

"Because I don't like being threatened, and Morton threatened me. Also, if he goes to jail he can't fire me."

"It seems funny," I said, "that someone from Bright Future would trail Smith to the canyon to kill him."

"What's funny about that? It's smarter than killing him in the executive toilet."

Before we left each other, Chloe invited me to dinner on Wednesday. She said she would try to have something for me by then. That was fine with me. I had plans for Tuesday night. Poker. And I thought one of my poker regulars might be a good source of information on the legalities of running a Bright Future type of business. My old friend Hal, bright young Berkeley attorney with friends in the D.A.'s office.

I drove back to the canyon thinking about the new information on Smith. Why had he quit his job? Had he been killed to cover up a scam of some sort? Even if Chloe wasn't trying to lead me astray for sinister reasons, wasn't it possible that she was indulging in wishful thinking? She had too much of a stake in getting rid of Morton.

So I was pretty preoccupied when I pulled into the canyon lot. I didn't even notice the car that pulled into the canyon a few seconds after me. I opened the door and stepped out, closing it behind me.

That was when the bullet ripped past my chest.

I dropped to the ground and bellied my way under my Chevy and out the other side. Good old high-riding Chevy. Solid car between me and the man with the gun—for the moment. But he didn't give me a lot of time to worry. He slammed into reverse and swerved back out of the canyon again. A blue Mercury. And when he was wrestling the wheel around to pull out onto the road, I caught a glimpse of elbow sticking out his open window. I couldn't be sure of the colors in the night-lighted lot, but the sleeve was definitely plaid, and maybe green and yellow.

I wasn't about to call the cops—although, for a moment, I thought of the solid presence of Sergeant Ricci, the sheriff's department detective I'd met on that first day in the canyon—and tell them that Bert Franklin had shot at me because I was investigating a murder they'd already solved. And no one else in the canyon was very likely to call them. Not for one measly gunshot.

I realized I was shaking, so I stood there for a while calming myself down. Then I went back to the other side of the car. The wing window looked like a spider web with a hole in the middle. The bullet must have come close to hitting me. I unlocked the door and got the flashlight out of the dash compartment. I found the little killer lodged in the dash near the radio. It took me a couple of minutes to find it, because my hands weren't working too well, but I dug it out with a pocket knife and dropped it into my pants pocket. Then I made my wobbly way up the steps to Rosie's room. I was remembering that, just a little while before, I had been skeptical about someone from Bright Future following Smith to the canyon to kill him.

Rosie must have noticed something when she opened the door.

"Jake? Are you all right?"

I walked past her and collapsed into the easy chair. "Didn't you hear the gunshot?"

"Yes, and Alice barked. But I thought it was just Hanley. It wasn't, huh?"

I told her. I also told her what Chloe had said about Smith.

"Well, gee," she said, "that kind of takes the edge off my news."

I stared at her. "Sorry," I said. I was about to get even huffier when I saw the look on her face. She was baiting me, slapping me out of my shakes. Good thing, too. I had an urgent phone call to make. I got up again and headed for the door.

"Where are you going?" Rosie squeaked.

"Got to call Chloe. Warn her."

"There's a phone upstairs. They're not home."

Chloe had given me her number, and her address, when we'd made our date for Wednesday night. I dialed it. There was no answer. I waited a few minutes and tried again. This time she picked it up on the fifth ring. She was a little short of breath.

"Are you okay?" I yelled.

"Of course I'm okay."

"You didn't answer right away."

"I was pulling in when I heard the phone."

I told her what had happened. "And if Franklin was following me he probably saw us together. You're in danger. Sit tight, I'm on my way."

"Hold it, Jake. Call the police. Don't you see how wonderful this is? It will lead them right to Morton."

I explained that I couldn't get mixed up with the police. If I did, I might never get a chance to find out who had really killed Smith.

She gave me an argument. "Morton has to be stopped."

"Then we'll stop him. I promise. Okay? Now lock up your place and wait for me."

"Look, Jake, I'm tired and I'm going to bed. There's no need to run around playing cops and robbers. Morton may be dangerous, but Bert's just a jerk. I work with him. I know. He got drunk and he tried to scare you off. He probably scared himself even more. I've got a dog and I've got a gun of my own. I don't need your protection."

"Don't you think you're carrying this big, strong woman act a little far?"

"No. Don't you think you're carrying the big, strong detective act a little far?"

"No!" I barked.

"Then I guess you'd better have a talk with Bert. He'll be sober tomorrow. See you." She rang off.

For several minutes, I sat looking at the phone, wondering what to do. I decided to take her word for it and go after Franklin at Bright Future the next day. Which reminded me of the call I'd meant to make to Hal.

As usual, I got his answering machine. I told him what I wanted to know and asked if he could try to get it for me in time for a prepoker dinner the next night. I told him to leave a yes or no about dinner at Artie's number. Then I went back down to Rosie's.

She was posted just inside her open door, with Alice, looking down the steps.

"Standing watch?" I asked.

"Yes. Did you get Chloe?"

I recounted the conversation.

Much to my irritation, Rosie laughed. "There's a woman who's used to doing things the way she wants them done. She'll be okay. Besides, I'm not so sure Morton is the killer, even if some drunk did take a shot at you for threatening his job." Rosie's tone, heavy with significance, alerted me.

"You said you had some news, didn't you?"

"You bet. Although I'm not terrifically happy about it." I waited for her to finish her dramatic pause. "Bill Smith's lover Andy was in town that weekend. He was meeting with some friends who have been planning a fund-raiser for his case. He was also talking to his lawyer. They had a new problem to deal with."

"Rosie, for God's sake, will you stop teasing me?"

130

"Okay, but you need some background. See, Andy's wife has custody of their daughter, and Andy has visitation rights. The child stays with him during vacations and sometimes on weekends."

I nodded rapidly. "Yeah? So?"

"So when the ex-wife found out Andy was gay, and, heaven forbid, living with his lover, she petitioned the court to change their custody agreement so Andy would never see the kid at all."

"And?"

"Well, the court started its investigation—those usually take about a month, and then there's a hearing where the evidence is presented and the judge makes a ruling."

"Rosie—"

"I'm getting to it. What happened was this—James Smith offered to give evidence against Andy and Bill. He was going to testify that they were unfit to have a child in their home. He never got the chance."

22

This time when I went to Bright Future I pulled into the lot. Sure enough, there was a blue Mercury parked right behind the building.

I walked in the door just about the time the receptionist was starting her first cup of coffee.

"Yes, sir?" She smiled professionally. "May I help you?"

"No, that's okay. He's expecting me. I'll just run right up."

Chloe's secretary wasn't at her desk. Chloe's office door was closed, but I could hear her talking or dictating. So she was okay, and she wouldn't have to have any part of what I was about to do.

I stomped into the editorial office. Bert was sitting at his desk, reading something. The green and yellow jacket was hanging from the back of his chair. When he looked up and saw me, he turned pastier than usual, but he didn't jump up and attack me or run away or anything. Maybe he was too hung over to move.

"Where can we talk privately, Franklin?"

The other two writers looked up briefly and went back to their work. After all, they were used to intruders by now.

"Why should we?" Franklin blustered. I just grinned nastily back at him and asked him if he'd rather talk right there. He got up and followed me out the door, down the hall away from the communications offices, and into a small vacant room. I closed the door behind us, grabbed a hunk of shirt and tie, and shoved him up against the wall.

"I don't like getting shot at, asshole. And I don't like the bullet holes you put in my window and my dash."

"You're crazy."

"What kind of car do you drive, you moron? That nice blue Merc that's parked in the lot outside?"

"There must be a thousand blue Mercurys in Marin County, what's mine got to do with anything?"

I gave him a poke in the gut. I was a little surprised he felt it through all that padding. "If you're going to shoot at people you should wear gray flannel. Not green and yellow plaid. And you should learn to drive without sticking your elbow out the window."

He started to cry. His nose got all red and runny and tears dribbled down his fat little cheeks. I didn't feel bad.

"Stop that," I told him, banging his head against the Sheetrock. He cried harder. His body turned to dead weight and I let him slide down to the blue carpeting. He hit with a bump, still crying. I stood over him.

"Did Morton tell you to follow me? Did he tell you to kill me?"

"I didn't kill you. I wasn't even trying to kill you. I just wanted to scare you. Really." He was looking at the floor. The tears had stopped falling. His eyes were puffy and his nose was still running.

"Blow your nose, fuck-up. Maybe you didn't mean to kill me but you came awfully damned close." He pulled a hanky out of his pants pocket, a real, white cloth hanky, and blew his nose delicately. "You didn't answer my question about Morton. Did he tell you to shoot at me? To scare me off, if not to kill me?"

He looked up, defiant. "No one told me to do anything. You're trying to close down Bright Future. I'd lose my job." His lip quivered pathetically in his ugly face. "How many jobs do you think there are for a man like me? I'm not a kid anymore, you know. I just wanted you to lay off." He could have been telling the truth, but I didn't let that stop me. I wanted to talk about Morton.

I squatted down in front of him and took hold of his shirt again.

"You're lying. I know you're lying. You're not exactly the self-starting type, Franklin. I can't see you playing hoodlum all on your own. Morton always tells you what to do, doesn't he? He brought you with him from that cosmetics company—why did that fold, Franklin? Who closed that down? He gave you a job here and you do what he says. Isn't that right?" I banged his head against the wall again, not very hard. He clamped his lips together like a fat little kid who wasn't going to tell the grownup anything and shook his head, once, from side to side.

I let go of his shirt. He unclamped his lips and said, "You can't prove anything, Samson. It's your word against mine." I wanted to kick him but even more, I wanted never to touch him again. So I made a few threats and left him sitting there.

And ran all the way to Morton's office, past his secretary and through his open door, trying to beat Franklin's warning call. Maybe I beat it and maybe I didn't, but Morton wasn't in. His secretary told me stiffly that Mr. Morton was out of town and was due back after lunch the next day if I wished to make an appointment. I told her no thanks.

My next stop was out on the street, at a pay phone near the corner. I put in a call to Chloe. Yes, she was fine. No, she hadn't seen Morton that day, he was out of town. Bert Franklin had not been his usual friendly self when she'd said good morning, but he hadn't pulled a gun or anything.

I told her I was coming back the next day to see Morton. She said fine, just don't stop by and visit me, and dinner is still on for tomorrow night.

Okay, that was all of Bright Future for the moment. Time to shift gears. I sat in my car for a while considering the day's work.

133

Rosie was doing the follow-up on Andy, and his presence in the Bay Area the weekend Smith was killed. I would be seeing Hal that night and he might have something for me on business scams. That left one other person I wanted to talk to. I had some questions I wanted to ask Mrs. James Smith.

I drove south to Mill Valley and got my second strike of the day. Morton had been out of town. Mrs. Smith wasn't home. I sat outside for a while before I went back to the canyon to take a nap. There was a note on my door from someone in the Perrine household. It said "Hal says sure. Six P.M."

23

When I pulled up in front of the Smith house that afternoon I caught myself glancing nervously around for Bunny, and was much relieved that she wasn't lurking anywhere in sight. Precocious is nice for spelling bees and science fairs. Other than that, I can live without it.

Mrs. James Smith was in. She raised her eyebrows at me with tremendous self-control and good breeding and said nothing about unexpected visits.

"I was just making some coffee, Mr. Samson. Would you like some?"

I didn't want any, but it seemed like a good idea to go along with her offer of hospitality. She asked me to "be seated" and went off to get the coffee. That gave me a few minutes to rehearse my approach.

She returned with a silver coffeepot, sugar bowl, and cream pitcher perched in the middle of a silver tray and accompanied by delicate flowered cups and saucers. I fought the urge to turn my cup over and check out its pedigree. She poured.

"And what can I help you with today, Mr. Samson?"

I smiled shyly. "I don't know quite how to approach this, Mrs. Smith."

"Be straightforward," she said coolly. If she had been another kind of woman she would have told me to spit it out.

"Okay," I said, taking a deep and boyish breath. "It's about your husband's relationship with Bright Future. I know he believed in that company. Yet I've just heard he was planning to quit. Gave his notice, as a matter of fact. Can you tell me why?"

Her eyes glazed over. "I'm afraid I don't see what relevance information of a personal nature could have to your magazine article."

I could see I wasn't going to get any help from this woman as long as she thought I was looking for a story. And I needed information from her.

"Mrs. Smith," I said, "I'm going to level with you. Do you want to see your husband's killer caught and punished?"

She set her cup carefully in its saucer, and looked directly into my eyes for the first time. "I don't know what you mean, Mr. Samson. The police have caught my husband's murderer."

"No," I told her. "They haven't."

"But I told them everything they asked. Are you a policeman? May I see your identification?"

"I'm not with the police, Mrs. Smith, but I am trying to find out who killed him."

"Why? Are you some sort of private detective?"

"In a way. I'm a friend of the accused man's family. I believe he's innocent."

"I see," she said. "You are neither a reporter nor a policeman." Although she didn't use the word "liar," her look was slightly accusing. At the same time, she seemed softer, as though she liked me better. Apparently a friend of someone's family, in her mind, had higher status than either journalists or cops. "Well, Mr. Samson, I would like to help you, but I'm not altogether sure why he made his decision, and I don't know why he made it when he did. He had been somewhat dissatisfied with his work for some time. He had made inquiries about other positions. A few weeks ago he received an offer to become headmaster of a private school in Southern California. It was a very good offer, complete with a lovely family home on the campus. Still, even then, he was reluctant to leave Bright Future. He was a very loyal man. He didn't want to leave this area, either. We were making plans to build a new home. We had decided to purchase a lot. In the canyon where he passed away, as I told you before."

I've always hated that particular expression, and it seemed especially inappropriate in this case. Passed quietly away while being stabbed with a hunting knife and tossed down a spillway. Sure.

She continued. "Then, just about two weeks ago, he made his decision. He would accept the new position and we would move south."

"So the decision surprised you?"

"Oh, not exactly surprised. But it did seem sudden."

"And you didn't question that?"

"Of course not. A man's work is very important to him. He must be happy—" she stopped, a flicker of pain crossing her face.

"I'm sorry, Mrs. Smith. I know this is hard for you."

"I'm quite all right, thank you." She sipped at her coffee. I swallowed the first mouthful of mine. Lukewarm, but good and strong.

"When I first talked to you," I said, "you told me that your husband was in the canyon that day because you were planning to buy property there. I don't understand. He made the decision to move days before that."

"Yes, but James was a shrewd businessman. We would have the money from the sale of this house to invest. He wanted to invest in real estate, either here or in Southern California. That morning, that Sunday, when he left the house, he said he wanted to have another look at the lot. To look at it and decide whether to withdraw the offer we had made or to go ahead with it."

"And you believe that's all there was to it?"

"Oh, yes. James always said the best decisions are made—let's see, how did he put it?—on the site of the issue. I suppose that's the sort of thing he meant. And there was his concern about the runoff."

It was possible. It was also possible that he had an appointment to meet his killer. I guessed I wouldn't know one way or the other until I knew who the killer was.

"One other thing, Mrs. Smith. Did you know your son's lover

136

was involved in a child custody fight with his ex-wife?" She flinched at the word lover, but her upper lip stayed stiff.

She frosted up again. "I had heard something about it. I believe there was something in the newspaper. But really, this is not a matter I wish—"

"Mrs. Smith, did you know your husband was going to testify against him? Did he know something about the man?"

She stood up. "I'm afraid I can't help you any more, Mr. Samson. I know no such thing. I know nothing about this man. I wish to know nothing about this man. I do not wish to discuss my son. It is simply too painful." I stood up, too.

"I'm sorry you feel that way."

"Please leave."

"Just one more thing, Mrs. Smith. It's not about your son. Can you tell me why your husband was dissatisfied with his job?"

"No, I cannot. He said he believed the company was moving in a direction he did not care for. That was all he said. That was enough for me."

I was sure that it was. I thanked her for her help.

Bunny was waiting at my car. Today she was wearing at least two sets of eyelashes, lavender pants that bunched up around the ankles, three-inch heels, and some kind of leather pullover, like a closed-up vest. Her lipstick was the color of ripe tomato. The sixteen-year-old lowered her eyelashes and smiled seductively.

"Barbara," I said, "don't look at me that way. It will get you nowhere. I'm not attracted to younger women."

She laughed. "Too bad. I sure like older men. How about another lift into town?"

"Sure. Get in." I wasn't crazy about carting her around, but maybe she could tell me things her mother wouldn't even think about.

She had one answer to all my questions, including the ones about her father's threatened intervention in the custody case. "Yeah," she said. "I could tell you a lot."

I was patient. "What?"

She ran her long red fingernail down my forearm. "I'll tell you if you'll go out with me."

137

"I do not go out with sixteen-year-old girls."

"Okay." She sat looking straight ahead, smiling to herself.

"This is extortion."

"I guess."

"Why are you playing this little kid game with me, Barbara?"

"Because I'm a bored little kid." She was still smiling that tiny smile.

"What do you mean by 'going out'?"

The smile got bigger. "We could go dancing."

"Forget it. Any place I'd want to go dancing wouldn't let you in."

"Fuck you, Samson." But she didn't stop smiling. We'd reached the center of town. "Still got my card, Jake?"

"Yeah."

"Well, if you want to know what I know, just give me a call. I'd settle for dinner. You won't be sorry."

Sure, I thought, I've heard that line from women before. And always from women who made me very sorry indeed.

Bunny got out of the car and headed for the bus station.

The kid made me tired. I didn't realize how tired until I was standing at the bottom of the canyon steps. They looked steep and damned near endless. Afternoon sunlight was sifting down through the redwoods. Gold and green and red brown. The water in the spillway ditch was shallow, and eddying around the rocks and outcrops of root-bound clay instead of crashing and foaming. But this was still March, and there would be more rain. Alan had been unlucky. That knife could easily have stayed hidden in the mud until May. Or even forever.

I didn't see Rosie sitting on the steps below my room until I got all the way up to the path-called-a-lane. She was holding a pair of binoculars in one hand and using the index finger of the other to give me the "shh" signal. I crept up and sat beside her.

"What's happening, Rosie?" I whispered. "What are you doing?"

She flashed me a grin. "I'm watching Hanley watching Carlota."

I laughed as quietly as I could. "Are you also watching Carlota?"

"Oh, every so often I take a look just to see what Hanley's seeing."

"What's he seeing?"

"Nothing very much. She's fully dressed, and she and Nona aren't rolling all over the floor in uncontrollable lust or anything. Nona's not even home. I don't know why he does it. Can't be all that entertaining."

"What's he doing while he's seeing nothing?" I bent over and peered around the corner of my room. Hanley was just visible on the other side of the bridge, crouching behind a fuchsia.

"The last time I looked he was drinking beer and belching."

"Wow."

"I know, Jake, but there must be something to it. He says he doesn't trust her. He must suspect her of something."

"Oh, hell, Rosie, that reminds me. I completely forgot to tell you what I found out yesterday." In all the excitement of the night before I'd neglected to mention my visit to the county building and my talk with Mary.

"That does make the canyon motive stronger, doesn't it?" she said thoughtfully, when I'd finished my story.

"Yeah, but there's more." I ran down the day's Bright Future events.

"So Mrs. Smith confirmed what Chloe said about Smith quitting."

"Right. And it was a very sudden decision."

Rosie shook her head stubbornly. "Maybe that's important and maybe it isn't, but it doesn't let the canyon off the hook." She jerked a thumb in the general direction of Hanley Martin.

I agreed. "Hey," I said, changing the subject, "I've got a poker game on tonight. Want to sit in?"

"Can't. Got a date."

"Same one as last time?"

"Uh huh. Her name's Carol. Really nice." She was peeking through her binoculars at Hanley.

139

"Nice? That could be serious."

Her smile reminded me a little of Bunny's, but she would not be deflected from her detective work. "He's still there, watching."

I stood up. "The hell with this bunch of freaks. I'm heading for the East Bay."

24

After two weeks, I was really looking forward to my poker game. Maybe it's part of my midlife crisis, but I seem to require a certain consistency in my life these days, a few habits. That Tuesday night game is one of the little habits that keeps me from floating off into outer space.

Those who have no trouble keeping their feet on the ground, and those who prefer life in outer space, will have no idea what I'm talking about.

Tigris and Euphrates came to meet me as I trudged up my gravel driveway with one large grocery bag tucked in the crook of each arm. Tigris rubbed against my leg, purring, and almost tripped me. Euphrates was a little cooler. He meowed once in irritated greeting. Then they both ran ahead, leading me to the house as cats will do. I hadn't been home in days. Rosie had been around a couple of times, I knew, and had given them some attention. But I noticed, as they trotted to the door, that their round bellies were rounder than ever. My neighbor, it appeared, had been taking good care of them.

Appearances were not deceiving. When I dumped my two bags on the kitchen table I noticed that their food dishes were full to overflowing. One large bowl of canned food, one large bowl of dry. Dinner had been served.

I unpacked the bags. Beer and chips for poker; steaks, salad makings, smoked oysters, canned clam chowder and French bread for dinner. Hal likes his food, and he's congenitally skinny no matter what he eats. But I like him anyway.

Then I got a towel from the bathroom and hung it on the

fence between my yard and my cat-sitting neighbor's. The prearranged signal. I was home. No need to cater the felines until the towel came down again.

I was gently stirring the vodka martinis, Hal's favorite drink, when he banged on the door.

"Hey, man," he said, slapping me on the back, "getting into trouble again, right? Another case?" For some reason, Hal finds me amusing. I poured his martini, straight up, and gave myself a short glass of beer.

"Can't seem to help it, Hal."

He plunked himself down in front of the Franklin stove and stretched out his long legs. "Don't suppose it has anything to do with Artie's nephew being in jail?"

"You heard."

"Sure. Is Artie going to be here tonight?"

"He said he would. I tried to convince him that sitting up in that canyon having a nervous breakdown wasn't going to help anything."

"Good. Now about your problem. I picked a couple of expert brains for you today, so ask me some questions."

I sat down across from him in my favorite chair, the one that tips over if you sit on the arm, and shoved the footstool halfway across the small room so we could share it.

"Bright Future, for starters. Did the people you talked to have anything on the company?"

"They sure knew the name. They've been trying to keep tabs, you know? Keeping an eye out. But they don't have anything solid."

"What about a company called Perfect Day?"

"California?"

"I don't know. Maybe not. Cosmetics, though, I know that."

"You didn't say anything about it in your phone message."

"I guess I forgot. I wasn't at my best that night."

He thought a minute. "Don't recall anyone saying anything . . . let me use your phone a minute." When he got his party, he asked him or her about Perfect Day. Then he said "Uh huh" once, recited my phone number, and said goodbye.

141

"She says it sounds familiar. She'll call me back. Now, ask me some more questions."

"I don't know. It's hard. The whole thing sounds so tricky, legally."

He grinned, and his face, which is the color of strong black tea, broke into a whole new set of good-looking planes. "I'll tell you, Jake, it seems to be a tricky issue. The laws are relatively new and they vary from state to state. And there's a whole lot of vagueness."

"Anything federal?"

"There's an FTC decision that's reasonably clear and pretty recent."

He dug in his hip pocket, pulled out a notebook, flipped past the first few pages, and shoved his glasses farther up on his nose.

"Now the FTC says multilevel marketing companies have got to concentrate on retail sales. They don't like big investments in front or any kind of purchase requirement of inventory. They'll land on any company that makes misleading claims about earnings or sells distributorships. And you got to let people sell product back to the company if they can't move it."

"What's that about retail sales—what does that mean?"

"Means you've got to have a product and you've got to sell to the public. You can't have a plan where the only real consumers—the only people who buy the product—are people participating in the plan. Distributors. In other words, the product has to be viable in its sales potential. You can't just go along making people buy twenty cases of goose grease nobody wants so they have to unload it on someone else just below them in the pyramid who has to unload it on someone else in the program. That kind of closed system is, as a matter of fact, called a pyramid. And it's illegal. Legal multilevel marketing doesn't involve a closed system."

I was beginning to see a little light. "In other words, you can't just circulate the product, whatever it is, among your own people, with the guy at the bottom sitting on goose grease he can't sell and everybody above him making money on what he paid for it."

"Yeah. That's part of it. Like a chain letter. And the buck

142

stops somewhere. Before it ever gets to the poor sucker who bought in last."

"That's it? You have to sell real product to real consumers and not tell lies about how much people can make doing it?"

"Don't forget the part about big investments. And telling people they have to buy a ton of product in order to get in on this hallelujah-once-in-a-lifetime opportunity. Got another martini?"

I went to the kitchen, trying to get it clear in my head. As far as I could tell, Bright Future and its sailors sold a more or less real product to real humans. Also as far as I could tell, they didn't require any big initial investments. About ninety dollars to get some demonstration materials, according to some of the stuff Morton had showed me. Was that okay?

I brought Hal his second martini and put the question to him.

"Sure. Most states say anything under a hundred dollars is okay for sales materials."

I was remembering that Bright Future had a lot of ranks in their navy. I showed Hal the chart Morton had given me. At the bottom were lieutenants, with commanders above them. Then every city had a captain, who was under a state commodore, who was under a regional admiral, who answered only to Howard Morton. And everyone made a percentage off sales. Hal said that was okay.

"That's what makes it multilevel. But legally, everyone's got to sell product. And everyone who makes a commission off someone else's sales has to be functioning as a supervisor in some way."

"Can that go on forever? I mean could you have a hundred levels?"

"No, not really. Because you have to sell retail. That's the catch. If you've got a hundred people divvying up the commissions you can only go one of two ways. You've got to have an awfully big markup to start with, or you've got to find people who are willing to work for nothing, or damned near it."

"You've lost me."

"Well, look. You've got, for instance, a fifty percent markup. Say you're selling books. You buy a book for five dollars from the company and the ultimate consumer gets it for ten. That means you've got five dollars to spread around in commissions. That will only spread so far before nobody wants to work."

I got that part. Then I had one of those flashes of insight that make me so valuable as an investigator. "And since you have to be able to sell retail, you can't get bigger commissions by pricing the book out of the market."

"Right. Exactly. The only way an endless chain would work is if nobody outside the company ever had to buy any of the company's product."

That was all pretty clear, but I still couldn't see where Bright Future was slithering over the legal edge.

"This company," I said, "has a so-so product. They did okay with it in the good old days, but then they started going downhill. I don't think they've improved the product, but they brought in this multilevel stuff and they're doing better. How would you explain that?"

"Could be better motivation of the sales people, bigger volume. Could all be legitimate. They making any big money claims?"

"Nothing specific. Just a lot of hype."

"That's standard. But you think there's something funny going on?"

"Yes."

"You think they're not selling to real people?"

"I don't know. I never got a straight answer on the number of students they have, and I wouldn't trust any 'proof' they showed me. But I can't believe they're running a straight business. The system's just too damned complicated."

"But that's how they work it. They dazzle the people with this mishmash of levels, with the downshoots and offshoots and money moving all over the place, and they dazzle them with figures. And the figures look good. All they can see is that this company offers them a whole lot of different ways of getting rich."

"And the company makes money by dazzling people with figures?"

"In a way. See, one of the things that happens is that the company does tend to sell more product, at least for a while.

144

Things look better because you've got people buying up batches of books, or courses, or whatever, because they've been hyped into believing they can sell them. The company can't make them buy the stuff, because that's against the law. But these guys look up the line, and see some—what is it, admiral?—driving a big car, and they get the idea. Go along with the program. Look good. Make an impression. Get up there yourself."

"Up the ladder," I said, remembering what Morton had said to me.

"Yeah. Sure, everybody's supposed to be selling to consumers, but the guys at the higher levels are also making a percentage off the guys below them, guys they bring into the program, for supervising and training. And the people they bring in bring in more people. Up, down, and sideways, money stacked on money. Or so they say. And the only way you can move up is by creating volume."

"So the company might actually make more money, at least for a while, if they got enough people hyped up enough."

"Sure."

Maybe that was all there was to it, but Chloe had implied that something more was going on. She'd said something about recruitment. Hal had said something about selling distributorships.

I mentioned that.

"You think there's a chance people are getting head-hunting commissions?"

"Head-hunting? Is that what they call it?"

"Yeah. And that's the big one. That's the one big no-no, in pretty much all the states. You can't make money from slave trade. Nobody pays to join the program, and nobody makes a fee for recruiting. It's product or nothing. But head-hunting, huh? Well, the fact is, that's where some big money can be made if you can get away with it long enough."

"Okay, but what I don't understand is this: Say some guy buys in. He pays a lot of money to get the job and he buys a lot of product and runs right out to recruit a bunch of people. And he fails. He can't sell the product and he can't find any suckers. Isn't he going to be a little bit upset?"

"Separate the product from the head-hunting. If it's a matter of product, remember this: You can't make people buy product to get into the program, and the company's required by law to buy back at least ninety percent of the investment of anyone who does buy product. In a legal operation, that's how it works. And if the product doesn't sell eventually, the company loses. Eventually. But if it's a matter of head-hunting, what you have is a totally under-the-table arrangement. Maybe a guy halfway up the pyramid pays a kickback to the guy below him for every new recruit he brings in. Or say the sucker being recruited doesn't know the law about recruiting and somebody tells him he's got to slip some cash—maybe a whole pile of cash—to the guy above him in order to be let in on the ground floor of the biggest thing since vitamins. Or in order to be promoted so he can make bigger commissions. If you have enough people slipping a thousand apiece up the line you've got something to divide that beats the hell out of selling some piddly product. Someone's going to make some real money."

I looked at my watch. It was time to start the steaks. Hal followed me into the kitchen.

"But to get back to my original question," I said. "People might go along with something like that for a while, but eventually, won't someone make a complaint?"

He nodded. "Great-looking steaks. Sure. Eventually, someone figures out he isn't getting rich and he's out some money. But one of the things that happens with these companies is that you're made to feel like a real asshole if you don't persevere. There's a lot of pressure, a lot of you-can-succeed-if-you-really-work-the-program kind of hype. And sometimes people are just plain embarrassed to admit they've been conned. But some day, somewhere, there's going to be a complaint. And when that happens the law begins to look into it. And eventually the company is run out of business. But before that happens, there might be a few people who make a lot of money, and the hell with the company."

"And that's happened?"

"It's happened."

The phone rang. I was busy with the food, and Hal went to answer it. He didn't seem to be saying much. Mostly, he was listening.

146

"You've got something there, all right," he said when he came back into the kitchen. "About Perfect Day cosmetics. Couple of years ago. Atlanta. Not a big deal, not a real big company. But it looked like there was head-hunting going on and when the Georgia law started having a look, the company just kind of faded away. What's the connection?"

I told him about Morton.

"No shit, Jake? I think some of my friends might be interested in hearing about that. Now, when do we eat?"

25

The next morning I puttered around the house for a few hours, watering plants, talking to the cats, sweeping the floor, and removing bowls and pots of moldy leftovers from the refrigerator.

Shortly after noon, I refilled the cats' bowls, pulled the towel off the fence, and pointed the Chevy north toward the San Rafael bridge, timing my arrival at Morton's office for 1:00 P.M. I made it with five minutes to spare. His office was open and empty; his secretary was not around. I walked in and sat in his visitor's chair to wait for him.

The secretary spotted me when she came back to her desk nibbling a cookie.

"Mr. Samson?" I nodded. "Mr. Morton said he was expecting you. He is at lunch. He should be back any moment now." She didn't say anything about my letting myself into her boss's office. She just stuck some paper into her shiny new typewriter and began tapping away.

Morton strolled in ten minutes later, looking cheerful and content, as though he'd just had a large, expensive meal and was about to have a friendly chat with a business acquaintance. He shook my hand and dropped smiling into his high-backed executive swivel. He asked what he could do for me. I told him to can the shit. He laughed.

"All right, Samson. Bert told me what happened. He got

147

scared and pulled a dumb stunt. Is there something you expect me to do about it?"

"Yeah. Explain it. Explain what Franklin's scared of. Explain what it is, exactly, that you're doing with this company. Explain what happened at Perfect Day. And then you can explain why you killed James Smith."

He laughed again. "Did you rehearse that? It's very good. I don't see that I have to explain anything to you, but obviously you're going to make a nuisance of yourself unless I do. Franklin's scared because Franklin is always scared, has led his whole life being scared. When Perfect Day went under, he lost a good job. He's not the kind of man who bounces back. Good enough at his work, loyal to his employer"—I snorted, but Morton just kept on talking—"but not strong, and not very smart. He has some idea that you can cause trouble for Bright Future, and that he'll lose another job. Pretty silly idea, but then a man's entitled to his fears, isn't he?"

Morton didn't look any different from the way he'd looked the last time I'd seen him, but he sure didn't sound the same. He'd dropped the hype, the sales clichés. He wasn't bothering to do his act for me, and the clothing and hairdo he wore for the sales vice-president's role suddenly looked more like a costume than plain bad taste.

I decided to try out some of my new sophistication.

"I don't think his fears are all that silly, Morton. Perfect Day 'went under,' as you put it, because it was operating outside the law. And Bright Future's next in line because you're running the same kind of head-hunting operation here."

"Head-hunting?" he smiled brightly at me. "Head-hunting? I'm not really sure exactly what you mean by that. But whatever it is, it doesn't sound like anything that's going on here. Not that I know of, anyway. And," he yawned, "if it has to do with sales, I'd certainly know about it."

"You don't just know about it. You started it and you're doing it. And that's why you killed Smith. Because he was threatening to blow the whistle."

He nodded thoughtfully. "I think I understand now, Samson.

You have some idea that I'm doing something illegal. You think Smith had proof of it and threatened to use that proof against me."

"Exactly."

"And you think I killed Smith to protect myself."

I was watching him carefully. He seemed perfectly relaxed. Was he considering bashing me over the head and dumping me in the bay?

"Tell me," he said, "have you told the police what you think?"

"They know what I know," I lied, continuing to watch him. I was disappointed. He just looked back at me and shook his head.

"Samson, my friend, you're bluffing. I don't know why. I guess we're all ambitious, and you're just looking for a big story to make your career. I don't blame you for that. Ambitious. Sometimes people go a little too far with that." He smirked. "I guess you've heard that the people at Perfect Day might have gone a little too far with that. But think about it. Even if I were doing something illegal here, James Smith would never have done anything to harm the company itself. He was resigning. Leaving the area. Moving on. An appropriate response for an executive who disagrees with company policy and has no hope of changing it. And that's all it came down to, you know, a slight disagreement on policy. And there's something else. If there were any lawbreaking going on here, do you think I'd want to call attention to the company, and to myself, by killing one of the executives? Doesn't make a lot of sense, does it?"

I'd listened to his monologue patiently, and now it was my turn again. "You didn't have any choice. You're a crook. You were covering your ass. You were desperate."

"I'm never desperate," he snapped at me. "And it's not true that the police know what you know. They know more. They know that I was leading a sales meeting right about the time Smith died. In Santa Cruz. And I had breakfast with the Santa Cruz people before that."

I shrugged. "Nice alibi. So Franklin killed him for you."

Morton laughed loudly. "Sorry, wrong again. Franklin was in Santa Cruz, too. Covering the meeting for the company newsletter." He leaned back in his chair and slitted his eyes at me. "I think I should warn you not to run around talking this kind of crap. About a crooked operation. About murder. I'll hit you with one hell of a lawsuit, and I'll win."

I thought about that. If he was covered on the murder—if he really was—that didn't mean he was covered on the scam he was running. "Now you're the one who's bluffing," I said, grinning at him.

He shook his head at me again. Then he put his elbows on his desk and leaned toward me. He wasn't smiling, not the slightest bit. "You'll know soon enough, Samson. Now get out of my office. I have a company to run."

I was finished with him anyway, at least for the time being, so I got. All the way down the hall to Bowen's office. I told his secretary I had something important to tell him. She looked at me skeptically, as though no one ever had anything important to tell Bowen, but she let him know I was there and he invited me in.

He was wearing the same suit as the first time, and was sipping a glass of sherry.

"Would you like some, Mr. Samson? Good for the digestion, after a nice lunch."

I told him no thanks. Then I told him there was a possibility that Morton was running a crooked sales force and maybe killed Smith to cover it up. He turned very pale and spilled some sherry.

"So maybe you can tell me, Mr. Bowen. Was Morton in Santa Cruz that weekend?"

Bowen stared at me a while longer, and set his sherry down on the desk. "I don't know. How would I know?" His voice shook. "Howard is always going somewhere on business. He travels all the time. I don't know where. He does his job very well. He's very conscientious. He's done wonders. Saved the company. I'm sure, Mr. Samson, that you are very, very wrong." His hands were trembling and he looked sick and shocked. He also looked old and not very strong. I was afraid that if I pressed the issue the man would have a heart attack right before my eyes. He spoke again. "I don't know why you would want to say a thing like that to me. James resigned because he wanted to work for a school down south. Be-

150

cause he was tired of the pressures of the executive life, and wanted to return to academia." The old man sounded wistful. I got the feeling he was wishing he'd done the same thing years ago. Then his mood, and his facial expression, changed abruptly. He was angry. "I've often felt that the state of modern journalism is deplorable. Sensationalism, lies, all kinds of destructive behavior. If you are fishing for scandal, you are fishing in the wrong pond."

I reeled in, threw away the bait, and left. I did try to get into Bill Armand's office, but he wasn't in.

26

At seven o'clock, 101 north was still clogged with commuters. I sat comfortably in my Chevy, plugging along mile by mile, looking at Marin County, trying not to care that Morton, my favorite suspect, had an alibi and that the alibi would probably hold. After all, the police hadn't been sitting on their hands between Smith's death and Alan's arrest. They'd talked to people at Bright Future. That was how they'd heard about Alan's argument with Smith.

Somewhere, though, they'd missed something. The something I had to find.

Meanwhile, I was looking forward to spending an evening with Chloe. I was glad she lived in the northern end of the county. I like it up there. It's peaceful.

Now that I'd spent some time, again, in Marin, some of the good memories were coming back, some of the fondness I'd always felt for this place. Not just the dank southern end of it, but all of it, in all its variety.

Each part of the Bay Area has its own, unique character. The East Bay is tough and political and has a hard urban maleness that keeps me moving and functioning. San Francisco is androgynous. And Marin, well, Marin always feels female to me. Like you could just pillow your weary head on those round, smooth hills.

Popular wisdom has it that Marin County is uniformly rich. I'd once heard a Berkeley radical use the county's name as a synonym for the other side in what he called, with great originality, "the class struggle."

It's true that Marin has a high per capita income, natural beauty, and, in some places, incredible wealth. Even movie folk live there. But back when I'd been drifting around this side of the bay, I'd come to know a whole different Marin, and some of it had to be there still. Rotting shacks in the woods inhabited by welfare mothers and their children. Leftover flower children growing tomatoes on the dusty backside of someone else's West Marin property. People who'd lived off those back roads and in those canyons and meadows so long that they remembered when you could buy a little place for under twenty thousand dollars, maybe even trade a hand-painted van for a down payment. A long time ago. Like about fifteen years.

I don't know. Maybe they're all gone now, moved to Sonoma or Mendocino or Humboldt County. Or L.A. or Fresno. Forced out by years of pay-anything demand for a chunk of Marin soil. But I doubted it. I wanted to believe those people were still around, the ones who'd been hiding in the wrinkles of Marin for twenty years. And that they would hide out there for another twenty years.

I turned off at the downtown Novato exit and headed toward Indian Valley Road, taking advantage of a stoplight to glance again at the directions. The address was on a road that angled off just before Indian Valley. You could even call it a street, because on one side were middle income tract homes and on the other, small ranches running about five acres. A dividing line between suburbia and country, all within the borders of the same town. The mail box was enameled in streaky red, like nail polish. A length of chain with a "Keep Out" sign tied to it with wire was strung between posts on either side of the entrance. The driveway was a dirt road that ran a good 200 feet back to a white frame house sheltered by two oaks and a huge old walnut. According to my directions, that was the landlord's house. I was to drive past it to a smaller one at the back.

I pulled up at the chain, got out of my car, unhooked one end of it, got back in my car and took the first few feet of mud in first gear. Then, also according to directions, I got out and hooked the chain to its post again. I nearly got stuck about halfway on, where the road dipped and the mud was especially deep and soft, spun my wheels a little, backed up, rocked a couple of times, and lurched ahead.

No wonder Chloe wasn't worried about unwanted visitors.

At my right was a rail fence lined with irises as yet unbloomed. I was supposed to call Iris soon, I remembered.

Beyond the frame house, I passed some kind of outbuilding—my headlights caused an eruption of crackling and crowing from within—and thirty or forty feet beyond that was a tiny house that looked like it, too, had once been an outbuilding. A perfect rectangle, sheltered by more oaks and surrounded by foot-high grass. I pulled in behind an old blue gray Volvo. A German shepherd shoved the curtains aside and glared at me, barking, through a big window. I started up the overgrown walk that appeared to be made of broken chunks of concrete and led to a concrete slab porch on the long side of the rectangle. The door opened, the shepherd lunged at me, and Chloe said, "Hi, come on in."

The dog sniffed my hands and feet, wagged once or twice, and led me inside, where he trotted off to a corner and curled up for sleep.

"Achilles likes you," Chloe said.

"He's too trusting." I handed her the bottle of Grand Marnier I'd brought. She thanked me, waved me to a chair with a "be right back," and went through a door into the kitchen. I sat down and surveyed the room, trying to get a fix on its inhabitant.

Real knotty pine paneling, probably done in the thirties or forties, whenever this box of a place had been converted from a bunkhouse, outhouse, stable, or chicken coop.

I was sitting in an oak rocking chair beside a small, hot potbelly stove, in the corner near the big window. Directly in front of the window was an oiled pine table with two straight-backed chairs. In the opposite corner there squatted a brown space heater so old it had a black stovepipe and rounded corners. It looked like an old radio. There was a big, multicolored braided rug, a navy blue couch with a red pillow squashed up against the arm, and, at

153

right angles to that, an overstuffed chair. Between them stood a brass lamp with a fringed shade. The wall to my left, on the other side of the door, was floor-to-ceiling books.

Chloe came back into the living room with an opened bottle of wine and two stemmed glasses.

Grey Riesling," she said. "I remembered that you like it." I nodded enthusiastically, even though I would have preferred beer.

Chloe turned the overstuffed chair around and dragged it closer to the fire. "I brought some things from the office for you to look at."

"Are they exciting things?"

"I don't know. I raided Morton's files. Grabbed a couple of handfuls of correspondence."

"How'd you manage that?"

"He was out of town. I just skulked around until his secretary was away from her desk, opened a drawer—"

"And pulled out a plum."

"I hope so. I needed some excuse to get you here, but it would be nice if something else came out of it."

I raised my eyebrows. That always makes people say more. Well, almost always. Chloe knew the trick, too. She raised her eyebrows at me. We were both silent, struck dumb by each other's technique.

Ever since I'd first met Chloe, some memory had nagged at me. The look she had, one-third amused, one-third hostile, one-third sexual. The dark, sharp-featured face. Now I remembered. About twenty-five years ago. A long time. I'd been just a couple of steps past the first catastrophes of puberty. A hot, midwestern Saturday afternoon at my parents' corner grocery. The heat, the dusty smell of the potatoes and onions in bushel baskets on the warped gray wooden floor, the sharp sugar scent of the penny candy and bulk cookies. My father was napping, my mother was out. I was in charge for an hour. I'd already neatened up the pyramids of apples and oranges in the front window. I was drinking an orange pop—I can taste it now—and thinking about turning on the fan in the transom over the door. But I knew I wouldn't. My mother had infected me with her own fear that the ancient, exposed blades would fly off their mounting and decapitate me.

154

"Hey, little Jakey!" Rachel swooshed in the screen door, wearing a red skirt and a peasant blouse. Beautiful Rachel. Five years older than I. A Gypsy who had arrived in the neighborhood only a month before, part of a caravan of old, rusty cars full of brightly dressed, dark-skinned, laughing, teasing, Romany-speaking people. I never did know exactly how many there were, about fifteen I thought, and they all lived in one apartment in a ratty building across the street. Rachel and I had talked a few times, and I'd been horrified to learn that she'd never been to school. The last time we'd talked we'd struck a bargain: I would teach her to read and write, she would teach me to speak Romany.

"Gimme a strawberry pop, Jakey. I came to say goodbye."

I jumped to my feet, pulled a bottle of strawberry from the cooler, opened it for her, waved away the dime she was offering, and croaked, "Goodbye?"

My face felt as if all the muscles had fallen, and the orange pop was piping itself back up my esophagus.

"We're going back to California today." She looked very happy.

"Why?"

She looked at me as though I'd just asked why trees have leaves. "We always go back there. Besides, we don't like it here. People look at you too much."

I guess I just stood there, staring at her, confused thoughts of our aborted teacher-student relationship almost but not quite making their way out my mouth in speech. She gazed back at me, bemused. Then she laughed, shaking her head. She stepped closer, and she had that look. Part amused, part hostile, part sexual. "Oh, Jake," she said, shaking her head again. Still holding the strawberry pop in one hand, she grabbed my waist with the other, pulled my pelvis up against hers, did a quick bump and grind, and swooshed back out the door again. She took the soda pop with her.

And there sat Chloe. She was wearing jeans, not a full red skirt. Her skin was Mediterranean olive, not Gypsy brown. Educated, literate, cynical, and more than twice the age Rachel had been. But by some trick of chemistry, some migration of spirit, she was Rachel. I was in trouble.

She refilled my wineglass. Dinner was popping and bubbling in the oven; it smelled like chicken.

"I didn't mean to scare you," she said. "Tell me what you've been doing." I told her about my encounters with Morton and Bowen. She digested the part about Morton's alibi slowly and reluctantly.

"Chloe," I said, "you run the communications department. Didn't you know Morton was out of town that weekend? And what about Franklin? He's supposed to be working for you."

"I don't bother with the newsletter," she said. "Franklin writes it and Morton checks it through. Sometimes I manage to avoid reading it altogether. But Jake, just because Morton says it's so doesn't mean it is. And the newsletter story might not be—quite accurate."

"That's true. Is there any way for you to check it out?"

"Yes. I'll call some people in Santa Cruz with some excuse or other." She looked sad.

"Sorry to bring you such depressing news."

"Well, hell . . . I have to do some things to our dinner, now."

"Anything I can do?"

"No, it's all under control. Want to read some of that correspondence while I cook?"

I nodded and she handed me a stack of paper that had been sitting on the bookshelf. She left the room. I began thumbing through the letters. Most of them were addressed to admirals and commodores, a few to captains. Most of it was congratulatory—keep up the good work, numero uno—or threatening—shape up or ship out, commodore. Pretty boring. I read through maybe half of it, put it aside in two neat piles, and strolled out to the kitchen. Chloe had just finished putting chicken, broccoli, and parsley potatoes on two plates. I picked up the plates and carried them to the table in the living room. She followed me with more wine and a bowl of salad. She lighted the candles and switched off the standard lamp.

I poured out two more glasses of wine and held up my glass. "To a pleasant evening." We touched glasses, smiled at each other, and began to eat.

"Good chicken," I said.

"Tarragon." She helped herself to salad.

"I got through about half the letters."

"Good. Have some salad. Find anything?"

"Not yet."

"Are you clear on the hierarchy, the levels?"

"Reasonably. But what's with the navy stuff?"

She laughed. "Multilevel companies tend to model their hierarchies on something traditional. The army, the navy, even British aristocracy. Anything with status and a sense of power."

"Any archbishops?"

"Not that I've heard of. No rabbis, either."

"Have you read any of Morton's correspondence?"

"No. That's for you to do. My department's clean—more or less—and I want to keep it that way."

We took the plates out to the kitchen, where dessert waited in the oven. Baked apples. I couldn't remember the last time I'd eaten a baked apple. She'd made real whipped cream, too. We sat in the chairs near the fire to eat them, and when we'd finished I offered to do the dishes. No, she said, the dishwasher would do that. So I went back to my reading while she filled the machine.

In a few minutes, she returned to the living room and lay down on the couch with a book. Another half an hour and I'd finished. Morton was a careful man. The way some of the letters read, there was more between the lines than on them, but with the possible exception of one letter, there wasn't much to go on. It was addressed to the captain of Los Angeles and it referred by name to a commander who was causing some kind of trouble about a "fee" that was due "with reference to" a new lieutenant, who was also named. I folded the letter and put it in my pocket. Then I put the rest of the correspondence back on the bookshelf.

Chloe glanced at me. "Finished?"

I nodded.

"What do you think?"

"Could be."

She sat up at one end of the couch and I joined her. "You

157

could still lose your job, you know," I said. "If there's an investigation, and if anything comes of it, the company might not survive."

"I know," she sighed. "But I could lose it anyway. Morton's never been too crazy about me, and now—it's a gamble, but a job's just a job. I've had a lot of those."

"Tell me about that. What it's been like for you."

"You want to hear my life story?"

"Yes."

"Especially the parts with Smith in them?"

"Those too."

At some point while I'd been reading, she had made the Grand Marnier appear magically on the table, along with two liqueur glasses. She got up, put another chunk of wood on the fire, and poured our drinks. When she brought them back to the couch, she sat closer to me.

"Friendship," I said, raising my glass.

"Friendship," she repeated, smiling softly. When she smiled that way, the crease between her eyebrows smoothed out and the sardonic lines at the corners of her mouth deepened into something happier. The firelight took the chill off a face that reflected a complicated life and a loss of faith. At that moment, I felt a kind of love for Chloe. What Iris and I had was good in its way, but she kept her emotional distance so we managed to avoid the real closeness that carries the threat of loss. There was nothing cool, that night anyway, about Chloe.

"Samson, what is it about you?"

"What? What about me?"

"You look at me with those big blue eyes, run your fingers through your graying yellow curls, and I want to beat you to death with my life as a woman. Maybe it's because you look so vulnerable. For a man." I leaned over and kissed her gently. She responded, briefly, then moved a few inches farther away.

"Once upon a time," she said, "there was a bright, ambitious, eager young woman. College editor. Crusader. Star. But she made a big mistake. She graduated. Out into the ugly, real world. A homesick kid five hundred miles from home. Like the song, you know? I used to sing it sometimes. Learning about life and love and pain and everything all at once." She smiled wryly. "Nothing was like it was supposed to be. The job I thought I'd prepared myself to do, wanted to do, was a Rosalind Russell movie. The job I was doing was an existential nightmare. I hated it. When the stories weren't stupid or senseless, they were painful. I was a 'girl reporter.' I begged for decent assignments but when I got them I seized up, paralyzed. I drank too much and I went to bed with too many men and I shattered, like the little porcelain receptacle I was."

"Where was this?"

"Chicago."

"Where was home?"

"Wisconsin."

"Couldn't you have worked there?"

"Sure. On what they used to call the Women's Pages."

"So you went to Chicago."

"They offered me a job. Wire service. I took it. I don't know why. Come to think of it, I don't know why I came to California."

"Because you got a job here." I poured some more Grand Marnier.

"Oh yes, that's right. I guess you know my life story, after all."

"Not enough of it."

"You have a nice, strong nose. Tell me about your life now."

"Thank you. My nose goes with my blue eyes and yellow curls. We can talk about me another time. I want to hear more about you. What happened next?"

"I left the wire service and started drifting. You want words? I do words. Public relations, magazines, textbooks. Then I ran out of luck. You can only drift for so long before you become what is known as unemployable."

"So, being unemployable, you went to work for Bright Future."

"Correct. But when they started making plans to move I decided not to move with them."

"Because you didn't like the job, or the company, or the management?"

"Does it sound like I liked any of my jobs? Temperamentally

unsuited to corporate life. Or just a little too crazy for it. Or too sane. And of course, even after the move, Smith would be my boss. I couldn't see moving all the way to California to keep on working for an asshole. I decided to write poetry, instead."

"Speaking of working for an asshole, there's something I've been meaning to ask you about. The Bright Future faculty. They worked with Smith. Did any of them have any problems with him?"

"Wrong tree, bloodhound. They all date back to Chicago days. The only one who doesn't still live back there is an old woman who retired to Arizona five years ago."

Well, I thought, it was just an idea, anyway.

"So," I said, "you didn't want to move to California to keep working for an asshole. But you're here."

"I changed my mind. It turned out I was also temperamentally unsuited to starvation. And Chicago's not a comfortable place to be poor in. I wrote Bowen a letter. He rehired me. Smith wasn't happy about it, but he went along with Bowen."

"So you never got along with Smith?"

"We got along. He made it clear I belonged in someone's kitchen, and I could barely stand the sight of him, but we got along. And you're not Sam Spade. You're a cop, and now that you know I had a motive, you're going to arrest me for murder, right?"

"No. I work for the attorney general's office and I'm going to arrest you for fraud."

"Good," she said cheerfully. "Fraud has more class." We had gotten to the point where a good dinner, good wine, and romantic firelight were combining to make us both feel attractive, witty, and compatible. Maybe there was a touch of adolescent memory in my attraction to her, but it was her real presence as Chloe that was doing me in.

It was all Iris's fault. If she were more reliable, I wouldn't have to travel all over the place chasing women. My stepmother was right.

"That's a look of speculation, Jake."

"The trouble with mature women is that they can pick up the

subtlest look, the tiniest nuance. But the look is not one of speculation. It is a simple, honest look of lust."

"That's the trouble with mature men. High expectations. I
suppose you think I invited you out here because I wanted to go to
bed with you."

I shook my head. "Never occurred to me. This was a business
dinner. Purely informational."

"That may be. But dinner is over."

27

I didn't get back to Mill Valley until the following afternoon.
Chloe called in late and we spent the morning making love, before
and after an omelet I threw together from some odds and ends
including leftover chicken, jack cheese, and mushrooms. Chloe
was as impressed with my cooking as I had been with hers.

By noon, she was getting anxious to replace the correspondence she'd lifted, minus the letter I was keeping. I borrowed an
envelope, a stamp, and a piece of notepaper, scribbled a note to
Hal, sealed it up with the Morton letter, and stuck it in my pocket,
ready to mail.

We said goodbye with the promise to be in touch by the weekend,
sooner if Morton discovered she'd been messing with his files.

On my way into Mill Valley, I dropped the letter in a box.
Then I found a phone booth and, shuffling through the accumula-
tion of business and personal cards in my wallet, extracted the
purple one Bunny had given me the first time I'd visited the Smith
house. The phone number was not the same one I had for Mrs.
Smith. After three rings I got a recorded message.

"Hey, this is Barbara." Thump thump thump went the new
wave music, fade back and voice over. "And you've probably
guessed I'm not home." Thump thump thump, fade back. "But I
don't know where I am so I can't tell you, right? So you tell me
where you are, and who you are, and maybe I'll call you when I
get back from wherever I am." Thump thump beep. I left my

name and Artie's phone number, figuring someone would probably be around there if Bunny should actually play back her tape and decide to call. Then I phoned Artie's house and warned Julia that she might get a strange call for me. I had this vision of messages going back and forth in space between me and Bunny for days. Maybe if I just parked in front of her house, she'd appear as she had each time before.

Rosie was working on the steps. She'd replaced one section of a stringer and was nailing redwood treadboards to it. There was a gap of about six steps, so I stopped.

"Glad I caught you, Jacob."

"Certainly did," I agreed, looking at the open stringers with mud behind them.

"You can crawl up the side. Listen, you've got to do me a favor."

"Okay."

"I've gotten myself stuck with an evening with Carlota and Nona. Dinner and a showing of Carlota's fil-ums."

"Poor baby."

"Yes. And I can't stand the thought of doing it all alone. Please?"

"Oh, shit, Rosie. You want me to be your date or something?"

"Something. Please, Jake. At least, if you're there, it will be bearable."

"Tonight?" I sighed.

"Tonight."

"What time?"

"You're a true friend. Six-thirty. The films are at eight-thirty."

"Lovely."

I grabbed hold of the railing and hoisted myself up along the stringer until I got to real steps again. Then I went to my room, locked the door behind me, and went to sleep.

28

Rosie came to get me at six-thirty and we descended together to Carlota's. Nona let us in—we knocked, we didn't use the gong—and offered us martinis.

"Got any beer?" Rosie asked. Nona scowled.

"Me, too," I said. Nona shrugged.

Carlota was draped across the grand piano, martini in one hand, cigarette in the other, martini pitcher at her elbow. She was wearing a black velvet lounging outfit, the tunic top cut low front and back, the pants tucked into the tops of some knee-high black glove leather boots. Very fetching. Nona was dressed in a baggy white suit that looked like something Peter Lorre might have worn in some steamy tropical movie, and a flowing red cravat.

Rosie and I were pretty dressed up, for us. I was wearing cords, and turtleneck, and a tweed jacket. Rosie was wearing an outfit similar to mine.

"How kind of you to come, Jacob," Carlota said.

"Kind of you to ask me, Carlota." She hadn't, but that was okay.

"Yes. Well," she waved airily, "sit down, please. Dinner will be a while. I hope you both like stroganoff."

Nona came out of the kitchen carrying a tray in each hand, one with our steins of beer, the other with hors d'oeuvres. She looked like a butler. Rosie and I had seated ourselves on the loveseat. Nona set both trays down on the coffee table in front of us.

"Do try the canapes," Carlota said. I picked one of the small toast rounds off the tray. Melted cheese with an anchovy embedded in it. Some kind of herb, too. I liked it. Rosie didn't take any. She hates anchovies. "Aren't they lovely?" Carlota asked. "They're one of Nona's specialties." Nona had retired again to the kitchen. Carlota had maneuvered herself onto the piano stool. "Would you like to hear something?"

We both said yes. I wondered if Rosie felt as trapped as I did. Carlota began clomping her way through an exercise in cacophony that seemed to consist mostly of jarring starts after patternless pauses.

Rosie leaned close to my ear. "I think I've got a lead to someone who might know where Andy was, or at least where he wasn't, when Smith was killed. I should know for sure in a couple of days."

I nodded, downing another appetizer. I hadn't eaten, after all, since about eleven.

"I haven't had a chance to tell you," I said. "It looks like Morton has an alibi."

Rosie made a face. She wasn't happy.

Carlota kept banging away, with much head-jerking. She didn't seem to notice our half-whispered conversation. In the relatively quiet parts of the piece, I gave Rosie a disjointed account of the evening with Chloe, with emphasis on the correspondence. I was about to start filling her in on my talk with Morton when the piece Carlota was playing ended abruptly. We waited a couple of seconds to be sure it was really over, then we applauded.

Carlota bowed, deeply and slowly, from the waist.

Nona appeared in the doorway. "Dinner is almost ready," she told Carlota, who looked startled at being brought out of her trance. "Perhaps our guests would like another drink." Then she turned and disappeared again into the kitchen.

Neither Rosie nor I had finished our first beer. Carlota poured herself another martini, no olive. She downed it in three gulps. Then she smiled brightly, said, "Must go help Nona," and left us alone.

"What kind of impression are you getting about Andy's whereabouts that day? Anything?"

"I've only found out one thing for sure. There was a small party on Saturday night. Organizers for the fund-raiser, friends. And I know Bill wasn't there. But the day of the murder? That's what I'm checking on now. Incidentally, the fund-raiser's this Sunday."

Carlota and Nona reappeared with a wood and brass serving cart. We took seats at the dining table. The napkins were real linen, the plates fine china, the candlesticks and flatware silver. The wineglasses were still discount store.

Somehow, knowing the temperaments of our hosts, I had expected an elaborate and possibly inedible dinner. But this was just ordinary old beef stroganoff with noodles, and a salad with artichoke hearts.

"Nona," I said, "this is very good."

She smiled. She had a surprisingly sweet smile. It occurred to me that she must have a good side to her personality, and that living with Carlota could put almost anyone in a permanent state of tension.

"And I've been admiring your artwork," I added. Actually, I hadn't really looked at it since the first time I'd been in the house.

"Thank you. I hope to be able to make it pay eventually."

"That's right," I said. "You were at work the morning that man was killed. What do you do?"

"I work in an art supply store." She said it simply, without embarrassment or pride. "We're open on Sunday mornings."

"Like a hardware store," Carlota said. "But it's only temporary and she gets her materials at a discount."

"Well," I held up my glass, "here's to your success."

Carlota smiled briefly and twitched, wrinkling her forehead. "She will be successful, I'm sure," she said, in an end-of-discussion tone. She added, with hardly a break between sentences, "I'm so glad you two are coming to my films tonight." The message was clear. This was her night, and it was her art we were going to concentrate on. Nona was glowering again.

"Yes," I said agreeably. "I read Eric's review. Quite a rave."

"Oh, yes. I was so pleased. And it's so terribly pleasant that we've become great friends, as well as colleagues."

Rosie stifled a yawn. "Colleagues?"

"Oh, Rosie, dear, have some more wine, please." Carlota poured some for herself and passed the decanter to Rosie.

Carlota continued to babble about her friendship with Eric. How much she admired him. How much he admired her work. How they often talked together about art. I wasn't really listening. I was thinking about Andy and Bill, wondering what Rosie would learn.

". . . we're developing something of a salon," Carlota was saying. "Nona joins us when she's at home. And not painting . . ."

I also wondered whether Bill would join Andy at the fundraiser.

Did he ever break his rule of no weekends away from the inn? If he actually had such a rule.

Carlota was still talking about her mentor. I thought she must be pretending he was famous, and that she, as his friend, shared his glory. ". . . and he's such a fine, sympathetic man. On that dreadful day, when I was so distressed, he brought me some lovely sherry. Our first real tête-à-tête . . ."

And what if Rosie learned that Andy was not covered for the time of the murder? Had been off somewhere on his own? If we had that information by Sunday, when Andy would be conveniently in town, could I force the issue with him in some way?

Rosie had asked something about the review. Her manners as a guest are always good. And Carlota babbled on. "Oh, yes, weeks and weeks ago. We spoke about it and he said he would try. But he couldn't promise. It was only after he'd seen them, you see . . ."

I would have to confront Andy with his presence in the area that weekend, and with Smith's plans to testify against him. But I needed more. I needed evidence. A witness to say that Andy was seen in the canyon. Anything.

Rosie and Carlota continued to chat while Nona watched them suspiciously. Carlota was obviously delighted with the attention Rosie was giving her. Nona was not. I shook myself out of my speculations about Andy and set myself to the task of being a good guest like Rosie.

"Nona," I said, "I'd love to see your studio. After dinner, maybe?" She pulled her watchful eyes away from the two women and muttered that she would be happy to show me everything except the work in progress. We finished the stroganoff and salad.

"Carlota," Nona said sharply, "would you mind getting the dessert?"

"Of course, darling. Do excuse me, Rose." She left the table.

"Would anybody like more wine?" Nona asked. When we said we wouldn't, she took the decanter across the room and tucked it away in the liquor cabinet. Then she did the same with the martini pitcher.

Carlota returned with a bowl of fruit and a wedge of cheese

166

centered carefully on a wooden board. She looked at the table, where the decanter had been, then her eyes shifted to the piano. After casting a slightly accusing look at Nona, she settled down to cutting an apple into very small pieces, all the while talking about the size of the audience she expected that night.

Suddenly she stood up. "It's time to go. We must get there early—in time to greet people, you know."

"If we have a few minutes," I said, "I'd like to see Nona's studio."

She sent a tender look Nona's way. "Do you mind doing that another time, darling?"

Nona shook her head and smiled a resigned smile. "Of course not. We should go."

We took two cars, mine and Nona's, and arrived at the film showing early enough to join the patrons in a glass of cheap champagne and late enough to make an entrance. Carlota swooped about greeting people, striking poses, and guzzling champagne until it was time for the show to start.

We seated ourselves along with the two dozen other film fans, the lights went out, and the projectionist let the first film roll.

It started with about ten seconds of blackness punctuated by the rhythmic flashing of a single very bright light. Then, suddenly, overexposed and backed up against a bank of ferns, there was Carlota.

"A star is born," Rosie whispered in my ear.

The film blacked out again, and came to somewhere on the floor of the forest, looking up through the trees at the wispy fog. This was followed by a shaky tilting of the camera, so the trees were horizontal. Then they were upside down.

Another blackout, and a car window view of a narrow road. Just the road. Then we were on Miller Avenue, watching the cars go by. That went on for a while, and was followed by a shot of a rainbowed pool of water and gasoline and another one of a mud puddle with a fast-food hamburger wrapper half submerged.

Still another blackout, and we were crossing the Golden Gate Bridge, its struts and cables quivering with the unsteadiness of Carlota's camera. This was followed by a series of stills of the ocean, and then another blackout. We were back in the woods again, staring at an underexposed fern.

The title came at the end: *Exposures*, a film by Carlota Bowman. The audience applauded mildly.

The projectionist had a little trouble getting the next film going. This one began with its title: *Dance*.

We were back in the woods once again, looking at ferns. Then a pair of feet, female, I thought, with painted toenails, flitted through the foliage. A slightly different pair of feet followed, running and mashing fronds into the clay. Still another pair of feet came next, doing basically the same things the other feet had done.

The feet, which were now a little muddy, continued to follow each other around for a while, tripping lightly, skipping, leaping, tippy-toeing. Then the camera backed up a little and we got to see the bodies that went with the feet. They were women, all right. Three of them. Holding hands. They were dressed in flowing robes, vaguely classical in style. No one I recognized. They spent the next fifteen minutes weaving in and out of the trees, wrapping sashes around each other, and getting their feet even dirtier. Then, with many silent exclamations, they discovered another woman lying on the ground and gathered around her. The film blacked out for a fraction of a second, and then the camera focused on the corpse, or sleeping woman, or whatever. It was Carlota. She opened her eyes and the film ended.

There was, the projectionist announced, one more to go, after a brief intermission. We went back out to the champagne bottles. Rosie and I did not dare speak to each other. Carlota and Nona, thank God, were busy talking to a bearded man wearing a black turtleneck sweater and filthy jeans. The rest of the audience was standing around looking self-conscious. Their facial expressions said these were art films, and heaven knows they appreciated art, and wasn't this all terribly interesting? I heard someone mention the review in the *Journal*, but I noticed that no one was talking much about the films.

The intermission ended and we all trudged back to our seats.

The last film was called *Mirrors*. It was an endless—twenty minutes? an hour? three days?—study of objects reflected in mirrors. I recognized two of the mirrors that hung in Carlota's living room. There was the one that hung near the French doors, reflecting one side of the living room, a window looking out onto the kitchen deck, and some of the steps leading up to the path above her house. I could even see a piece of my room across the path and under Charlie's house.

Then there was the one that hung near the grand piano. That reflected the piano, some of Nona's artwork, and some of the hillside along the stairway.

I stopped watching after the first ten minutes or so, and let my mind work on the problems of Andy and Bill and Howard Morton. And Bunny. I was going to have to cope with Bunny again.

When the film finally ended, we drifted back out again to the reception table. There was no champagne left. Carlota was surrounded by a small circle of enthusiasts—Nona, two other women, and the bearded man. A few other people looked like they thought they should speak to the filmmaker, and hovered around the outside of the circle looking confused, but most of the audience just walked slowly out the door. Rosie and I agreed that was the best course. We congratulated Carlota on the showing, and said we had some errands to run that night.

Then we escaped to a soda fountain in San Rafael. Rosie had a hot fudge sundae; I had a banana split.

29

At nine the next morning, Julia came and knocked on my door to tell me someone named Barbara was on the line.

"She sounds pretty eager, Jake. What's your secret?"

"Wrinkles."

Bunny wanted to know why I'd kept her waiting so long. "What did you do," she demanded, "shave first?"

I explained that I wasn't living near my telephone, gritted my teeth, and apologized.

"Oh, that's okay. No pressure. You ready to take me out?"

"For lunch," I said. "Just lunch. Can I pick you up at school?"

"I'm not in school today."

I did a quick run-through of my mental calendar. "Is it a holiday?"

"No. Just lunch, huh?" I could almost feel her shrug. "Well, maybe you'll change your mind after lunch."

"I won't change my mind."

"Meet me at the Casbah at twelve-thirty."

I thought she must be kidding. "You an old movie fan or something?"

"Huh?" I gathered from that answer that she wasn't. "It's no movie, Samson, it's a restaurant. On Throckmorton. It's not far from the movie, though."

"See you there at twelve-thirty."

"Yeah, you will."

But I didn't. I was there at 12:35 and she wasn't. The Casbah was a pleasant and expensive looking place with dark gold plaster walls hung with Oriental carpets, a few wooden booths alongside the front window, a few tables in the center, and about half a dozen archways hung with beads along the left side. They did a good lunch trade.

A slender dark man approached me. "Name?"

"Samson." Terrific, I thought, he's going to tell me there's an hour wait for lunch.

"This way, Mr. Samson." He led me to one of the beaded archways, pulled back the beads, and showed me into a cozy little hideaway, a platform with a low table and cushions for sitting.

"Did I have a reservation?" He nodded solemnly.

"And Miss Smith said she would be about fifteen minutes late. May I bring you a drink?" I glanced at the wine list. They had retsina.

"Greek wine?" I asked.

170

He smiled. "The owner's wife is Greek. You will see from our menu that we are quite cosmopolitan here. Greek dishes, Arab dishes. We like to think of ourselves as Eastern Mediterranean. You would like a glass of retsina?"

My love for retsina dates from my Chicago days. I'd gone through a belly-dancer period in my early twenties and I used to spend half my evenings hanging around the old Greek Town area. It's a funny thing about retsina. If you don't like it, you think it tastes like furniture oil with the furniture still in it. If you love it, as I do, it reminds you of the forest the resin came from. Unique, this resinous wine of Greece, like feta cheese and wrinkled black olives. When I drink it, I imagine myself sitting in a cafe overlooking the Aegean, dreaming out my days in useless philosophy.

After a while, I stuck my head and arm through the beads and ordered another glass of wine. A few minutes later, Bunny arrived. She was playing a new role. Her hair looked a little less like Elvis Presley's. She was wearing loosely fitted green velvet pants that stopped halfway down the calf, high-heeled boots, a fishnet shirt with something satiny under it, and a green velvet jacket, darker than the pants, with short embroidered sleeves. I wondered where she'd left her coat. The day was chilly for bare arms. She slid into the cubicle beside me, and moved in close.

"Sit around on the other side of the table, Barbara," I said.

"Come on, Jake, no one can see us here."

"Just the patron saint of little children."

"You Catholic or something?" she snarled and moved to the other side of the table, nearly colliding with the waiter, who was bringing our menus. He did not ask her if she wanted something to drink. She asked for a Turkish coffee; I continued working on my second retsina. The menu was extensive for lunch. Since Artie was paying, I tried to keep the overhead down by ordering egg-lemon soup and a falafel sandwich with hummus. Bunny ordered the soup and stuffed grape leaves.

"Two avgolemono, dolmades, falafel with hummus," the waiter repeated, writing it all down very carefully while he gave Bunny several long looks. After he finished checking out Bunny, he gave me an approving leer, I guess for being tucked away in this little den with an adolescent. I glared back at him and he went away.

"Okay, Barbara," I said, all business. "Why don't you tell me what you have to tell me?"

"Before lunch?" she whined. "How do I know you won't just take off and leave me here?"

I sighed. "I wouldn't do that."

"You won't because I'm not talking until we eat."

I surrendered. "Fine. How's school?"

She snorted. "You mean what am I studying and what do I want to be when I grow up? Jesus, Jake."

"Well, you must be interested in something."

"Lots of things. Right now, I'm interested in who you think killed my father."

I decided to shake her up a little. "Maybe your brother did it."

She laughed, but the laugh wasn't real. "Billy? Don't be stupid. He wouldn't kill anyone. He's real sweet."

"He had some good reasons for hating your father. I talked to him. He's pretty angry about your father's reaction to his being gay."

She screwed up her face, thinking hard. "He wouldn't kill him for that."

"Maybe you're right," I said. "But your daddy was also trying to fuck up Andy's life. Wouldn't he kill him for that? Or maybe Andy would. What do you think? What do you know about Andy?"

"I only met him once. He seemed real nice."

"Did you know what your father was planning to do before I asked you about it?"

"Yeah. Billy told me."

"When?"

"Well, right after he found out. We keep in touch."

The soup arrived. It was thick and yellow and it smelled wonderful. It tasted wonderful, too. Best I'd had since Chicago. Egg-lemon soup is not easy to make. The base is chicken broth, to which you add a mixture of egg and lemon. A chef once told me you beat the egg whites first, then add the yolks and beat some more, then you add the lemon juice very slowly, beating the hell out of the whole mess while you're mixing the eggs and lemon. If you don't do it that way, the lemon will curdle the egg. Anyway, it goes something like that. There's rice in the soup, too.

Bunny tasted hers. "This is weird."

"I thought you were a sophisticate, ordering stuffed grape leaves and everything. You mean you've never had avgolemono soup?"

"Never had grape leaves, either. I just liked the way it sounded." She plodded along with her soup-eating. I waited until my sandwich and her dolmades had arrived before I got back to picking her brain.

"Okay, Barbara," I said, "I seem to be pretty much committed to paying this check, now. You ready to let loose of some information?"

She poked at one of the sauce-covered cylinders on her plate, unrolling a little of the grape leaf, cutting it off with her knife, and tasting it.

"What's this sauce?" she asked suspiciously. "Tastes like the soup."

"That's because it's egg-lemon sauce."

"Grody. And this really tastes like a leaf." She hacked away at her food until the spiced meat stuffing was exposed. She liked that all right. Little savage. She picked up her Turkish coffee and slugged about half of it down. She liked that, too.

The falafel sandwich was good, with the hunk of falafel, lettuce, and pieces of cherry tomato inside a pocket of pita bread along with the hummus, a kind of dip made of ground-up chickpeas and I don't know what else. The hummus seemed a little thin. Sure enough, three bites into it the stuff soaked through the bottom of the half-circle of pita and the whole mess dropped down into my plate. I went after it with my fork.

"I'm waiting, Barbara. What do you know?"

"Can I order one of those?" she asked, after she'd polished off those parts of her lunch she'd decided to eat.

"Sure. After a little conversation."

173

"Oh, all right. What did you ask me?"

"One of the things I'd like to know is how Bill knew what your father was planning to do. I can't imagine one set of lawyers passing on that information to the other set of lawyers."

"You don't understand my father at all. He wrote Billy a letter, telling him what he was going to do. He believed you could do all kinds of shitty things if you told people what you were doing. Kind of like warning them, you know? So he sent this letter saying he was going to help Andy's ex-wife keep him away from the kid. He was going to do it by telling the judge that Andy was unfit and so was Bill."

"Let me get this straight. Andy's ex-wife found out he was gay and started the custody fight. How did your father come into it?"

Bunny sneered. "He saw this piece in the paper about how some gay people were trying to help Andy raise money for court. Bill's name was in it. And Andy's ex-wife, too. My father called her."

"So what did your father know that she didn't know?"

"Nothing, as far as Bill could see from the letter. He just said he was going to testify that the guys were unstable or nuts or something and would screw in front of the kid. I mean he didn't use those words."

"Is that true?"

"Can I order one of those sandwiches now?" I hailed the waiter and ordered her falafel. "No, it's not true, for Christ's sake, Jake. Of course it's not true."

"Your father was going to lie?"

She sighed wearily. "He never lied. He thought that's how it would be. He was pretty ignorant."

"How did Bill feel about that?"

"He was pissed off. Nobody likes to have their own dad saying things like that, you know. But he wasn't real worried. He said he didn't think the judge would listen to that kind of crap, without proof or anything. He said he wasn't even sure the other lawyer would want to use it."

"Did Andy agree with him?" I didn't. Maybe the judge wouldn't have bought it—maybe—but I was willing to bet there

174

would have been some attempt to use James Smith's statement.

Her falafel arrived and she took a huge bite. I waited while she chewed.

"Don't know. Didn't ask him."

I was wondering what Andy's lawyer had told him. I was also wondering whether Andy—or Bill—had been enraged enough by the man's viciousness to strike out at him no matter what they thought the legal effects of his plan would be.

"There's another thing," I said. "Your mother seemed to think your father's decision to take the new job was pretty sudden. But she says she didn't question him about it. Is that true? Do you know anything about that?"

"Boy, you sure expect a lot for one lunch. I already answered all the stuff about Andy and Bill. Maybe I should make you take me out again—"

"Barbara," I said, pulling her plate over to my side of the table. "How much do you want the rest of this sandwich?"

"Okay." She was laughing, but she was also hungry.

"Tell me when you found out you were going to be moving."

"Yeah, you know that was really something. It was on my birthday. Some birthday present, huh? He came home with this present for me—you know, that journal—and he handed it to me and wished me happy birthday and then he said to my mother that he'd decided to take the new job, and that we were going to be moving down south."

"How did your mother react to that?"

"She was upset."

"How do you know?"

Bunny laughed unpleasantly. "Because for once she didn't say 'Yes, dear, whatever you say, dear' or some kind of shit like that. She said she didn't want to take me out of school here, and that our whole lives were here, and all that. And she wanted to know why."

I leaned forward, keeping my fingers locked onto her plate. "What did he say?"

"He said he couldn't tell her everything because it wouldn't be good for her to know, whatever that meant, and that she had to trust him. He said it was personal. She asked him if something had happened at work that day, and he said no. But he thought it would be best if he took the other job."

I asked Bunny if she thought he'd been telling the truth.

"Oh, sometimes he wouldn't tell you everything you wanted to know. But he didn't lie."

30

A light rain had begun to fall as I got out of my car and started up the steps. Rosie, wearing a yellow slicker, was nailing the last new boards into place on the landing outside her room. Alice was sitting just inside the door, well out of the drizzle.

"How about some coffee, pal?" I said. She nodded, whacked in a few more nails, and followed me up to my room. I filled the kettle at the outdoor faucet and plugged in my hot plate.

Alice came in, shook herself, and flopped, sighing, in a corner.

I told Rosie about my lunch with Bunny, and we talked for a while about odds and ends of the case. She said she'd probably know by Saturday night whether Andy could account for himself on the morning of the murder.

"He was staying," she told me, "with a friend of a friend of a friend."

She caught my skeptical look.

"No, Jake, it's more reliable than it sounds. And it's better to approach things indirectly, anyway. References, you know. What I've done is passed the word that I'm interested in having a fundraiser for a woman I know and I want to talk to the guy Andy was staying with because he's one of the organizers for Andy's. He's supposed to get back to me Saturday."

"It's going to take some fancy chat to steer the conversation the way you want it to go," I said.

Rosie tasted her instant coffee and made a face. "I can handle it, Jacob. If the man is at all friendly he'll want to talk about how

176

Andy is taking this, and that leads us right into the time Andy spent at his place."

I hoped so, but I knew that if anyone could do it, Rosie could. Charm goes a long way, sometimes.

She returned to the subject of lunch with Bunny.

"He said it was personal?" she asked. "That could mean almost anything. But if something at the company didn't rush him into a decision . . ." She was thoughtful.

"Personal might have to do with Andy and Bill."

"It might. But there are other possibilities."

"Sure, but let's not get too imaginative until we've exhausted the ones we know about."

"Why not? We really ought to wrap this thing up soon. I can only stretch the work on the steps so far, you know. I'm beginning to look like the world's slowest carpenter."

Just then, Julia stuck her head in the open door. "Phone call, Jake. Chloe—I didn't quite catch the last name. And another woman, Iris, called about an hour ago. I didn't have a chance to leave a note. The next woman who calls, I'm going to tell her to take a number."

I walked back along the lane with her.

Chloe sounded very sad, so I could guess what was coming.

"He was in Santa Cruz. So was Franklin. Neither one of them could have been in Mill Valley."

"I was afraid of that. And trouble about the files?"

"No. He hasn't been around. Got to get off. Talk to you later."

I called Iris. She wanted to see me that night. Wanted to go to a movie. I accepted. I was just about to leave when Julia stopped me.

"I almost forgot this message, Jake. Probably because it was from a man. Here's the note."

The message was from Hal, who had received the Morton letter that morning. It said, "Pretty vague stuff, but it's being passed along. Thanks."

It was raining a little harder when I started back, and the footbridge was slippery. I managed to cross it without falling, but

177

nearly took a tumble in the mud on the other side. About the only thing more slippery than wet clay is ice.

Rosie had made herself another cup of coffee. I did the same and gave her the news. She just nodded.

"Since you're going to the East Bay, could you give me a lift? The truck's acting cranky and I want to let it rest. If you could drop me off at Carol's and pick me up again in the morning."

"Can I meet Carol?"

She smiled. "Okay." She finished her coffee. "I want to go do some thinking now. See you around five?"

I wanted to do some thinking, too. I wondered if Rosie's thoughts and mine were moving along the same lines. With Morton out of it for good, none of the alternatives were ones I liked very much.

We were both still thinking on the drive over, and hardly talked to each other.

Rosie's friend Carol lived in South Berkeley, near the Oakland line, in a brown shingled house with two housemates, a large mongrel, and three cats. She kissed Rosie and greeted me warmly, saying she'd heard a lot about me and she was glad to meet me. We drunk a beer and sat around for half an hour. I liked the way she was with Rosie, affectionate and thoughtful. And I liked the way she was with me. She cared enough about Rosie to respect her choice of friends. She had red hair and freckles and bright blue eyes and was altogether gorgeous and delightful. When I left I was sure I'd see her again.

I stopped at home for a while to shower and visit the cats, and got to Iris's house at seven-thirty. She wanted to have dinner at a very expensive French place that I'd taken her to when I'd gotten paid for the last job. I told her it was beyond my budget at the moment, but she convinced me that it was her turn to pay, anyway. Iris has a solid practice and I don't usually have any objections to her spending money on me now and again. It makes her feel good and I don't have any illusions about being a big, macho provider. I had a little problem with it this time, though, because I was also seeing Chloe. Even though Iris likes to keep our relationship open, I occasionally have twinges of monogamous guilt. Still, like I said, she convinced me.

The food was great. The movie—we caught the nine-thirty show—was funny. And Iris was in a terrific mood, witty, flirtatious, and even more beautiful than usual. I managed to forget about the case for a while. Mostly.

After we'd gone back to her house, and drunk herb tea, and made love, she wanted to know what was happening with the case. I told her I was chasing my tail. She didn't ask if I was chasing anyone else's tail and she dropped the subject, realizing I didn't want to talk about it or didn't know what to say. She curled up against my shoulder and fell asleep. I, on the other hand, couldn't stop thinking. I figure I got about two hours of sleep all night.

31

Rosie was cheerful enough when I picked her up the next morning, but the closer we got to Mill Valley, the more thoughtful she became.

"Rehearsing your phone call?" I asked.

"That, too."

"Andy might be okay."

"He might. But where does that leave us?"

"With other leads to follow, other calls to make. Are you thinking what I'm thinking, Rosie?"

She told me what was on her mind. I wasn't surprised. While Rosie was waiting for her phone call from San Francisco, we both had work to do. For her part, she said, she was going to have a talk with Hanley. And she was going to spend some time with Carlota, too.

There was a note on my door to call Chloe. She had phoned the night before. I dropped off my overnight stuff and went over to Artie's.

Chloe had news about Bright Future.

"Morton's quit," she announced. "Armand called me in yesterday to tell me. He looked terrible. He said Morton was going to Seattle, where he has an interest in a new company."

"Is he taking Bert with him?"

"I guess not. After I talked to Armand I mentioned it to Bert and I thought he was going to faint."

"Maybe Morton didn't want any gunslingers in his new operation. What about Bowen?"

"Armand said Bowen was upset about losing Morton, but I haven't seen him myself."

"What about Armand? Do you think he suspected something might be going on?"

"I think he suspected, just like Smith did. He looks scared. But he's not leaving. I think he wants to try to hold things together."

"But he's the man who's been handling the money."

"The money that's been recorded. Not Morton's money. He says he's going to talk to all the admirals, try to straighten things out, find a replacement for Morton."

"Do you think Morton took off because he discovered his files had been raided? Or because I walked into his office and talked like I knew what he was doing?"

"I don't know, but it sounds like he's been planning the move for a while. At least Armand had that impression. About that letter you took—if it leads to an investigation, how much time do you think we have before the truth sets us free? From our jobs, I mean."

"I don't have any idea. I'd guess this kind of thing takes time."

"Well, maybe there'll still be a company in six months and maybe there won't. Think I'll start looking around. So, what about this weekend? Want to have dinner?"

"I'd love to, maybe tomorrow. But a lot's happening right now. Can I give you a call back on it?" She said that was fine.

Just as I was hanging up, Artie came in.

"Hi, Jake. Could we talk? I feel like I don't know what's going on." I felt a little guilty. I'd been avoiding reporting to him, preferring to plunge ahead on my own without endless explanations. But that was pretty selfish.

"Sure. Just let me make a couple more phone calls." The first call I made was to Bill Smith in Mendocino. He said he was glad to hear from me, had, in fact, been thinking of giving me a call.

There was this fund-raiser tomorrow night, and maybe I'd be interested in going.

"How much?"

"Fifty dollars."

"Well, I do want to talk to you, but I think I'll have to pass on the fifty bucks."

He laughed. "I'm not surprised you want to talk to me. Bunny called to let me know you think Andy and I killed Crusader Rabbit. Can't let you go around thinking a thing like that. Tell you what, I'll be in Mill Valley Monday to see my sister. And my mother. How about I drop by then?"

I gave him directions to Charlie's house and he said he'd be there around noon. I was about to say goodbye when he stopped me.

"Wait a minute. That description you gave me. Is that by any chance the place where my father died?"

"Yes."

"Hm. Interesting."

I made two more calls after that, one to Bunny and one to Mrs. Smith. I asked them both the same question, a question I hadn't asked Bill. Bunny didn't know the answer and Mrs. Smith gave me part of the right one.

Then I sat down with Julia and Artie and filled them in on what had been happening since we'd last talked.

"My God," Julia said. "Is this ever going to end?"

"I hope so," I told her. "And soon."

Rosie and I got together again late that afternoon. She'd gotten the call we'd been waiting for. Andy was clear. He'd slept in San Francisco the night before the murder and had spent the morning hours working on plans for the fund-raiser. His host said Andy had been up and around the apartment early, anxious to get things done. Bill had not been with him.

Her talk with Hanley hadn't given us what we'd hoped, even though he'd been more willing to talk to Rosie than he had been to me. He still insisted that he hadn't been around on the day of the murder, hadn't done anything, and hadn't seen anything. But at least he admitted why he'd been watching Carlota. He was

Mary's friend, he said. And he suspected Carlota of having an affair with Mary's husband.

"So much for that," I said. "You don't think, maybe . . ."

Rosie laughed. "Nona would kill her. Carlota's proud of their friendship, but the only favors she wants from him are artistic."

None of that really mattered, though. The real treasure came from Carlota herself. Rosie had spent two hours with her, digging through the nonsense, patiently plowing through the woman's astounding egocentricity, and found out what we wanted to know. Carlota had seen a lot more the morning of the murder than she realized, even if she did spend most of her time looking in mirrors.

We went out for Chinese food and laid plans for the next couple of days. Then we found a bar with a pool table and slammed the balls around long enough and hard enough to work off some of our misery. Neither of us was happy about what had to be done.

32

Sunday was a day of rest.

Rosie spent it in the East Bay. I spent most of it holed up in my room, going around in moral circles. I had brunch with Julia, Artie, and Jennifer. I guessed they felt as though they had to be hospitable, but only Julia really tried. Artie sat around looking depressed and Jennifer barely spoke to me. I got the impression she thought I was one lousy detective.

But I couldn't very well tell them what we had. There were too many ifs, too many bad-luck turns our strategy could take.

After the meal, I crept off to use the phone in the bedroom. First I called Chloe to tell her I'd pick her up at six; then I gave my father a call, as I'd promised to do. When in doubt, my mother had taught me, be a good boy.

"Yeah?"

"Hi, pa. I said I'd call."

"Good thing. I tried calling the Italian but there was no answer. We're coming in September, you should have lots of notice."

"That's great. But you know it can get pretty hot out here in September."

"And in June it's too cold. Some climate you got." I didn't make the obvious comparisons between the weather in northern California and the weather in Chicago. "But September's best for the niece."

"Niece?"

"The niece, the niece. Eva's niece. The one you should meet. She's running around Europe all summer."

"Oh, yeah. The niece."

"Listen, you got a place we can stay at your house a couple days?"

That could mean anywhere from three days to two weeks. "You can sleep in the living room. I can rent a bed."

"The living room. That's it? How many rooms you got?"

I'd told him before, but he found the reality so unbelievable he kept forgetting.

"Four, pa. A living room, a bedroom, a kitchen, and a little closed-in back porch. It's too small for a bed."

He laughed. "The toilet's inside?"

I laughed too. "No, you got to dig a hole."

"That's a good one. I'll tell Eva. She'll love it. She'll be sorry she missed your call."

"She's not home?"

"No. Sunday she plays cards. With the *yentas*." My stepmother had been playing cards with the same group of women since the Great Depression. "So," he continued. "We'll stay in your living room. I'll be a sport, I'll rent the bed. Just the same, Jake, a man your age, his house should have a couple bedrooms."

"I got to go, now, pa." There's only so much talk about my age I can take.

"He's busy, the big shot? Okay. When you going to be home again?"

"Soon. Maybe. I'll let you know."

I got time and charges for the call and went back out to the

183

living room. Artie was reading the paper, Julia was doing a crossword puzzle, Jennifer was watering the plants. I tried to give Artie the money for the call, but much to my surprise, he refused. He said something about how hard I'd been working.

"Why didn't you call on a Saturday," Jennifer snapped. "Isn't it cheaper on a Saturday?"

"I think it's the same on Sunday," I said. Then I told them the same lie I'd told my father. "I have to go now. See you later. Thanks for brunch."

I went back to my room and sat down on my cot.

At five-thirty I went to get Chloe. We drove north into Sonoma County, to Santa Rosa, and had a family-style Basque dinner. A lot of food served by a large, motherly woman. Perfect for my mood.

"Tell me what you're thinking of doing about work," I asked.

"I don't know what I'll do," she said. "What's worse, I don't know what I want to do. But I've been making good money. I can hang on for a while until I find something."

"What about your staff? They might need to start looking, too. What are you going to tell them?"

"The truth. They're young. They'll do okay. Except for Bert."

"Betrayed and abandoned," I said.

"The man's pathetic, Jake. I would have expected you to feel more pity."

She was right. The problem was, I figured the best course at the moment was to feel pity for no one but Alan—that was hard—Artie, Julia, Jennifer, and me.

After dinner we drove into Petaluma, about halfway between Santa Rosa and Novato. Petaluma used to be called the chicken capital of the world. I don't know what it's the capital of now, but that night we heard some great bluegrass at a cafe there.

"When this case is over," Chloe said later, "you'll be going back to the East Bay, won't you?"

"Sure. But it's not like I live in Santa Barbara or someplace. We'll see each other. Often." I meant it. "Besides, maybe you won't be staying in Marin."

"Maybe."

I did everything I could that night to reassure Chloe that this was a relationship, not a convenient affair. And she did everything she could to reassure me.

33

Bill arrived promptly at noon. He looked like he'd had a good weekend. I could hear Rosie hammering away down below.

"Fund-raiser go okay?"

"Real good. We're almost out of debt."

I told him I was glad to hear it, and offered him a beer. I'd borrowed two cans from Rosie's cooler. We talked for a while about the coming custody hearing, but he got impatient with that.

"This isn't what you wanted to talk to me about, Samson. Why don't we just get to it?"

"Okay, but first I want to show you something. Come on." I led him out the door and down the lane. By the time we got to the footbridge he was getting a little fidgety.

"Is this the spillway, where—"

"Yeah."

We climbed the path all the way up to the crevasse. "This is probably where it happened, Bill," I told him. "Here's how it went. The killer met your father here. Maybe they fought, maybe it happened suddenly. The killer stuck the knife in your father's gut. Maybe he died right away, maybe not. Then the killer took him and dumped him into the spillway somewhere up here."

Bill was very pale. "What are you telling me this for? I didn't ask for a tour. I don't need this—"

"I think maybe you do." He shot me an angry look. "There was a lot more water in the spillway then. It carried your father all the way down. It was a rough trip. Somewhere along the way, the knife fell out."

"Look, you son of a bitch . . ."

"All the way down to the bottom." I pointed down the course of the spillway to the ditch, barely visible through the brush.

"Down to that ditch. Where he got stuck in some branches. That's where they found the body. In the ditch."

Bill turned abruptly and started down the path. I caught up with him.

"Come on back to my place for a few minutes, Bill. We've got more to talk about."

"I don't think we do."

"You left your jacket there. Come on. We'll have another beer."

"I don't want your fucking beer." But he came with me. He was looking sick.

We walked back across the bridge and along the lane to my room. I sat him down but he stood up again, reaching for his jacket.

"I'm sorry I had to do that, Bill. I just thought you ought to know, see it for yourself."

"Very sensitive of you, Samson. I think I'll just go, now. Unless you've got more games in mind. Like showing me a run-over cat."

"Bill, no one deserves to die that way. And the kid the police are holding doesn't deserve what's happened to him. I think you can help."

He quieted down. He was looking at me suspiciously, but he was interested. "What am I supposed to do about it," he demanded. "Confess?"

"Just give me a few more minutes of your time."

"All right," he snapped, "talk."

"Sure. But I think I need another beer." I really did. "How about you?"

He shrugged, watching me coldly, still standing and getting skittish again.

"Here," I said, tossing him my copy of the *Marin Journal of the Arts*. "Just let me go get the beer. Relax. Get a little culture. Bunny says you like films. Read a film review. I'll be right back."

"You're stalling. What are you stalling for?"

"I'm not stalling. I just want to get a beer."

"Oh, for Christ's sake," he said. But he opened the magazine and sat.

186

Rosie was sawing on a piece of railing on the landing near her door. She looked at me. I nodded. She stopped sawing and trotted down to where her truck was parked on the canyon floor. Then I waited a couple of minutes, standing just inside her room.

I would either have to take two more beers back upstairs or—I didn't have to. Someone was running down the steps. He passed the landing. Bill. He couldn't see me. I let him get all the way down. I waited until I heard a car start and churn gravel out of the canyon. I ran downstairs. Rosie was standing beside her truck.

"White Toyota!" she yelled. "And I'm not going with you."

I envied her. I swung my Chevy around and skidded out the entrance. No white Toyota in sight. I drove too fast for the narrow, winding road, and, after a quarter of a mile, spotted the car taking a curve ahead of me. I managed to stay one curve behind him all the way to Miller Avenue. When he pulled out into the sparse traffic, I let three cars fill the gap between us.

He pulled in at a meter in the municipal parking lot near the bus station, not stopping to feed it a quarter.

I gave him a couple of minutes, then I followed him into Mary's Bookstore.

The two men were facing each other. They didn't notice me come in.

"You didn't know your old teacher was living here, did you Bill?" I said. They both swung toward me.

Bill was whiter than he'd been at the spillway. Eric was gaping at me. I was glad to see that Mary wasn't around. After all, she had told me that Monday was her usual day off.

But Sergeant Ricci was there, a book in his hands, standing near a rack of best-sellers.

"Carlota told you," Eric croaked.

Bill closed his eyes. "No," he said softly. "I'm the one who told him. It looks like I told him. Again."

34

When I'd called Sergeant Ricci that morning to tell him everything Rosie and I had learned, he'd been skeptical. When I'd laid
out our plan for tricking Bill into identifying his former teacher,
he'd said it was a dumb-ass idea and had given me the required
earful about amateurs messing with law enforcement. He'd also
said he'd do some checking around himself.

So I'd been very relieved to see him at the bookstore. I
couldn't very well expect Eric to fall into my arms and let me lead
him quietly away, but he didn't give Ricci much of an argument.
He didn't give him anything else, either. Not right then. After his
initial indiscreet remark about Carlota, he clamped his mouth shut
and didn't open it again until his lawyer told him to.

Aside from all the other evidence against him, the law found
it hard to believe that Eric hadn't lied to the sheriff's people, way
back at the beginning, when they'd asked all the canyon residents
if they knew the victim.

Eric would have found it hard to forget James Smith, even
after twenty years. Like Bill, all he had needed was the face and
the right name to go with it.

The face of a student's father. The face of a man who came to
him, and accused him, and told him he was going to lose his job.
Because Smith believed in warning people of his intentions. Not
the kind of meeting that slips a man's mind later on. Especially
when the threat is real, and the man loses his job, his home, and
his family.

First the job went, then the home. Eric had trouble finding
work, and his wife had trouble dealing with his emotional problems and with the gossip that was inevitable in the small suburb
where they lived. Their teenage daughter had an even harder time.
The family moved to Chicago. The kid started getting in trouble at
school. Eric tried to talk to her. She accused him of ruining her
life. He broke, and went off on a two-week bender. By the time he
got back home, his daughter had run away. To California, the
goodbye note said.

Eric left his wife in Chicago and went off to find the girl. After a month of futile wandering, a letter from his wife caught up with him at the home of a friend in Los Angeles. She was filing for divorce. He never found his daughter, and he never went back to the Midwest. He met Mary, who took him in and supported him, held him up until he could stand on his own a little better, and made him a partner in her bookstore.

They bought a house in the canyon.

One day, while he was checking out the spillway for winter damage, he found a hunting knife on the trail. The knife was engraved with the owner's initials. He had a neighbor with those initials. Artie. A.P. But no one was home at the Perrine house, and he didn't want to leave a good knife out in the damp, so he took it home and forgot about it.

A few days later, James Smith walked into the store to buy a birthday present for Bunny.

"And Smith recognized Eric?" Chloe interrupted my storytelling. The three of us—Rosie, Chloe, and I—were sitting around Chloe's living room waiting for a pizza to be delivered. Alice and Achilles, the German shepherd, were sleeping butt to butt in front of the potbelly stove.

"No," I said. "Not right away. He brought one of the journals up to the counter and asked Eric if he thought it would be a good present for his sixteen-year-old daughter. Eric said he thought it would be. Then he took a second look at his customer."

"And knew who he was?" Chloe obviously wanted to get to the good part faster. She knew a lot of it already, of course. Some from me, some from news coverage. But we had the full story now, and she was eager for details.

"He wasn't sure," I told her.

He rang up the sale and initiated a friendly "do-you-live-around-here" conversation. Smith said yes, as a matter of fact, his family liked the area so much he was planning on building a new house just outside town.

That was when Eric was sure that the odd coincidence in names he'd run across recently was not a coincidence at all. James Smith was an almost ridiculously ordinary name. He'd had no

189

reason until that moment to think that the man who was buying a lot in the canyon was the James Smith he had known twenty years before and two thousand miles away.

"I'm glad you still have a daughter to buy presents for," Eric had said. "I haven't seen mine for a long time. You used to live in Chicago, didn't you?"

Yes, Smith admitted. He had moved to California with his company. Did he know Eric from somewhere? He looked familiar, but . . .

Eric couldn't take it. The man had ruined his life and then had just forgotten him. He told him who he was.

"And you're James Smith," he said. "The same damned James Smith." He accused him of causing trouble everywhere he went. "But that's all right, this time I've got the law on my side. I know what you're doing and I'm going to stop you." Then he told him to get out of his store and never come back.

For weeks, Smith had been agonizing over the situation at Bright Future, over his suspicions about Morton's sales empire. Although he had heard that there might be some question about the availability of the lot, it never occurred to him that what he was "doing" had anything to do with the canyon. When you work for a crooked company, and someone who hates you starts yelling about the law, you're going to assume that's what he's yelling about.

So Smith got scared. He decided right then that he'd better take the headmaster offer and get out fast. He went home and announced to his family that they would be moving. And as Bunny had said, he wasn't lying when he told his wife that it wasn't because of anything that had happened that day at work.

"Wait a minute," Chloe objected. "How do you know that Smith thought Eric was talking about Bright Future?"

I didn't get a chance to answer right away because the pizza arrived. We moved our conversation to the table.

"Because of something Smith said later on, to Eric," Rosie explained.

"Yeah," I said. "Give me a chance to get to it." I took a big bite of pizza.

"Now that his mouth is full," Rosie said, "I'm going to tell some of this."

She picked up where I'd left off. Eric said later that seeing Smith again had caused him to do "some brooding" about his lost daughter. But he insisted that he calmed himself down and concentrated on keeping Smith from getting the canyon property. He talked to both Mary and Hanley and offered them any help he could give them—Hanley testified to this—in preparing their case against the sale.

In the canyon a couple of days after that meeting with Smith, he ran into Mike, whom he recognized vaguely as Artie's son. He remembered the hunting knife, mentioned that he had something of Artie's and would drop it by. He'd said "had," not found, and both Mike and Artie had assumed it was something he had borrowed, maybe from Julia.

He didn't get around to returning the knife until the following Sunday morning. He'd been crossing the footbridge on his way to Artie's when he'd seen Smith walking up the trail. He'd followed him.

Not, of course, with anything violent in mind, he said. All he wanted to do was tell Smith he might as well give up any idea of buying the lot because the canyon residents were going to fight him. They hadn't yet found the documents they needed, but Mary was sure they existed and would be found.

At the top of the trail, near the lip of the spillway, Smith turned to see Eric coming up behind him.

Eric started to say what he'd planned to say. But Smith, he said, started jabbering about his job, for some reason Eric didn't understand. He told Eric he couldn't threaten him any more, that there was nothing he could do to him because he'd resigned. Eric, he said, could do anything he wanted to do about Bright Future.

"Ah hah!" Chloe said. "And then?"

Rosie was starting her third wedge of pizza, so I picked up the narrative.

"And then Smith got nasty."

According to Eric, Smith called him a bum and a criminal. He asked Eric what had happened to his daughter, the one he hadn't seen in years. Had he managed to ruin her life, too? Like he'd ruined Bill's?

Eric was sickened and enraged by the reference to his child. He started to feel dizzy, he said, and confused. And still the tirade went on. Something about how Bill was trying to pass his sickness on to another child, but he, Smith, was going to save her. Something about saving a little girl from the likes of Eric.

Anderson says now he has no idea how it happened. He says he went crazy, found the knife in his hand, and used it. He doesn't remember anything about throwing the body in the water, but he admits that he must have. He does remember falling in the mud afterward, picking himself up and running away.

There's no way to know whether his story was true. Rosie thinks it is, but I'm not so sure. In any case, his version of things didn't get him off with the voluntary manslaughter verdict his lawyer was trying for. The jury did go along, though, with second degree murder, because the prosecution couldn't prove premeditation.

"And Rosie," I concluded, turning the floor over to my friend, "was the one who really got things moving along the right lines."

Rosie explained that all the time she'd been working on those steps, she'd wondered about Eric's visits with Carlota. She said they looked like duty calls. He obviously wasn't having an affair with her. Just as obviously, he didn't really like her all that much.

Then Carlota referred to him as a "colleague," and that made her wonder even more. He reviewed films, but he didn't make them. If he were also a filmmaker, Rosie was sure, the blurb under his review would have said so. Did artists think of critics as colleagues? She didn't think so. Then she saw the lousy films he'd said were so great. Including the one that showed Carlota had a good view of the lane from her living room mirror.

When she finally hit Carlota with some solid questions, she got some interesting answers. Carlota made her living as a teacher. Eric was an ex-teacher, and therefore a colleague.

And Carlota had been spending a lot of time with her mirrors the morning of the murder. She had, as a matter of fact, seen Eric rushing home along the lane, beyond her own reflection, earlier that morning. She had wanted to talk to him about the review he had said he would do of her films. She dashed out to her kitchen deck, hailing him. He had hesitated, yelling back that he would talk to her later, and continued on to his house.

She had assumed, she told Rosie, that he wanted to go home because he was all muddy. At least she remembered seeing some mud.

Carlota, it seemed, had begun her wine drinking early that day. If the films were any indication, Carlota's "creative sparks" were often alcohol-fueled. So she missed something that Eric was sure, once he got home and saw it himself, she must have seen. A splash of blood on his shirt. Along with the mud.

He went back to see her that afternoon and told her all about the wonderful review he was going to write. She didn't mention the blood. He thought if he took good care of her ego, she never would.

Carlota had never felt, she said at the trial, that his appearance on the path had any significance. It was his job, after all, to inspect the spillway in the spring.

When Rosie and I sat down, at the last, to put things together, a fairly clear picture emerged. "A neighbor" telling Mike he had something that belonged to Artie, whose initials, like Alan's, were A.P. Eric, at the hot tub meeting after the murder, telling Artie that he didn't have anything of his, after all. Just a trowel he'd realized actually belonged to someone else. Eric, spillway inspector, wandering around the trail, the week before the murder, where the knife had been lost. Mary, his second wife, confiding that she'd met him when he was searching for a runaway daughter—not significant in itself, but consistent with the picture Bill had given me of an ex-teacher whose life had fallen apart. There was the location of Eric's house; he had to pass Carlota's to get to it. Then there was Smith's sudden decision to quit his job and leave the area, made on the day he visited the bookstore, a day when Mary wasn't there.

A lot of interesting bits and pieces.

And while Rosie had been talking to Carlota, I told Chloe, I'd been talking to Bunny and Mrs. Smith on the telephone. Bunny had never known the name of the teacher in Chicago. Mrs. Smith wasn't quite sure. It was something Scandinavian, she said. Johnson? Peterson? No, maybe it was Anderson. Yes, that sounded right.

We finished the pizza. Rosie had to leave so she could get home to the East Bay in time for a date. Chloe and I had a date, too. For the weekend.

What it all came down to in the end was getting Bill to identify Anderson. I didn't think he'd do it voluntarily, and Eric certainly had no reason to admit a connection with a murdered man. The police had checked out every likely suspect they knew about, concentrating on Morton, but they'd never taken the conflict over the lot very seriously and they'd never heard the story of the teacher back in Chicago. Sure, there was a lot of circumstantial evidence, but it can take a long time to follow a twenty-year-old trail, and meanwhile, Alan was sitting in jail.

While I was waiting for Bill to pay me a visit, Ricci was following my tip by checking with Mrs. Smith and with Carlota.

And we set Bill up. The review had a picture of Eric, as well as a byline. It said he was a partner in Mary's Bookstore, in Mill Valley. If we could get Bill to take a look at that review, I thought we might be able to bring the whole mess to a head.

Eric will spend a few years in prison, but maybe it's worth it to him. I don't think it's worth it to Mary. She's given up plans to open another store, but she's keeping the one in Marin open so when he gets out he'll have a job.

There were a few other side effects, too. The law went after Bright Future. They couldn't pin anything on the company, but they found head-hunting in the field, all right. And with the loss of the corporate good name, Bowen and Armand closed up shop. Artie helped Chloe get a job as copy editor at *Probe*, which she likes very much. Arlene Shulman went off to New York to become a free-lance book designer, and Hanley Martin stayed in the canyon. He gets drunk more often, and shoots trees more often, but the other residents try to be understanding.

Alan wrote a series on life in the Marin County Jail. He and

194

his family have their own place, now, an apartment in San Francisco.

Bunny and her mother are doing fine on Smith's investments.

Howard Morton is probably connected with a company up in Seattle, but no one seems to know for sure.

And no one knows what became of Bert Franklin.

As far as I know, no one else has ever reviewed Carlota's films.

The county accepted the canyon's report, and the lot belongs to the residents.

A couple of weeks after Eric's arrest, a judge ruled that Andy's ex-wife would have to be satisfied with the original custody agreement, and Andy kept his visitation rights.

Before that happened, though, I took a drive up to Mendocino to see how Bill was doing. I couldn't seem to get through to him on the phone.

Andy was working the desk at the inn.

He looked up when I walked in, but he didn't say a word. "I came to see Bill," I said.

"Let's go outside and talk about it, Samson," Andy growled. We went outside. Andy was gripping my arm hard.

"Bill's in his room. He spends most of his time there, ever since we got back. He talks a lot about betrayal. For a while he couldn't sleep and he would hardly eat. But it's okay. The doctor says he's coming out of it. He'll be better soon." Andy was still clutching my arm. I could feel the bruises turning color.

"I'd hoped that if I showed him how his father died, he wouldn't—" I began.

That was when Andy slugged me. Then he picked me up and slugged me again.

It hurt like hell, but it helped.

195